The Willow and Other Stories

Anton Chekhov

Translated by Stephen Pimenoff

ALMA CLASSICS

ALMA CLASSICS
an imprint of

ALMA BOOKS LTD
Thornton House
Thornton Road
Wimbledon Village
London SW19 4NG
United Kingdom
www.almaclassics.com

This edition first published by Alma Classics in 2024
Translation © Stephen Pimenoff, 2024

Cover: Nathan Burton

Extra Material and Notes © Alma Books Ltd

Printed in Great Britain by CPI Group (UK) Ltd, Croydon CR0 4YY

ISBN: 978-1-84749-917-2

All rights reserved. No part of this publication may be reproduced, stored in or introduced into a retrieval system, or transmitted, in any form or by any means (electronic, mechanical, photocopying, recording or otherwise), without the prior written permission of the publisher. This book is sold subject to the condition that it shall not be resold, lent, hired out or otherwise circulated without the express prior consent of the publisher.

Contents

Introduction

The stories in this collection are representative of each of the three main periods of Chekhov's all-too-short writing career: the early 1880s, when he wrote mostly short, light-hearted stories, some of them very funny; the late 1880s, when his focus changed and he wrote stories of a darker, more pessimistic hue; and the period towards the end of his life, when the stories became more like psychological studies.

Many of the early humorous stories carry overtones of satire. 'Fat and Thin' vividly conveys an idea of the deference shown by *chinovniks*, or civil servants, towards those who stood above them in the hierarchy of ranks, while 'Misfortune' and 'A Confession' gives some idea of the blatant corruption that was endemic among such functionaries. A few early stories might be classed as pure humour, containing no underlying "message", like 'The Custodian in Custody', 'The Lost Ones', 'The Fiancé' and 'The Guardian'.

Other early stories, such as 'In Autumn',* 'The Thief' and 'The Willow' – all of which were written in 1883, when Chekhov was twenty-three – not only show a level of maturity beyond his years, but already give intimations of the darker side of his nature. But even such stories are not without humour, though where the humour appears it tends to be black, as in 'The Avenger' and 'The Wallet'. The dark side became more pronounced a few years later in the stories 'Terrors', 'The Coroner', 'Despair' and 'The Conundrum', although some stories about social and family relations from this period, such as 'A Father', 'The Unwanted', 'A Slander', 'A Serious Step' and 'The Wedding' (deemed by Tolstoy to be Chekhov's best story), have a gentler air of resignation and acceptance.

'The Fiancée' was Chekhov's last story. Repeatedly revised by him, it dates from 1903, when he was writing *The Cherry Orchard*, and bears many similarities to that play. The heroine,

Nadya, a thoroughly modern young woman living at the home of her well-to-do grandmother, is engaged to be married to the idle, self-satisfied and materialistic Andrei, a pathetically inadequate dilettante quite unworthy of a woman of Nadya's character. She falls under the influence of the intensely idealistic dreamer Sasha, who persuades her to abandon her useless way of life, escape to St Petersburg and enrol in university. (Her name is short for Nadezhda, which means "hope".) His tirade against the futility, stagnation and immorality of her life of leisure, enjoyed at the expense of servants who are forced to work in overcrowded conditions of poverty and filth, closely mirrors that which Trofimov in *The Cherry Orchard* delivers to Anya, a young woman very much like Nadya.

Sasha, who suffers from consumption, is clearly modelled on Chekhov himself, who died of consumption a year after completing 'The Fiancée'. Sasha's plea for change, and his utopian vision of a new society built on the ruins of the corrupt and immoral old one, are revolutionary in nature, and ominously prefigure the upheavals in Russia that were to come within a few short years. It is hardly surprising that Chekhov was enthusiastically embraced by the Communists as being one of them.

The doubts and longings to which Nadya is subject also assail young female characters in Chekhov's three other late great plays. In *The Seagull*, Nina, the daughter of a wealthy landowner, leaves home to become an actress. Olga, Masha and Irina at the end of *The Three Sisters* are close to despair in frustration at the thought of their idle, useless lives, yet still cling to the hope that life will get better: "Time will pass... and our sufferings will turn to joy for those who will be living after us, happiness and peace will come on earth, and they will remember with some gentle word those who live now, and will bless them." Their dream is to go to Moscow, but the reader is left with the suspicion that they probably never will. Sonya, in *Uncle Vanya*, suffers badly from a sense of the futility of life, yet also echoes the optimism of Sasha in a moving speech at the end of the play: "We shall rest! We shall hear the angels, we shall see the whole sky all diamonds, we shall see how all earthly evil, all our sufferings, are drowned in the mercy that will fill the whole world. And our life will grow peaceful, tender, sweet as a caress..." These ideas were clearly very much in Chekhov's mind towards the end of his life.

Other recognizably Chekhovian characters also make an appearance in *The Fiancée*. The eccentric and endearing Father Andrei, always on the point of making a humorous remark; Granny, the matriarch of the house; and Nadya's mother, Nina Ivanovna, a lost soul tearfully given to spiritism and homeopathy. They are all presented as parasites, and seem to do nothing but talk, drink tea, play a little music and wander around aimlessly in a typically Russian manner. Their lethargy and the stagnation of their ideas provide a springboard for Sasha's denunciation of the life they lead, and his passionate calls for change.

In the course of his writing life Chekhov wrote many stories about love, marriage and relations between the sexes. He himself always enjoyed good relations with women, though he tended to keep them at arm's length, possibly fearing entanglements, and only married a few years before he died. But he was observant enough to write convincingly about these relations in such stories as 'A Failure', 'The Fool', 'The Pink Stocking', 'Two Letters', 'Champagne' and 'On the Approach of the Wedding Season'.

Many of the stories in this collection have, to the best of my knowledge, either never or rarely before been translated. Of the ones that have, I nevertheless thought a new translation to be justified. I believe there is no such thing as a definitive interpretation of a literary classic, any more than there is of a musical work. Such things as choice of words, syntax and even punctuation can subtly alter the effect of a piece of writing in much the same way as lighting can affect one's impression of a painting.

My approach throughout the book has above all been to convey the spirit of Russianness of the works, and not have them read as if written in English and set in Scotland, Texas or the Australian outback. To this end I have avoided introducing any dialect or pronunciation specific to a class or to people of another region or country. I have avoided the common or vulgar speech of any nation, feeling that it always grates in some translations to read Russian peasants talking like Cockney draymen or Billingsgate fishmongers.

I have kept my translations faithful in the sense that I have taken no unwarranted liberties with the text. Some earlier translators seem to have felt Chekhov's vocabulary to be too simple, not "literary" enough. For example the simple line literally translated as "everyone writes as he wants to and as he can" is rendered in one earlier translation as "everyone writes in accordance with his desire and his capacity", which is quite un-Chekhovian. The effect of Chekhov's prose lies partly in its simplicity, and wherever possible I have tried to preserve that feature.

Another quality of Chekhov's prose that is often remarked upon is its conciseness. "The way Chekhov... begins a story is wonderfully good," writes Somerset Maugham in the preface to his own *Complete Short Stories*. "He gives the facts at once, in a few lines; he has an unerring feeling for the essential statements, and he sets them down baldly, but with great precision, so you know at once whom you have to deal with and what the circumstances are... In his shorter stories Chekhov attained the concision he aimed at in a manner that is almost miraculous."

The tendency in some translations to "improve" Chekhov's language may be what has led to his works being considered "difficult". (Some years ago an advertisement for "Britain's Biggest Bottled Beer" carried the tag line "HEAVIER THAN CHEKHOV".) One critic complained that a new translation, when read aloud, sounded "clunky" (his word). This may have been because the translator was being *too* faithful to the text. Russian punctuation *can* impart a certain clunkiness to prose. More commas are used than in English, and sentences are often strung together, separated by commas rather than full stops or semicolons. So the punctuation often has to be changed in order to achieve the ideal of English prose – a sentence that reads smoothly with as little punctuation as possible, and does not have to be reread for its meaning to be grasped. Russian syntax being very different from English, the word order also usually has to be changed.

I have avoided words of modern coining, whether British or American, such as "edgy", "feisty", "gutsy", "fantabulous", "no-brainer", "stitch-up", "uptick" and thousands of others; contemporary idiomatic expressions like "going forward", "silver bullet", "good to go" and "to tick all the boxes"; and exclamations of contemporary coining, such as "give me a break". I felt that such ephemeral expressions with only modern associations would jar upon the reader's sense of fitness. I have also avoided certain all-purpose words, overworked today, like "totally", "absolutely" and "incredibly", and have not employed any sporting images that are so popular in common speech, like "to up one's game", "to knock for six", "to kick into the long grass", "to step up to the plate" and so on. In short, I have avoided any language that would be out of keeping with the period in which Chekhov wrote.

I have rendered literally some expressions that are not idiomatic English and are usually translated freely. For example, when a person dies, a Russian will say, "May the Kingdom of Heaven be his", or "Peace to his ashes". These are often given as "May he rest in peace", but I believe the literal translations to be wonderfully evocative of the Russian spirit, and so have kept them. Examples may be multiplied.

Russian words that may be puzzling to some readers, but have no precise English equivalents, have been italicized in the text and annotated. These are mostly items of food and units of measurements. Certain unfamiliar customs and historical references and personalities have also been annotated.

There is frequent reference in the stories to the decorations awarded to state officials. These are (in order of importance): The Orders of St Vladimir, St Anna and St Stanislav. An even higher decoration was the Order of the White Eagle.

A table of the ranks into which officials were classed in pre-revolutionary Russia, and which play an important part in some of the stories, is provided at the beginning. Readers may find it helpful to know that civil servants and generals in the first four ranks were entitled to be addressed as "Your Excellency". Independent of ranks, four classes formed the social hierarchy of Tsarist Russia: the nobility, the clergy, the merchant class – equivalent to the bourgeoisie or middle class – and the peasantry. Of the four groups, the last was by far the largest.

Characters in the stories are often referred to with their given name and patronymic. In 'The Fiancée', Nadya's mother is repeatedly referred to as Nina Ivanovna. In English versions the Ivanovna is often dropped, especially if it recurs repeatedly, but I have kept it wherever Chekhov used it, as I feel it imparts a more authentic colouring to the story.

Some readers may be confused by the variety of diminutive nicknames Russians can have. In the story 'The Lost Ones', a woman named Vera has no fewer than four diminutives: Verochka, Verunchik, Veryevunchik and Verka. These are terms of endearment or affection, and might be translated as "little Vera" or "Vera dear", but again I thought it more authentic to keep such terms as in the original, provided they did not lead to confusion. Likewise I have kept the words "mama" and "papa", rather than changing them to "mum" and "dad", which is sometimes done, and which do not sound at all Russian.

Once again, I wish to express my thanks to Mrs Masha Lees, an immensely erudite scholar of Russian, whom I have been privileged to know for many years, for checking my translations. The discussions I have had with her about the Russian language, its literature and history, have been enjoyable as well as enlightening.

– Stephen Pimenoff, 2024

The Willow
and Other Stories

Table of Ranks

	Civil Service	*Military*	*Court*
1)	Chancellor	Field Marshal/ Admiral	
2)	Active Privy Councillor	General	Chief Chamberlain
3)	Privy Councillor	Lieutenant General	Marshal of the House
4)	Active State Councillor	Major General	Chamberlain
5)	State Councillor	Brigadier	Master of Ceremonies
6)	Collegiate Councillor	Colonel	Chamber Fourrier
7)	Court Councillor	Lieutenant Colonel	
8)	Collegiate Assessor	Major	House Fourrier
9)	Titular Councillor	Staff Captain	
10)	Collegiate Secretary	Lieutenant	
11)	Ship Secretary*	*Kammerjunker*	
12)	Government Secretary	Sub-Lieutenant	
13)	Provincial Secretary*		
14)	Collegiate Registrar	Senior Ensign	

* *(abolished in 1834)*

The Avenger

SOON AFTER CATCHING HIS WIFE in flagrante delicto,* Fyodor Fyodorovich Sigayev was standing in the Shmucks & Co. gun store, choosing for himself a suitable revolver. His face was showing anger, grief and irrevocable determination.

"I know what I have to do..." he thought. "Family foundations have been shaken, honour trampled in the mud, vice celebrated – and that is why I, as a citizen and honourable man, must take vengeance. First I shall kill her and her lover, and then myself..."

He had not yet chosen a revolver, and had not yet killed anyone, but his imagination was already picturing three bloodstained corpses, smashed skulls, streaming brains, chaos, crowds of idlers, autopsies... With the malicious pleasure of an outraged man, he imagined the horror of relatives and the public, the death throes of the traitress, and mentally was already reading leading articles dealing with the disintegration of family ties.

The shop salesman – a lively Gallic figure with a paunch and a white waistcoat – laid out revolvers in front of him and, deferentially smiling and shuffling his feet, said:

"I would advise you, m'sieur, to take this lovely revolver. The make is Smith & Wesson. It's the latest word in firearms science. Triple action, with an extractor, it will kill at six hundred paces with a direct hit. I draw your attention, m'sieur, to the fine finish. The most up-to-date make, m'sieur... Every day we sell up to a dozen for thieves, wolves and lovers. Very reliable and strong action, it kills at great distance and will shoot right through a wife and her lover. And with regard to suicide, m'sieur, I don't know a better gun..."

The salesman raised and lowered the cocking piece, breathed on the barrel, took aim and seemed to gasp with delight. Looking at his rapt face, one could think that he himself would willingly have blown out his brains if only he possessed such a beautiful make of revolver as a Smith & Wesson.

"How much is it?" asked Sigayev.

"Forty-five roubles, m'sieur."

"Hm!... That's a lot for me!"

"In that case, m'sieur, I recommend another make, much cheaper. Here, would you like to see it? We have the widest range, at various prices... For example, this Lefaucheux revolver costs only eighteen roubles, but..." The salesman contemptuously screwed up his face. "But, m'sieur, the make is already obsolete. Only female psychopaths and the intellectual proletariat buy it now. To blow your brains out or kill your wife with the Lefaucheux is now considered a sign of bad taste. Good taste only recognizes the Smith & Wesson."

"I have no need either to blow out my brains or to kill anyone," Sigayev sullenly lied. "I shall buy it simply for the dacha... to frighten thieves..."

"It's no business of ours what you buy it for," smiled the salesman, discreetly lowering his eyes. "If in every case we tried to find the reason, then, m'sieur, we would have to close the shop. The Lefaucheux is no good for frightening off thieves, m'sieur, because it gives a soft, muffled sound, so I would suggest to you the standard-percussion-cap Mortimer pistol, the so-called duelling pistol..."

"Should I challenge him to a duel?" flashed through Sigayev's head. "But that's too good for him. Such a swine should be killed like a dog..."

The salesman, graciously turning and mincing back and forth, ceaselessly smiling and chattering, placed before him a whole pile of revolvers. The Smith & Wesson looked the most appealing and impressive of all. Sigayev picked up one revolver of this make, dully fixed his gaze on it and became absorbed in thought. His imagination visualized how he would smash the skulls, how the blood would flow on the carpet and parquet floor, how the leg of the dying traitress would twitch... But for his most indignant soul this was not enough. Bloody scenes, wailing and horror did not satisfy him. He had to think up something more horrible.

"What if I kill him and myself," he thought, "and keep her alive? Let her wither away with remorse and the contempt of those around her. For such a sensitive nature as hers it would be by far the most excruciating death..."

And he imagined his own funeral: he, the wronged one, lies in the coffin with a gentle smile on his lips, while she, pale, tormented by remorse, follows the coffin like Niobe* and does not know where to hide from the withering, contemptuous looks cast on her by the indignant crowd...

"I see, m'sieur, that you like the Smith & Wesson," the salesman said, interrupting his reverie. "If it seems to you too expensive, then, if you like, I can take off five roubles... Otherwise, we have other makes, less expensive."

The Gallic figure turned gracefully and got from a shelf another dozen cases of revolvers.

"This one here, m'sieur, is priced at thirty roubles. It's not expensive, especially as the exchange rate has seriously fallen, and customs duties, m'sieur, rise by the hour. M'sieur, I swear to God, I am a conservative, but even I am already starting to grumble! For goodness' sake, the exchange rate and customs duties mean that firearms now can be acquired only by the rich! Paupers must make do only with Tula* weapons and phosphorus matches, but Tula weapons – they're a disaster! Try shooting your wife with a Tula revolver, and you'll get hit in the shoulder..."

Sigayev suddenly felt pain and self-pity at the thought that he would be dead and would not witness the torment of the traitress. Vengeance is only sweet when you have the opportunity to see and feel its fruits – but what is the point if he will be lying in a coffin, aware of nothing?

"Maybe I should do it differently," he reflected. "I should kill him, then stay and watch the funeral, and kill myself after the funeral... However, they would arrest me before the funeral and confiscate the weapon... So then: I shall kill him and let her live. I... I for the time being shall not kill myself, but be arrested. I shall always be able to kill myself. Arrest would be even better, so that on interrogation

I would have the opportunity to disclose to the authorities and society the baseness of her behaviour. If I kill myself, then perhaps she, with her characteristic mendacity and impudence, will accuse me before everyone, and society will excuse her behaviour and, perhaps, laugh at me. But if I stay alive, then…"

A minute later he thought:

"Yes, if I kill myself, then perhaps they will judge me and will suspect me of small-mindedness… And besides, why kill myself? That's the first point. Secondly, to shoot oneself is to be a coward. So then: I shall kill him, keep her alive and myself go to trial. They will judge me, and she will appear in the capacity of a witness… I imagine her confusion, her shame, when my attorney cross-examines her. The sympathies of the court, the public and the press will of course be with me…"

He pondered, while the salesman laid out the goods before him, considering it his duty to interest the buyer.

"These are English of a new make, only recently received," he chattered. "But I assure you, m'sieur, all these makes pale beside the Smith & Wesson. The other day – you've probably already read – an officer acquired from us a Smith & Wesson revolver. He shot the lover, and – what do you think? – the bullet went right past, then passed through a bronze lamp, then the piano, and from the piano ricocheted to kill the lapdog and graze his wife. The effect was brilliant, and made the honour of our firm. The officer is now under arrest. They will prosecute him, of course, and exile him to hard labour. First of all, we still have too much obsolete legislation; secondly, m'sieur, the court is always on the side of the lover. Why? Very simple, m'sieur! Judges, barristers, prosecutors and defence attorneys themselves live with other women, and for them life would be more peaceful if there was even one fewer husband in Russia. Society would be pleasant if the government exiled all husbands to Sakhalin.* Oh, m'sieur, you don't know what indignation I feel about the contemporary corruption of manners! To love someone else's wife is now just as accepted as to smoke his cigarettes or to read his books. With each year our trade becomes worse and worse – it does not mean that there are fewer lovers, but that husbands accept their circumstances and fear prosecution and penal servitude."

The salesman glanced around him and whispered:

"And whose fault is it, m'sieur? The government's!"

"To go to Sakhalin because of some swine is also not rational," thought Sigayev. "If I'm sent to hard labour, it would only give my wife the opportunity to marry again and dupe her second husband. She will rejoice… And so: I shall let *her* stay alive, shall not kill myself, and *him* also… I shall not kill. I must think up something more intelligent and subtle. I shall punish them with contempt and initiate a scandalous divorce case…"

"Here, m'sieur, is an even newer make," said the salesman, getting down a dozen revolvers from the shelf. "I draw your attention to the unusual design of the lock…"

After his decision, Sigayev no longer needed a revolver, but the salesman nevertheless became more and more animated, and kept putting samples before him. The wronged husband grew ashamed that because of him the salesman's efforts had all been in vain… he had got carried away to no purpose, smiled, wasted his time…

"Very well, in that case…" he muttered, "I shall call in later or… or send someone."

He did not see the expression on the face of the salesman, but, so as to ease the awkwardness a little, felt obliged to buy something. But what on earth could he buy? He looked at the walls of the shop, seeking something cheaper, and his gaze rested on a green net that was hanging near the door.

"That… what's that?" he asked.

"It's a net for catching quail."

"And how much is it?"

"Eight roubles, m'sieur."

"Wrap it up for me…"

The wronged husband paid eight roubles, took the net and, feeling even more wronged, left the shop.

Fat and Thin

TWO FRIENDS MET AT THE NIKOLAYEVSKY railway station.* One was fat, the other thin. The fat one had only just dined at the station, and his lips, still smeared with butter, shone like ripe cherries. He smelt of sherry and *fleur d'orange.** The thin one had only just stepped out of a carriage and was loaded with suitcases, packages and boxes. He smelt of ham and coffee grounds. From behind his back peered a slim woman with a long chin – his wife – and a tall student with a half-closed eye – his son.

"Porfiry!" exclaimed the fat man, having sighted the thin one. "Is it you? My dear fellow! How many years has it been!"

"Good lord!" exclaimed the thin one in amazement. "Misha! Friend of my childhood! Where have you come from?"

The friends kissed three times and fixed their eyes tearfully on each other. Both were pleasantly stunned.

"My dear man," began the thin one after kissing. "So unexpected! What a surprise! Well, let me have a good look at you! Such a handsome man, as you always were! Such a dear soul and a bit of a dandy! Good gracious! Well, how are you? Rich? Married? I am already married, as you see. This is my wife Louisa, née Wanzenbach... a Lutheran... And this is my son Nafanayil, a third-year student. This, Nafanya, is a childhood friend of mine! We were at school together!"

Nafanayil hesitated for a moment and took off his cap.

"We were at school together," repeated the thin one. "Remember how we teased you? We called you Herostratus,* because you once burned a schoolbook with a cigarette, and I was called Ephialtes,* because I loved to snitch on people. Ho-ho-ho. We were rogues! Don't be shy, Nafanya! Come a little closer... And this is my wife, née Wanzenbach... a Lutheran."

Nafanayil thought for a moment and hid behind his father's back.

"Well, how are things, old fellow?" asked the fat one, looking delightedly at his friend. "Where do you work? How have you got on?"

"I am in the civil service, old man! This is already the second year that I have been a collegiate assessor, and I have been awarded the Order of St Stanislav. The pay is bad, but... well, it doesn't matter! My wife gives music lessons, and I make wooden cigarette cases on the side. Excellent cigarette cases! I sell them for a rouble apiece. If someone takes ten or more, I give a discount. We get along somehow. I've now been transferred here, you know, as head of my section... I shall be working here. Well, what about you? I suppose you are already a state councillor? Are you?"

"No, dear man, raise me a little higher," said the fat one. "I am already a privy councillor... I have two stars on my decoration."

The thin one suddenly grew pale. He froze, but his face soon creased into the widest of smiles. He felt as if sparks were pouring from his face and eyes. He shrivelled up, bent and grew thinner. His suitcases, packages and boxes shrivelled up and looked battered... The long chin of his wife became even longer. Nafanayil stood to attention and began doing up the buttons of his tunic.

"I, Your Excellency... Very honoured, sir! The friend, I may say, of my youth has suddenly turned into such a dignitary, sir. Hee-hee-hee!" He giggled obsequiously.

"Well, enough of that," grimaced the fat one. "Why adopt that tone? We are childhood friends – so why the servility?"

"For goodness' sake... That you, sir..." giggled the thin one, shrivelling up even more. "The kind attention of Your Excellency... is like a refreshing dew. This here, Your Excellency, is my son Nafanayil... wife Louisa, a Lutheran, as it were..."

The fat one seemed to want to protest, but so much reverence, sweetness and respect was written on the face of the thin one that the privy councillor felt sick. He turned away from the thin one and extended his hand in farewell.

The thin one squeezed three of his friend's fingers, bowed ingratiatingly and giggled like a Chinese: "Hee-hee-hee." His wife smiled. Nafanayil clicked his heels and dropped his cap. All three felt pleasantly overwhelmed.

The Wallet

THREE STROLLING PLAYERS – Smirnov, Popov and Balabaykin – were walking one beautiful morning along the railway tracks when they found a wallet. Opening it, they saw to their great amazement and delight twenty banknotes, six winning tickets of the second lottery and a cheque for three thousand roubles. They cried "hurrah", then sat down on the embankment and abandoned themselves to rapture.

"So how much of this does each of us get?" asked Smirnov, counting the money. "Friends! Five thousand, four hundred and forty-five roubles each! My darlings, this really is money to die for!"

"I'm not so glad about it for myself," said Balabaykin, "as I am for you, my dear fellows. Now you'll not starve or go barefoot. I am glad for art... First of all, friends, I shall go to Moscow, straight to the best tailor, who will make me, my friends, a wardrobe... I don't want to play the role of peasants... I shall switch to the role of fops and dandies. I shall buy a top hat. Fops wear a grey top hat."

"First, we should celebrate this good luck by having something to drink and eat," suggested the *jeune premier** Popov. "After all, for almost three days now we have lived on cold foods, so we should have something like... Well?..."

"Yes, it wouldn't be bad, my darlings..." agreed Smirnov. "There is a lot of money, but nothing to eat, my precious ones. Here's what, Popov my treasure. You, as the youngest and fittest of us, be an angel, take a rouble from the wallet and go for provisions... The village is over th-e-r-e! Do you see the church glimmering white behind the burial mound? It would be about five versts, not more... Do you see? It's a big village, and you'll find everything there... Buy a bottle of vodka, a pound of sausage, two loaves of bread and some salted herring, and we'll wait for you here, dear boy..."

Popov took a rouble and prepared to leave. With tears in his eyes, Smirnov embraced him, kissed him three times, made the sign of the cross and called him a darling, an angel, a sweetheart... Balabaykin also embraced him, swearing eternal friendship, and only after a stream of the tenderest and most touching outpourings did Popov set out from the embankment and direct his steps towards the darkening village in the distance.

"This really is such luck!" he reflected on the way. "I didn't have a penny, and now I have a fortune. I shall go to my home in Kostroma,* get together a company and build my theatre there. However... for five thousand nowadays you can't build even a decent barn. Now, if the money were all mine, well, then it would be a different matter... I could build such a grand theatre that it would do me honour. Strictly speaking, Smirnov and Balabaykin – what kind of actors are they? They are untalented, pigs in skullcaps, blockheads... They would waste the money on trifles, but I would bring benefit to my homeland and immortalize myself... That's what I would do... So I shall go and put poison in the vodka. They will die, but then there will be a theatre in Kostroma such as Russia has never known. Someone, I think it was Mac Mahon,* said that the end justifies the means, and Mac Mahon was a great man."

While he was walking and reasoning thus, his companions Smirnov and Balabaykin were sitting and talking as follows:

"Our friend Popov is a fine fellow," said Smirnov with tears in his eyes. "I love him, and highly rate his talent... I love him, but... do you know?... this money will destroy him... He'll either turn to drink or engage in shady practices and come to grief. He is still too young to have such money, my darling, my own dear friend..."

"Yes," agreed Balabaykin, kissing Smirnov. "Why give this money to a silly youth? You and I are another matter... We are family men, responsible... To us an extra rouble means a lot." He paused. "Do you know what, brother? Let's not stand here talking and sentimentalizing: let's just kill him!... Then you and I will get eight thousand each. We'll kill him and say in Moscow that he fell under a train... I love him too, I adore him, but surely the interests of art, I think, come before everything else. Besides, he is third-rate and stupid, like this sleeper."

"What are you saying?!" Smirnov said, frightened. "He is such a fine man, honourable... Though, on the other hand, frankly speaking, my dear fellow, he is a complete pig, a f-o-o-o-l, a schemer, a scandalmonger, a scoundrel... If we were indeed to kill him, he himself would thank us, my dear, my good friend... And so that it would not be so hurtful to him, we shall place a moving obituary in the Moscow newspapers. It would be the comradely thing to do."

It was no sooner said than done. When Popov returned from the village with the provisions, his comrades embraced him with tears in their eyes, kissed him, assured him for a long time that he was a great artist, then suddenly fell on him and killed him. So as to hide the traces of the crime, they put the body on the rails... After dividing the money, Smirnov and Balabaykin, deeply moved, exchanging tender words, began to eat, in full confidence that their crime would remain undetected... But virtue always triumphs, and vice is punished. The poison that Popov had put into the bottle of vodka was fast-acting: no sooner had they had a second glass each than they already lay lifeless on the sleepers. An hour later, crows were flying over them, cawing.

The moral: when actors with tears in their eyes talk about their dear comrades, about friendship and mutual "solidarity", when they embrace and kiss you, don't get too carried away.

Misfortune

THE DIRECTOR OF THE REGIONAL BANK Pyotr Semyonych, a bookkeeper, his assistant and two employees were sent for the night to jail. The day after the commotion, the merchant Avdeyev, a member of the bank's auditing committee, was sitting with his friends in his shop and saying:

"It's really God's will. One cannot escape fate. Now we are eating caviar, but tomorrow, look – prison, the beggar's bowl and perhaps even death. Anything can happen. Take now, for example, Pyotr Semyonych..."

He was talking and screwing up his small drunken eyes while his friends were drinking, eating caviar and listening. After describing the shame and isolation of Pyotr Semyonych, who even yesterday was influential and respected by all, Avdeyev continued with a sigh:

"The cat will cry for the mouse's tears.* It serves them right, these crooks! They knew how to rob, the sons of bitches, so let them now answer for it."

"Watch out, Ivan Danilych, that you yourself aren't caught!" observed one of his friends.

"What could I be caught for?"

"For this. The others robbed, but what was the auditing committee doing? After all, surely you signed the accounts?"

"So what, wasn't it a simple thing?" smirked Avdeyev. "I signed! They brought the accounts to me in the shop, so I signed. Was there really anything to understand? Whatever they give me, I sign it all. If you now write that I murdered a man, I shall even sign that. I don't have time to look into everything, and I don't see without glasses."

After discussing the collapse of the bank and the fate of Pyotr Semyonych, Avdeyev and his friends set off to a party at the home of an acquaintance whose wife was celebrating her name day.

At the party all the guests spoke only about the collapse of the bank. Avdeyev got more excited than anyone, and assured them that he had long had a foreboding of the collapse, and even two years before knew that all was not well at the bank. While they ate *pirog*,* he described some ten illegal operations that were well known to him.

"If you knew, why didn't you report them?" asked an officer who was present.

"Not just I, but the whole town knew..." smirked Avdeyev. "But there was no time to go to court. There you are!"

Having rested after the party, he dined and rested once again, then set off to vespers at his church, where he was an elder. After vespers he again went to the party and played préférence* until midnight. All seemed to be well.

But when Avdeyev returned home after midnight, the cook, opening the door for him, was pale and trembling and could not utter a single word. His wife, Yelizaveta Trofimovna – a fat, podgy old woman with dishevelled grey hair – was sitting on the sofa in the reception room, her whole body trembling and eyes staring vacantly like a drunk's. Near her, with a glass of water, also looking pale and extremely worried, bustled her eldest son, the schoolboy Vasily.

"What is it?" asked Avdeyev, looking angrily askance at the stove. (His family was often affected by the fumes.)

"An investigator has just been here with the police," replied Vasily. "They searched the house."

Avdeyev looked around. Cupboards, drawers, tables – all bore traces of a recent search. Avdeyev stood motionless for a moment, as if in a stupor, understanding nothing, then all his insides began to tremble and grow heavy, his left leg became numb, and, unable to bear the shaking, he lay face downwards on the sofa. He could hear how all his insides were turning over and how, against his will, his left leg was knocking against the back of the sofa.

In a matter of two or three minutes he recalled all his past life, yet could not find a single transgression that would warrant the attentions of the judicial powers...

"This is all just nonsense..." he said, rising. "I must have been slandered. I shall have to lodge a complaint tomorrow, so that they don't dare to do this same thing again..."

The next morning, after a sleepless night, Avdeyev, as always, set off to the shop. The customers brought him the news that the preceding night the prosecutor had sentenced his friend the director, and the bank's clerk, to prison. This news did not trouble Avdeyev. He was sure he had been slandered, and that if he now lodged a complaint the investigator would have to answer for the search of the night before.

After nine o'clock he ran to the office of the secretary, who was the only educated man in the whole department.

"Vladimir Stepanych, what's this all about?" he began, stooping to the ear of the secretary. "Some people have been stealing, but what has this to do with me? What's the reason? My dear man," his voice dropped to a whisper, "last night my house was searched! Really and truly... Were they mad, or what? Why did they trouble me?"

"Well, you shouldn't have been a fool," quietly replied the secretary. "Before signing, you should have looked..."

"What do you mean, 'looked'? If I'd looked at those accounts for even a thousand years I wouldn't have understood anything! I don't understand a damn thing! What kind of bookkeeper am I? They were bringing them to me and I was signing."

"I beg your pardon. Besides that, you and your whole committee were seriously compromised. You took nineteen thousand from the bank without any security."

"Good lord!" said Avdeyev in amazement. "Am I the only one in debt? Surely the whole town is in debt! I pay interest and will return the loan. For Heaven's sake! And besides, let's be honest, could I really have taken this money by myself? Pyotr Semyonych insisted that I take it. 'Take it,' he says, 'take more. If,' he says, 'you don't take it, then it means you don't trust us and should step aside. You,' he says, 'take it and build your father a mill.' So I took it."

"Well, there you are: only children and fools can reason like that. In any case, *señor*, there's no reason for you to worry. You won't avoid trial, of course, but you'll probably be acquitted."

The indifference and calm tone of the secretary had a soothing effect on Avdeyev. Returning to his shop and finding his friends there, he again drank, ate caviar and philosophized. He had already almost forgotten about the search, and was concerned about only one thing, which he could not fail to notice: his left leg was somehow strangely growing numb, and for some reason his digestion was troubling him.

In the evening of that same day, fate delivered one more heavy blow to Avdeyev: in an extraordinary session of the Duma,* all the bankers, including Avdeyev, were barred from the council, as persons on trial or under investigation. In the morning he received a notice inviting him to relinquish immediately the position of church elder.

Then Avdeyev lost count of the blows that fate gave him. Strange, unprecedented days quickly flashed by, one after another, and each day brought with it some new, unexpected worry. Among other things, the investigator brought him a summons. He returned home offended, red-faced after seeing the investigator.

"He badgered me without mercy: why did I sign? I signed, that's all there is to it! Did I really do it on purpose? They brought it to the shop, so I signed it. I can't read very easily."

Some young people with expressionless faces arrived, sealed up the shop and made an inventory of all the furniture in the house. Suspecting that this was part of a plan, and again not feeling any guilt, the offended Avdeyev took to running to the office and complaining. For whole hours he waited in entrance halls, composed long petitions, cried, swore. In reply to his complaints, the prosecutor and investigator spoke to him calmly and reasonably:

"Come when you are summoned, but we have no time now."

And others replied:

"It's nothing to do with us."

The secretary himself, an educated man, who Avdeyev thought would be able to help him, only shrugged and said:

"It's your own fault. You shouldn't have been such a fool."

The old man kept busy, but his leg suffered numbness as before, and his digestion grew worse. Wearied by idleness and compelled by need, he decided he would go to his father at the mill, or to his brother, and occupy himself in the milling trade, but he was not permitted to leave the town. His family left to stay with his father, and he remained alone.

Day after day flashed by. Without his family, without work and without money, the former elder, a venerable and respected man, for whole days frequented the shops of his friends, drank, ate and listened to advice. In order to kill time, mornings and evenings he went to church. Gazing at the icons for whole hours, he was not praying, but thinking. His conscience was clear, and he explained his situation as being due to an error and misunderstanding. In his opinion it was all because the investigators and officials were young and inexperienced – it seemed to him that if some old judge could talk to him heart to heart and in detail, all would get back to normal. He did not understand his judges, and the judges, he felt, did not understand him...

Day after day flew by, and finally, after a long, exhausting delay, the time of the trial arrived. Avdeyev borrowed fifty roubles, stocked up on alcohol for his leg and herbs for his stomach, and went to the town where the court of justice was to be found.

The trial lasted a week and a half. All during the trial Avdeyev, as becomes a venerable and innocent victim, sat unhappily, but with composure and dignity, among his co-accused and listened, understanding nothing at all. His mood was hostile. He was angry that they kept him so long in court, that there was nowhere to get Lenten food and that his lawyer did not understand him and spoke at cross-purposes. He thought the judges acted improperly. They paid almost no attention to Avdeyev, and addressed him only once in three days. The questions they asked him were of such a kind that, answering them, Avdeyev each time roused the public to laughter. When he tried to talk about his expenses, his losses, and even how he hoped to recover his legal costs, his lawyer turned away and made an incomprehensible grimace. The public laughed, and the chairman severely ruled that it be dismissed. In his final statement, he said not what he had told his attorney, but quite the opposite, which also aroused laughter.

In those terrible hours when the jurors were deliberating in their room, he sat angrily in the buffet without thinking at all about the jurors. He did not understand why they were deliberating so long if it was all so clear, and what they needed from him.

When he got hungry, he asked the usher to bring him something cheap, suitable for Lent. For forty copecks he was given some cold fish and carrots. He ate and immediately felt how the fish lay in his stomach like a heavy lump. He began to belch, and felt heartburn and pain…

Then, when he was listening to the foreman of the jury, who was reading some of the points at issue, his entrails turned over, his body was bathed in cold sweat, his left leg went numb. He did not hear, understood nothing and suffered unbearably from finding it impossible to listen to the foreman either sitting or lying. Finally, when they told him and his co-accused to sit down, the court prosecutor rose and said something incomprehensible. As if springing up from the ground, policemen with drawn swords appeared from somewhere and surrounded all the accused. Avdeyev was ordered to stand and go.

Now he understood that he had been convicted and was being taken into custody, but he was neither frightened nor surprised. His stomach was in such disorder that he was not at all bothered about custody.

"Does it mean they now won't let us return to the room?" he asked one of the others who had been convicted. "I have three roubles of cash in the room and a hundred grams of fresh tea."

He spent the night in detention, felt discomfort all night because of the fish and thought about the three roubles and hundred grams of tea. Early in the morning, when the sky was getting blue, he was ordered to dress and go. Two soldiers with bayonets took him to prison. At no other time had the streets of the town seemed to him so long and endless. He walked not on the pavement, but in the middle of the road, through melting, muddy snow. His insides were still warring with the fish, his left leg was numb. He had forgotten his galoshes either in court or while in detention, and his feet were cold.

Five days later all the accused were brought to court to hear the sentence. Avdeyev learnt that he had been sentenced to exile for life in Tobolsk Province. But this neither frightened nor surprised him. For some reason it seemed to him that the trial had not yet ended, that the delay was being further extended, and that the real "decision" was still to come... He remained in prison and every day awaited this decision.

It was only six months later, when his wife and son Vasily came to say goodbye to him, when in the gaunt, badly dressed old woman he barely recognized the formerly well-fed and stout Yelizaveta Trofimovna, and when instead of a school uniform he saw his son wearing a short threadbare jacket and rough cotton trousers, that he understood his fate was sealed, and that whatever new "decision" there yet would be, he would no longer recover his past. And for the first time in the whole period of the trial and his imprisonment, his face lost its serious expression and he began to cry bitterly.

The Custodian in Custody

HAVE YOU EVER SEEN how they load up a donkey? Usually they pile everything imaginable on the poor donkey, without considering either the weight or the volume: kitchen stuff, furniture, beds, barrels, babies in sacks... so that the loaded animal resembles a huge shapeless lump where the tips of its hooves are barely visible. A similar sight was presented by the prosecutor of the Khlamov circuit court, Alexei Timofeyevich Balbinski, when, after the bell had rung for the third time, he hurried to find a place in a carriage. He was loaded from head to foot... bundles of provisions, boxes, tins, suitcases, a bottle of something, a woman's cloak and... the devil only knows what else! The sweat was streaming from his red face, his legs were bent, his eyes showed the suffering he was undergoing. Behind him, carrying a multi-coloured umbrella, walked his wife Nastasya Lvovna, a small freckled blonde with a lower jaw that jutted prominently forward and bulging eyes exactly like a young pike's when it is pulled from the water on a hook... After wandering for a long time through the carriages, the prosecutor at last found a place. He piled the baggage up on the bench, wiped the sweat from his brow and made for the exit.

"Where are you going?" his wife asked him.

"I want to go to the station, my dear... to have a glass of vodka..."

"Don't even think about it... Sit down..."

Balbinski sighed and obediently sat down.

"Hold this basket... It's the crockery..."

Balbinski took the big basket in his hand and gazed sadly out of the window... At the fourth stop his wife sent him into the station for hot water, and there at the buffet he met his friend Flyazhkin, a colleague of the chairman of the Plinsk circuit court, who had persuaded him to go abroad with him.

"My dear man, what is all this?" said Flyazhkin, homing in on him. "This really is a swinish trick, to put it mildly. You suggested we go together in one carriage, but for some devilish reason you're in third class! Why are you travelling third class? Are you short of money, or what?"

Balbinski waved his hand and blinked.

"It's all the same to me now," he muttered. "I would even go in the tender. When I look at my situation, I think I'm going to end up… I shall throw myself under a train… You can't imagine, my dear man, how my better half has worn me out! I mean, she's so worn me out that it's amazing I'm still alive. My God! The weather is splendid… this air… this whole expanse, nature… all the conditions for a delightful life. Just the thought that we're going abroad should be enough to send me into ecstasies of happiness… But no! Evil fate had to fasten that treasure on my neck! And how that same fate has mocked me! In order to get away from my wife I claimed to have a liver disorder… I wanted to make off abroad… All winter I dreamt of freedom, and even in my daydreams I saw myself as a bachelor. And what happened? She insisted on going with me! I tried everything I could – nothing worked! 'I shall go, and that's the end of it,' she said. Nothing I said made any difference! Well, so we went… I suggested we go second class… Not for anything! 'How can we waste money like that?' she said. I gave her all the reasons… I told her we had the money, and that our prestige would suffer if we were to travel third class, that it was stuffy and stank… She wouldn't listen! She was gripped by the demon of economy… Now, take our baggage, for example… Why do we have to take such a load of things with us? Why all those bundles, boxes, trunks and other rubbish? It's not enough to put ten *pood** in the baggage wagon, we even have to occupy four benches in our carriage. The conductors keep asking us to clear a place for others – the passengers are angry, she starts to argue with them… It's shameful! Can you believe it? I feel as if I'm burning in some fire! But to get away from her – God forbid! She doesn't let me get a step away. I sit beside her with a huge basket on my knees. Now she's sent me for hot water. Well, is it seemly for a court prosecutor to walk around carrying a copper teapot? After all, some of my witnesses and defendants are probably travelling on the train. Prestige goes to the devil! But this, dear man, is a lesson to me for the future. Now I know what personal freedom means! Sometimes, you know, you're moved to have a person arrested for no reason at all. Well, now I understand… It's been driven home… I understand what it means to be under arrest! Oh, how I understand!"

"You'd probably be glad to be released on bail?" smirked Flyazhkin.

"Delighted! Would you believe it? Though I'm not rich, I would happily pay a bail of ten thousand… But I'm going… I have to rush… to be reprimanded!"

At Verzhbolovo,* Flyazhkin, walking on the platform early in the morning, saw the sleepy face of Balbinski through the window of the third-class carriage.

"Wait a moment," the prosecutor said, motioning to him. "My wife is still asleep, she has not woken up. When she's asleep I'm relatively free… I can't leave the carriage, but for the moment at least I can put the basket on the floor… Thanks for small mercies. Oh, yes! Didn't I tell you? I'm delighted!"

"Why?"

"Two boxes and one bag were stolen from us… So the load is all the lighter… Yesterday we ate the goose and all the *piroshki*… I ate more on purpose, so that there would be less baggage… And what air we have in the carriage! You could cut it with a knife… Pfff… This is not travelling, but sheer torture…"

The prosecutor turned around and looked angrily at his sleeping spouse.

"My Varvarka," he whispered. "You are such a tormentor, Herodias!* Will I, an unfortunate one, ever escape from you, Xanthippe?* Would you believe it, Ivan Nikitich? Sometimes I close my eyes and dream – and if wishes could come true, she would fall into my clutches as a defendant. I think I'd banish her to penal servitude! But… she's waking up… Shhh…"

In an instant the prosecutor assumed an innocent look and took the basket in his hands.

At Eidkuhnen,* going for hot water, he looked happier.

"Two more boxes have been stolen!" he boasted to Flyazhkin. And we've eaten all the *kalatches*...* The load's even lighter now..."

At Königsberg he seemed transformed. Running in the morning to Flyazhkin's carriage, he collapsed on the seat and burst into happy laughter.

"My dear man! Ivan Nikitich! Let me embrace you! Excuse me for treating you so informally, but I am so happy, so wickedly happy! I... am... free! Do you understand? Freeee! My wife has gone!"

"What do you mean, 'gone'?"

"She left the carriage during the night, and until now there's been no sign of her. She may have run away or fell under the carriage, or perhaps remained at some station... In a word, she's gone!... My angel!"

"But listen," said Flyazhkin in alarm. "In that case, you have to send a telegram."

"God forbid! I mean, I now feel such freedom that I can't even describe it to you! Let's go and walk on the platform... breathe the air of freedom!"

The friends left the carriage and strode back and forth on the platform. As the prosecutor walked, he accompanied each deep breath with the exclamation: "How good it is! How easy to breathe! Are there really people who always live like this?"

"Do you know what, brother?" he suggested. "I'll now move to your carriage. We'll lounge around and start to live like bachelors."

The prosecutor dashed to his carriage to get his things. Two minutes later he emerged from the carriage no longer beaming, but pale and stunned, with the copper teapot in his hands. He tottered and clutched his chest.

"She's back!" He waved his hand when he saw Flyazhkin's enquiring look. "It seems that during the night she mixed up the carriages and by mistake ended up in another. It's all over, brother!"

The prosecutor stood in front of Flyazhkin and fastened on him a gaze full of sadness and despair. Tears welled up in his eyes. A minute passed in silence.

"Do you know what?" Flyazhkin said, tenderly pulling him by a button. "If I were in your position... I would leg it..."

"What do you mean?"

"Run away – that's all... Otherwise, to look at you, you'd just wither away."

"Run... run..." thought the prosecutor. "That's an idea! Here's what I'll do, brother: board the oncoming train and be off! Later I can tell her I got onto it by mistake. Well, goodbye... We'll meet in Paris..."

Terrors

DURING ALL THE YEARS that I have lived in this world, I have only been really frightened three times.

The first real fear, which caused my hair to bristle and my flesh to creep, was caused by a trivial but strange phenomenon. Once, having nothing better to do, I drove on a July evening to the posting station for the newspapers. The evening was calm, warm and almost sultry, like all those monotonous July evenings which, once they have set in, follow one another in a regular, continuous succession for a week or two, sometimes even longer, and then suddenly are brought to an end by a wild thunderstorm and a drenching downpour that refreshes everything for a long time.

The sun had already long before set, and an unbroken grey shadow lay over all the earth. A honey-sweet scent of grass and flowers hung in the motionless, stagnant air.

I was driving a simple dray-cart. Behind me, with his head resting on a sack of oats, quietly snored the gardener's son, Pashka, a boy of about eight whom I had taken with me just in case I needed someone to keep an eye on the horse. Our route lay along a narrow track, as straight as a ruler, which lay hidden like a big snake in the tall, thick rye. The glow from the sunset was growing dim; a bright streak of light cut through a narrow, clumsily placed cloud that resembled now a boat, now a man wrapped in a blanket…

I drove two or three versts, and there, against the pale background of the twilight, tall, shapely poplars began to appear, one after another. Behind them shone the river, and before me suddenly, like magic, stretched out a rich panorama. I had to stop the horse, as our straight road came abruptly to an end and went down along a steep incline bordered by shrubbery. We stood on the mountain, and below us was a big pit, a large expanse full of dusky, fantastic shapes. At the bottom of this pit, on a wide plain guarded by poplars and caressed by the glow from the river, huddled a village. It was now asleep… Its huts, belfried church and trees emerged from the grey twilight and were reflected darkly on the smooth surface of the river.

I woke up Pashka, so that he would not fall out of the cart, and carefully began to descend.

"Have we arrived at Lukovo?" asked Pashka, lazily raising his head.

"Yes. Hold the reins!…"

I led the horse down the mountain and looked at the village. From the very first glance my attention was drawn to something strange: at the very top of the belfry, in a tiny window between the dome and the bells, glimmered a little light. This light, like the light from a dying icon lamp, now faded away for an instant, now brightly flared up again. Where was it coming from? I could not understand what was producing it. It could not have been burning behind the window, because there could be neither icons nor icon lamps up there in the belfry: there, as I knew, there were only beams, dust and cobwebs. It was hard to get up there, because the way through the tower must be securely sealed.

The most likely explanation was that this little light was the reflection of another one outside, but however I strained my eyes I could not see, besides this light, a single speck of any other light in the vast expanse that lay before me. There was no moon. It could not have been the reflection of the last pale ray of sunset, because the window with the little light did not face west, but east. These and other such thoughts passed through my mind while I was leading the horse down the slope. At the bottom, I sat on the cart and once again looked at the little light. As before, it was glimmering and flashing.

"It's strange," I thought, lost in conjecture. "Very strange."

And, little by little, I was seized by an unpleasant feeling. At first I thought that this was annoyance at being unable to explain a simple phenomenon, but then, when I suddenly turned away from the little light in horror and grabbed Pashka with one hand, it became clear that I was overcome with fear... I was gripped by a feeling of loneliness, melancholy and horror, as if I had been thrown against my will into a dark pit, where I stood face to face with the bell tower, which was staring at me with its red eye.

"Pasha!" I cried, closing my eyes in terror.

"What is it?"

"Pasha, what is that, shining on the belfry?"

Pasha looked over my shoulder at the belfry and yawned.

"Who knows?"

This short exchange with the boy calmed me a little, but not for long. Pashka, noticing my agitation, directed his big eyes at the light, looked once more at me, then again at the light...

"I'm afraid!" he whispered.

Right away, beside myself with fear, I put one arm around the boy, pressed myself to him and gave the horse a flick with the whip.

"It's silly!" I said to myself. "I am frightened by this only because I can't understand it... Anything we can't understand is mysterious and therefore frightening."

I tried to convince myself, but at the same time did not stop urging on the horse. After arriving at the posting station I intentionally spent a whole hour chatting with the supervisor and read two or three newspapers, but my disquiet still did not ease. On the return trip the little light was no longer visible, but then the silhouettes of the huts, of the poplars and the mountain, which we had to ascend, appeared in clearer outline. But to this day I still do not know why the light was there.

Another fear I experienced was caused by no less trivial an occurrence. I was returning from a romantic rendezvous. It was one o'clock in the morning, a time when nature is usually plunged into the deepest and sweetest early-morning sleep. But at this particular time nature was not sleeping, and the night could not have been called "peaceful". Corncrakes, quails, nightingales and sandpipers were calling; crickets and burrowing insects were chattering. A light mist was drifting over the grass, and in the sky clouds were racing past the moon as fast as they could. Nature was not asleep, as if fearing to miss the best moments of its life.

I was walking along a narrow path on the very edge of a railway embankment. The moonlight was gleaming on the rails, on which a dew was already lying. Big shadows of the clouds were continually running past along the embankment. Far in the distance a dim green light was peacefully glowing.

"It means all is well," I thought, looking at it.

My soul was quiet, calm and at rest. I was walking from my rendezvous; there was nowhere for me to hurry to; I was not sleepy, and felt health and youth with every breath and each step that I took, and I heard indistinctly the monotonous hum of the night. I do not remember what I was feeling then, but I remember that I was happy, very happy!

After walking no more than a few versts, I suddenly heard behind me a monotonous rumble like the murmur of a big stream. With each second it grew louder and louder, and sounded nearer and nearer. I glanced back: a hundred paces from me was the dark outline of the grove from which I had just emerged. There the embankment turned to the right in a graceful semicircle and disappeared into the trees. I stopped in perplexity and stood waiting. Just then there appeared at the bend a big black shape that came rushing noisily towards me and flew past along the rails with the speed of a bird. Less than half a minute later the shape vanished, its rumble mingling with the hum of the night.

It was an ordinary goods wagon. In itself, it was nothing special, but its appearance on its own, without a locomotive, and moreover at night, puzzled me. Where could it have got the power to rush with such terrible speed along the rails? From where and to where was it flying?

Had I been superstitious, I would have believed that it had been demons and witches on their way to a witches' sabbath, and would have kept on walking, but I could not explain the incident at all. I could not believe my eyes, and was tangled in conjecture, like a fly in a cobweb...

I suddenly felt that I was alone, all alone in a vast expanse, that the night, which was by now hostile, was looking me in the face and directing my steps. All sounds, the cries of the birds and the whispers of the trees now seemed sinister, existing only in order to frighten my imagination. I rushed from the scene like a madman, and, failing to understand, kept running, trying to go faster and faster. And just then I heard what I had not paid attention to earlier: namely, the mournful humming of the telegraph wires.

"The devil knows what this is!" I said, feeling ashamed of myself. "It's faint-heartedness, stupidity!..."

But the faint-heartedness was stronger than common sense. I eased my pace only when I reached the green light, where I saw a darkened signal box and, near it on the embankment, a human figure, probably a guard.

"Did you see it?" I asked, panting.

"See what? Who are you?"

"A wagon went by here!..."

"I saw it..." the man said reluctantly. "It broke away from a goods train. There is an incline a hundred and twenty-one versts from here. The train was pulling it up the mountain. The chains on the rear wagon didn't hold, so it broke away and rolled back down... Just try and catch it now!..."

The strange incident was explained, and lost its air of surrealness. I regained confidence and continued on my way.

The third intense fear I happened to experience occurred once in early spring when I was returning from hunting. It was at dusk. The forest road was covered with puddles from the rain that had just stopped, and the mud made a squelching sound under my feet. The crimson glow of evening was filtering through the trees, illuminating the white trunks of the birch trees and their new leaves. I was weary, and could hardly move.

Five or six versts from home, going along the forest road, I unexpectedly came upon a big black dog of the Newfoundland breed. As it ran past, the hound looked intently at me, straight in my face, and ran further on.

"Fine dog..." I thought. "Whose is it?"

I looked back. The dog was standing ten paces away, its eyes fixed on me. For a minute we silently studied each other; then the dog, probably flattered by my attention, slowly came up to me wagging its tail...

I walked on. The dog followed.

"Whose dog is this?" I asked myself. "Where has it come from?"

I knew all the landowners for thirty or forty versts around, and knew their dogs. Not one of them had a Newfoundland dog like this. So how did it come to be here, in a dense forest, on a road along which no one travelled and which was only used for gathering firewood? It could hardly have become separated from some passer-by, because on that road there was nowhere for the local inhabitants to go.

I sat down on a stump to rest and began to look closely at my travelling companion. He also sat down, raised his head and stared fixedly at me... He looked at me without blinking. I do not know whether it was the influence of the stillness, the forest shadows and sounds, or perhaps the result of exhaustion, but the fixed look of this ordinary dog's eyes was suddenly terrifying to me. I remembered about Faust and his bulldog, and that nervous people suffering from fatigue are sometimes susceptible to hallucinations. That was enough to make me rise quickly and continue hurriedly on my way. The dog followed me...

"Go away!" I shouted.

The hound probably liked my voice, because it gaily leapt up and ran on ahead of me.

"Go away!" I cried once again.

The hound glanced back, looked intently at me and gaily wagged its tail. It was evidently amused by my menacing tone. I should have patted it, but I kept thinking about Faust's bulldog, and the sense of fear became more and more intense... Darkness was setting in, and finally I felt disorientated, and each time the dog ran up to me and beat its tail against me I closed my eyes like a coward. I felt the same as I had with the incidents of the belfry and the railway wagon: I could not bear it, and ran off…

At home I found a guest waiting, an old friend, who, after greeting me, complained that when he was coming to see me he had lost his way in the forest and had become separated from his fine, precious dog.

The Lost Ones

A DACHA SETTLEMENT, shrouded in the darkness of night. The village bell tolls one. Government barristers Kozyavkin and Layev, both in an excellent mood and swaying slightly, come out of the forest and make for the dachas...

"Well, glory to the Creator, we've arrived..." says Kozyavkin, taking a deep breath. "To come five versts from the railway station on foot in our state was heroic. I'm exhausted! And, as if to spite us, not a single cab..."

"My dear fellow, Petya... I can't go on! If I'm not in bed in five minutes, I think I shall die..."

"In b-e-e-d? Why, you're joking, brother! We'll first have supper, drink a little red wine and then maybe go to bed. Verochka and I will not let you sleep... It's a fine thing, my friend, to be married! You don't understand that, you callous man! I am arriving at home tired, worn out... A loving wife will meet me, will give me tea and something to eat – and, in gratitude for my labour, out of love, will gaze at me so tenderly and affectionately with her delightful black eyes that I shall forget, my dear man, the tiredness and the burglary and the legal chamber and the court of appeal... It's g-o-o-d!"

"But... I think my legs are giving way... I can hardly walk... I'm terribly thirsty..."

"Well, here we are at home."

The friends go up to one of the dachas and stop at the far window.

"It's a splendid little dacha," says Kozyavkin. "You'll see tomorrow what views we have! The windows are dark. Verochka must already have gone to bed, didn't want to wait. She's lying in bed and must be worrying that I've not yet arrived..." He pushes the window with his walking stick, and it opens. "She's one brave girl, to go to bed without locking the window." He takes off his cape and throws it, together with his briefcase, through the window. "I'm hot! Let's strike up a serenade, make her laugh..." He starts singing. "'The moon floats through the night-time sky... faintly wafts the gentle breeze... faintly lulls the gentle breeze...' Sing, Alyosha! Verochka, shall we sing you Schubert's serenade?" He sings: "'My song-g-g-g... goes with entreaty-y-y-y'..." His voice is broken by a convulsive cough. "Tfoo! Verochka, kindly tell Aksinya to unlock the gate for us." He pauses. "Verochka! Come, don't be lazy – get up, my dear!" He stands on a stone and looks through the window. "Verunchik, my darling, Veryevunchik... my little angel, my incomparable wife, get up and tell Aksinya to unlock the gate for us. I know you're not asleep! Mamochka, truly, we are so weak and weary that we are not at all in the mood for jokes. We really have come from the station on foot. Do you hear me or not? Oh, the devil take it!" He tries to climb through the window and falls. "These are unpleasant tricks to play on visitors! I see, Vera, that you are just as much a schoolgirl as ever, always being naughty..."

"But maybe Vera Stepanovna is asleep," says Layev.

"She's not asleep. She probably wants me to make a noise and disturb all the neighbours. I'm starting to get angry now, Vera! Oh, the devil take it! Help me, Alyosha, I'll climb in. You are a silly girl, a schoolgirl, and nothing more!... Help me up!"

Layev, panting from the effort, helps Kozyavkin up. The latter climbs through the window and disappears into the darkness of the room.

"Verka!" Layev hears a minute later. "Where are you? What the dev-v-vil... Tfoo, I've soiled my hand on something! Tfoo!"

A rustle is heard, a flapping of wings and the desperate cry of a hen.

"Good lord!" Layev hears. "Vera, since when have we had hens? The devil take them, where did they come from? There's a little basket with a turkey-hen... It pecked me, the scoundrel!"

Two hens come flying noisily out of the window and, cackling loudly, go racing along the street.

"Alyosha, we've come to the wrong place!" says Kozyavkin in a broken voice. "There are all kinds of hens here... I must have made a mistake... To the devil with them, they're flying all over the place, the villains!"

"Well, come out quickly! Understand? I'm dying of thirst!"

"In a moment... I first have to find my cape and briefcase..."

"Light a match!"

"The matches are in my cape... What made me climb in here? All the dachas look the same – the Devil himself couldn't distinguish them in the dark. Oi! A hen has just pecked me on the cheek. D-d-despicable creature..."

"Get out quickly, or they'll think we're stealing hens!"

"In a moment... I can't find my cape. There are a lot of rags lying around here, and I can't see where my cape is. Throw some matches up to me!"

"I don't have any matches!"

"I'm in a mess, that's for sure. What can I do now? I can't leave without my cape and briefcase. I have to find them."

"I don't understand how it's possible... not to know one's own dacha," Layev says indignantly. "Drunken swine... If I'd known this would happen, I wouldn't have come with you for anything in the world. I should be at home now, peacefully sleeping, but here, thanks to you, I'm feeling so bad... I'm terribly tired, thirsty... my head's spinning round!"

"In a moment, in a moment... you won't die..."

A big cockerel flies over Layev's head with a cry. Layev sighs deeply and, with a despairing wave of his hand, sits down on a stone. His throat is burning with thirst; he cannot keep his eyes open, and his head is drooping... Five minutes go by, ten, then twenty, but Kozyavkin is still busy with the hens.

"Pyotr, will you be long?"

"In a moment. I found my briefcase, but lost it again."

Layev props his head up on his fists and closes his eyes. The cackling of the hens grows louder and louder. The residents of the empty dacha fly out of the window and seem to him to circle like owls over his head in the darkness. Their cries ring in his ears, filling his soul with terror.

"The swine!..." he thinks. "He invited me to visit, promised to entertain me with wine and thick country sour cream, and instead of that makes me come from the station on foot and listen to these hens..."

Feeling indignant, Layev thrusts his chin into his collar, lays his head on his briefcase and gradually calms down. Weariness overtakes him, and he dozes off.

"I found my briefcase!" comes Kozyavkin's triumphant cry. "I'll find my cape in a minute and then – that's it, we'll go!"

And now, through sleep, he hears the barking of a dog. First one dog barks, then another, a third... and the barking of the dogs mixes with the cackling of the hens to create a sort of wild music. Someone comes up to Layev and asks about something. Then he hears others climbing over his head up to the window, knocking, shouting... A woman in a red apron stands near him with a lantern in her hand and asks about something.

"You have no right to say that!" he hears Kozyavkin's voice. "I am a crown barrister and graduate at law, Kozyavkin. Here is my visiting card!"

"What do I care about your card!" says someone in a hoarse bass voice. "You've driven away all my hens, you've crushed all the eggs! Look at what you've done! The eggs were due to hatch any day now, and you've crushed them. So why do I need your card, sir?"

"Don't you dare bully me! No, sir! I won't have it!"

"I'm thirsty..." thinks Layev, trying to open his eyes and sensing how, over his head, someone is climbing down from the window.

"I am Kozyavkin! My dacha is here, everyone here knows me!"

"We don't know any Kozyavkin!"

"What are you saying? Call the village elder! He knows me!"

"Don't get excited, the constable will be here in a minute... We know all the local residents, but we've never seen you before."

"I've lived for five years already in a dacha in Gniliye Vysyelki!"

"What! Do you think this is Visyelki? This is Zhilovo. Gniliye Vysyelki is to the right, behind the match factory. About four versts from here."

"The devil take me! It means I took the wrong road!"

The shouts of the people and the cackling of the hens blends with the barking of the dogs, and from the mixture of noisy chaos, Kozyavkin's voice is heard:

"Don't you dare threaten me! I shall pay! You'll learn whom you're dealing with!"

Finally the voices, little by little, die away. Layev senses someone shaking his shoulder.

A Failure

ILYA SERGEICH PEPLOV and his wife Kleopatra Petrovna were standing at the door, listening intently. A declaration of love was evidently taking place in the little sitting room behind the door. This was between their daughter Natashenka and a teacher at the district school, Shchupkin.

"He's biting!" whispered Peplov, trembling with impatience and rubbing his hands. "Listen, Petrovna,* as soon as they start to talk about their feelings, immediately take the icon off the wall and we'll go and give them our blessing... We'll seal it... A blessing given with an icon is sacred and inviolable... He'll not wriggle out of it even if he takes us to court."

But behind the door the following conversation was taking place.

"Don't behave like that!" said Shchupkin, striking a match against his checked trousers. "I certainly wrote you no letters!"

"Of course you did! As if I don't know your handwriting!" said the girl, shrieking with affected laughter and glancing at herself from time to time in the mirror. "I recognized it at once! What a strange man you are! You're a teacher of calligraphy, yet your handwriting looks like a hen's footprints! How on earth do you teach writing if you yourself write so badly?"

"Hm!... That's not important. In calligraphy it's not handwriting that matters, but ensuring that the pupils don't doze off. Some you hit on the head with a ruler, others you get to kneel in the corner... Forget about handwriting! It's irrelevant! Nekrasov* was a writer, and his handwriting was a disgrace. You can see it in his collected works."

"You're not Nekrasov," she said with a sigh. "I would go for a writer with pleasure. He would always be writing me poems!"

"Even I can write you poems, if you wish."

"What on earth can you write about?"

"About love... about feelings... about your eyes... You'd go crazy when you read them... You'd weep endless tears! If I write you a poem, will you let me kiss your hand?"

"How daring!... You can kiss it now, if you like!"

Shchupkin jumped up and, wide-eyed, pressed his lips to her soft, plump, egg-soap-scented hand.

"Get the icon!" Peplov said. He nudged his wife and sprang into action, pale with excitement as he buttoned up his frock coat. "Let's go! Come on!"

And, not pausing for a moment, Peplov flung open the door.

"My dears..." he muttered, raising his hands and tearfully blinking. "God bless you, my dears... Be fruitful... multiply... replenish the earth..."*

"And... I too bless you..." said Mama, crying with happiness. "Be happy, my dear ones! Oh, you are taking away my only treasure!" she added, turning to Shchupkin. "Just love my daughter, be good to her..."

Shchupkin gaped at them with amazement and alarm. The intervention of the parents was so sudden and bold that he was unable to utter a single word.

"I've been trapped! They've married me off!" he thought, overcome with horror. "You've had it now, brother! You won't escape!"

He humbly lowered his head, as if to say: "Take me, I'm defeated!"

"I... I bless you," Papa continued, and also started to cry. "Natashenka, my dear... Stand next to him... Petrovna, hand me the icon..."

But now the father suddenly stopped crying, and his face became distorted with anger.

"You clod!" he said angrily to his wife. "You're a dimwit. Is this the icon?"

"Ah, good Heavens!"

What had happened? The calligraphy teacher cautiously raised his eyes and saw that he was saved: instead of the icon, Mama had hastily taken from the wall a portrait of the writer Lazhechnikov.* Old man Peplov and his spouse Kleopatra Petrovna, with the portrait in their hands, were standing disconcertedly, not knowing what to do or say. The calligraphy teacher took advantage of the confusion and escaped.

A Story Without an End

SHORTLY AFTER TWO O'CLOCK one night long ago, the cook, pale and anxious, rushed suddenly, unexpectedly into my study to announce that Mrs Milyutikha, the old woman who owned the neighbouring cottage, was sitting in her kitchen.

"She asks, *barin*,* that you come to her," said the cook, breathing heavily. "Something bad has happened to her lodger... He has shot or hanged himself..."

"What can I do about it?" I said. "Let her fetch a doctor, or the police!"

"How can she find a doctor? She can hardly breathe, and out of fear has taken refuge under the stove... You should come, *barin*!"

I dressed and went to Milyutikha's house. The gate that I made for was open. After standing awhile in indecision and not finding the caretaker's bell, I entered the yard. The porch, dark and shabby, was also not locked. I opened the door and entered the hall. Inside, it was utterly dark, with no light at all, and there was in addition a perceptible smell of incense. Groping for the exit from the hall, I hit my elbow against something metallic and stumbled in the dark on some sort of board which almost fell to the floor. Finally I found the door, which was covered with torn felt, and entered a little reception room.

Now, I am not writing a fairy tale, and am far from wanting to frighten the reader, but the sight I saw from the hall was surreal, and one I shall remember till my dying day. Right in front of me was a door leading to a little room. Faded, slate-coloured wallpaper was faintly lit by three five-copeck wax candles standing in a row. In the middle of the room lay a coffin on two tables. The wax candles illuminated a little, dark-yellow face with a half-open mouth and a sharp nose. From the face to the toes of the two slippers were arranged disorderly folds of gauze and muslin, and from these folds peeped out two pale, motionless hands holding a wax cross. The dark, gloomy corners of the little room, the icons behind the coffin, the coffin itself – all, except for the silently flickering lights, were deathly motionless, like the grave itself...

"What an astonishing thing!" I thought, stupefied at the unexpected sight of death. "How did such a sudden end come about? The lodger has only just hanged or shot himself, yet he is already in the coffin!"

I looked around. On the left was a door with a glass panel, on the right a decrepit stand with a shabby fur coat.

"Give me some water..." I heard a groan.

The groan came from the left, from behind the door with the glass panel. I opened this door and entered a little room. It was dark, with a solitary window through which shyly crept the weak light from the street lamp.

"Is anyone here?" I asked.

And, without waiting for a reply, I struck a match. While it burned, I saw the following sight. A man was sitting on the bloodstained floor at my very feet. Had I taken a longer step, I would have trodden on him. With his legs stretched out and his hands supporting himself on the floor, he was making an effort to raise his handsome face, which was deathly pale beneath a thick beard that was as black as Indian ink. In his large eyes, which he raised to me, I read inexpressible terror, pain, entreaty. Big drops of cold sweat were streaming down his face. The sweat, the expression on his face, the trembling of the hands that were supporting him, his heavy breathing and clenched teeth, spoke of unbearable suffering. Near his right hand, in a pool of blood, lay a revolver.

"Don't leave..." I heard a weak voice say when the match went out. "A candle is on the table."

I lit the candle and, not knowing what to do, stopped in the middle of the room. I stood and looked at the man, who was sitting on the floor. And it seemed to me that I had seen him before somewhere.

"The pain is unbearable," he whispered, "but I can't bear to shoot myself again. My indecision baffles me!"

I threw off my coat and attended to the injured man. Raising him from the floor like a child, I placed him on the oilcloth sofa and carefully undressed him. He was shivering and cold when I took off his clothes. As for the wound, which I saw, it bore no relationship either to the shivering or the expression on the wounded man's face. It was not serious. The bullet had passed between the fifth and sixth ribs on the left side, piercing only the skin and flesh. The bullet itself I found in the pleats of the frock coat lining near the rear pocket. After stopping the blood as much as I could and making a temporary bandage from the pillowcase, a towel and two handkerchiefs, I gave the injured man a drink and covered him with the fur coat that was hanging in the hall. In all the time that I was applying the bandage, neither of us said a word. As I worked, he lay motionless, looking intently at me through screwed-up eyes, as if ashamed of his failure at shooting himself and the trouble he was causing me.

"Now be so good as to lie still," I said after finishing the bandaging, "and I shall run to the chemist's and get something there."

"It's not necessary!" he muttered, clutching me by the sleeve and opening his eyes wide.

In his eyes I read fear. He did not want me to leave.

"It's not necessary! Stay another five minutes... ten... If you don't mind, then stay, I beg you."

He begged me and shivered, his teeth chattering. I acquiesced and sat on the edge of the sofa. Ten minutes passed in silence. I said nothing, but looked around the room into which fate had so unexpectedly brought me. What poverty! The man, who had a handsome, pampered face and a thick, well-trimmed beard, lived in surroundings that would not have been envied by an ordinary workman. A sofa with its shabby torn oilcloth, a plain greasy chair, a table piled with discarded paper and a hideous-looking oleograph on the wall – that was all I saw. The room was damp, gloomy and drab.

"What a wind!" muttered the wounded man without opening his eyes. "How it moans!"

"Yes," I said. "Listen. It seems to me that I know you. Didn't you take part last year in some amateur dramatics at General Lukhachev's dacha?"

"So what?" he asked, quickly opening his eyes. A little cloud seemed to pass over his face.

"I'm sure I saw you there. Are you not Vasilyev?"

"Even if I am, so what of it? I'm none the better for you knowing me."

"None the better... I was just asking you by the by."

Vasilyev closed his eyes and, as if offended, turned his face to the back of the sofa.

"I don't understand this curiosity!" he muttered. "All I need now is for you to start interrogating me about what drove me to suicide!"

Not even a minute passed before he again turned to me, opened his eyes and began to speak in a tearful voice:

"Excuse me for adopting this tone, but you'll agree that I'm right! To ask a prisoner why he's in prison, or a suicide why he shot himself, is mean and... indiscreet. It's to satisfy one's idle curiosity at the cost of someone else's nerves!"

"You are wrong to be upset... It did not occur to me to ask about the reasons."

"But you would have asked... It's in the nature of people. But why ask? If I told you, either you would not understand or you would not believe me... I confess that even I myself don't understand... There are terms in newspaper reports like 'hopeless love' and 'desperate poverty', but the reasons are unknown... They are known neither by me, nor by you, nor by the editorial staff who dare to write 'from the diary of a suicide'. Only God understands the state of a man's soul when he takes his own life, but people don't know."

"That's all very well," I said. "But you shouldn't talk so much."

But my suicide was warming to his theme. He propped his head up on his fist and continued in the tone of a tedious professor:

"Man will never understand the psychological subtleties of suicide! What are the reasons? Today one reaches for a revolver for a reason, while tomorrow that same reason seems not worth a half-eaten egg... It all depends, probably, on the particular feelings of the subject at a given time... Take me, for example. Half an hour ago I longed terribly for death, but now, with the candle burning and you sitting next to me, I don't even think about the hour of my death. Try and explain that change! Have I become rich, or has my wife risen from the grave? Was I influenced by the light, or by the presence of someone else?"

"The light certainly has an influence," I muttered, in order to say something. "The influence of the light on man's body..."

"The influence of the light... It's accepted! But surely people shoot themselves even by candlelight! And there would be little honour to the heroes of our novels if such a trifle as a candle were to change the course of the story so suddenly. Perhaps all this nonsense can be explained, but not by us. It's no good asking about, or trying to explain, what you don't understand..."

"Excuse me," I said, "but... judging by the expression on your face, it seems to me that now you are just... showing off."

"Yes?" Vasilyev said suddenly. "It may well be! I am by nature terribly vain and foppish. Well, now explain, if you believe in reading people's faces! Half an hour ago I was shooting myself, and now I'm showing off... Try and explain that!"

Vasilyev delivered the last words in a weak, dying voice. He grew tired and stopped talking. Silence fell. I began to examine his face. It was pale, like a corpse's. It seemed that life in it had drained, and only traces of the suffering that the "vain and foppish" man had endured showed he was still alive. It was terrible to look at that face, but it was the same Vasilyev who had had enough strength to philosophize and, were I not mistaken, to show off.

"Are you here?" he asked, suddenly raising himself a little on his elbow. "My God! You only have to listen!"

I began to listen. The rain lashed on the dark window without ceasing for a moment. The wind moaned mournfully and drearily.

"And I shall be whiter than snow, and my ears will hear gladness and rejoicing."* Mrs Milyutikha, who had returned, was reading in the drawing room in a lazy, tired voice, not raising or lowering her monotonous, dreary voice.

"Isn't it true that there will be rejoicing?" whispered Vasilyev, turning his frightened face towards me. "My God, the things a man has to see and hear! This chaos should be set to music! 'It would confound the ignorant,' as Hamlet says, 'and amaze indeed the very faculties of eyes and ears.'* How I would then understand this music! How deeply I would feel it! What time is it?"

"Five to three."

"Still long till morning. And the funeral's in the morning. A charming prospect! You walk behind the coffin through the mud, in the rain. You walk and see nothing but the cloudy sky and the dreadful scenery. The muddy torch-bearers, taverns, woodyards... trousers wet to the knees. Streets endlessly long, time dragging by like eternity, crude people. And on your heart lies a stone, a stone!"

After a short silence, he suddenly asked:

"Is it long since you've seen General Lukhachev?"

"I haven't seen him since the summer."

"He loves to get on his high horse, but he's a dear old man. And do you still do a bit of writing?"

"Yes, a little."

"Now... Do you remember how like a bleating, excited calf I leapt to join these amateur performances when I was courting Zina? It was stupid, but good, light-hearted fun... Even in recollection I can smell the spring... But now! What a harsh change of scene! There is a subject for you! Just don't think to write 'the diary of a suicide'. That's passé and trite. Think up something humorous."

"Again you... are showing off," I said. "There is nothing humorous about your situation."

"Is there nothing amusing? Do you say there's nothing amusing?"

Vasilyev raised himself a little, and tears began to glisten in his eyes. An expression of bitter resentment spread over his pale face, and his chin began to tremble.

"You laugh at cheating cashiers and unfaithful wives," he said, "but surely not a single cashier, not a single unfaithful wife ever cheated as fate has cheated me! I have been deceived more than any bank depositor, any cuckolded husband, has ever been! Only realize how I number among ridiculous fools. Last year, in your eyes, I didn't know what to do with myself out of happiness, but now, in your same eyes..."

Vasilyev's head fell on the pillow, and he burst out laughing.

"It's impossible even to imagine anything funnier or sillier than such transition. Chapter one: spring, love, honeymoon... honey, in a word; chapter two: the striving for a position, a secured loan, poverty, the chemist's shop and... tomorrow the trudge through the mud to the cemetery."

He again burst out laughing. I felt terrible, and decided to leave.

"Listen," I said, "you lie down and I'll go to the chemist's."

He did not reply. I put on my coat and left his room. Passing through the hall, I looked at the coffin and at Mrs Milyutikha, who was still reading. However I strained my eyes, in the yellow, dark-complexioned face I was unable to recognize Zina, the lively, attractive *ingénue** of Lukhachev's company.

"*Sic transit*,"* I thought.

Then I went out, not forgetting to take the revolver with me, and set off to the chemist's. But I shouldn't have gone. When I returned from the chemist's, Vasilyev was lying on the sofa in a fainting fit. The bandage had been roughly torn off, and blood was flowing from the exposed wound. I was unable to bring him round until morning. Till then, he continued to rave feverishly, trembling and casting his eyes wildly around the room, and did not hear the chanting of the priest, who had started the *panikhida*.*

When Vasilyev's flat was filled with old women and torch-bearers, when the coffin had been taken out and carried from the yard, I advised Vasilyev to stay at home. But he did not listen, despite his pain and the grey, wet morning. He walked to the cemetery behind the coffin without a hat, silently, dragging his feet with difficulty and from time to time convulsively picking at his wounded side. His expression was one of complete apathy. Only once, when I roused him from his pensive state with some insignificant question, did he look round at the road and the grey fence, his eyes flashing for an instant with dark anger.

"'Weelrite Shoppe'" he read on a signboard. "Illiterate louts, the Devil take the lot of them!"

From the cemetery I took him home with me.

* * *

Just one year has passed since that night, and Vasilyev has barely had time to wear out the boots in which he plodded through the mud behind his wife's coffin.

Just now, as I am finishing this story, he is sitting in my drawing room and playing the piano, showing the ladies how provincial young girls sing sentimental romances. The ladies are laughing loudly, and he himself is laughing. He is in a joyful mood.

I call him into my study. Evidently displeased that I have deprived him of pleasant company, he enters my room and stands before me in the attitude of a man who has no time. I hand him this story and ask him to read it. He, always indulgent about my authorship, suppresses a sigh, the sigh of a reader's laziness, sits down in the armchair and starts reading.

"The Devil take it, how dreadful," he mutters with a smile.

But the more he becomes absorbed in reading, the more serious his face becomes. Finally, under the stress of intense recollection, he grows terribly pale, gets up and continues reading while standing up. On finishing, he starts to pace back and forth.

"So how does it end?" I ask him.

"How does it end? Hm..." He glances around at the room, at me, at himself...

He sees his new fashionable suit, hears the laughter of the ladies and... collapsing on the armchair, begins to laugh, as he laughed on that night.

"Well, was I not right when I told you this is all amusing? My God! I bore on my shoulders as much as an elephant can bear on its back, suffered the devil knows how much, more than it seems possible to suffer, but where are the traces of that? It's astonishing! It would seem that the impression made on a man by his torments must be eternal, indelible and inviolable. But what happens? This impression wears out as easily as a pair of cheap shoes. Nothing remains, not a thing! It's as if I was not suffering, but dancing a mazurka. Everything in the world is change, and change is amusing! A wide field for humorists!… Add a humorous end, brother!"

"Pyotr Nikolayevich, are you coming?" the impatient ladies call my hero.

"Just a minute!" says the "vain and foppish" man, adjusting his tie. "It's amusing, brother, and sad, sad and amusing, but what can you do? *Homo sum…** But all the same, I praise Mother Nature for her ability to adapt. If we had been left with the excruciating memory of toothache and those fears we all experience, and if they were to last for ever, our fellow man would find it horrible to live in this world!"

I look at his smiling face and am reminded of that despair and that terror with which his eyes were filled when, a year before, he had looked at the dark window. I see how he, playing his usual role of learned windbag, is preparing to flaunt before me his empty theories like adaptability, and at the same time I recall how he was sitting on the floor in a pool of blood, with imploring eyes filled with pain.

"How does it end?" I ask myself aloud.

Vasilyev, whistling and adjusting his tie, goes out to the drawing room, and I follow him with my eyes, feeling vexed. For some reason I regret his previous suffering – regret all that I myself experienced for the sake of this man on that bad night. It was as if I had lost something…

The Wedding

THE BEST MAN, IN A TOP HAT and white gloves, puffing from the effort, throws off his coat in the entrance hall and, looking as if he wants to communicate something dreadful, runs into the reception room.

"The groom is already in church!" he announces, taking a deep breath.

Silence falls. Everyone suddenly becomes sad.

The bride's father, a retired lieutenant-colonel with a gaunt, haggard face, probably feeling his slight military figure in riding breeches to be insufficiently ceremonial, pompously puffs out his cheeks and straightens himself. He takes an icon from a little table. His wife, a little old lady in a tulle cap with wide ribbons, takes bread and salt* and stands next to him. The blessing commences.

The bride, Lyubochka, noiselessly, like a shadow, kneels before her father. This causes her veil to rustle and catch on the flowers that cover her dress; several hairpins come loose from her coiffure. After bowing to the icon and exchanging kisses with her father, who is puffing out his cheeks even more imposingly, Lyubochka kneels before her mother. Her veil again rustles, and two young ladies worriedly run up to her, pull it down, adjust it, fasten it with pins...

There is silence. Everyone is quiet – no one stirs. Only the ushers, like spirited trace-horses, impatiently shift from foot to foot, as if waiting to be allowed to dart off.

"Who will carry the icon?" someone asks in an anxious whisper. "Spira, where are you? Spira!"

"Coming!" replies a child's voice from the entrance hall.

"God bless you, Darya Danilovna!" Someone quietly comforts the old lady, who is pressing herself to her daughter's face and sobbing. "For Heaven's sake, do you really have to cry? You should be happy, my dear, and not cry."

The blessing ends. Lyubochka, looking pale and so solemn and serious, exchanges kisses with her friends, after which all the guests noisily, jostling each other, rush to the entrance. The ushers, hurrying anxiously, and unnecessarily crying "Pardon!", attire the bride.

"Lyubochka, let me look at you just one more time!" groans the old lady.

"Ah, Darya Danilovna!" someone sighs reproachfully. "You should be happy. God knows what it is you're imagining..."

"Spira! Where are you? Spira! That boy is such a nuisance! Come here!"

"Coming!"

One of the ushers lifts the train of the bride's dress, and the procession starts to descend. On the banisters of the staircase and at all the doorposts cling various maids and nannies. They devour the bride with their eyes. A buzz of approval can be heard from them. From the back rows come the sounds of anxious voices: someone forgot something, someone has the bride's bouquet. The ladies scream, begging that something not be done, because "it brings bad luck".

A carriage and a coach have been waiting a long time by the entrance. Paper flowers adorn the horses' manes, and all the coachmen's arms are wrapped to the shoulder with coloured scarfs. On the box of the carriage sits a huge fellow with a broad, thick beard, wearing a new kaftan. His extended hands with clenched fists, thrown-back head and unusually wide shoulders make him appear not a living human being: it's as if he's turned to stone...

"Tprrr!" he voices in a high tone, and at once adds more deeply, "I'll have none of your tricks!" (From this it seems there are two throats in his wide neck.) "Tprrr! No nonsense, now!"

The street on both sides is crowded with people.

"Drive up!" cry the ushers, though there was no need to drive up, as the carriage had long ago driven up. Spira, who carried the icon, and the bride with two bridesmaids get into the carriage. The door slams, and the street resounds with the clatter of the carriage.

"Ushers' carriage! Drive up!"

The ushers jump into their carriage. As it sets off, they raise themselves a little and, writhing as if suffering from cramp, pull on their coats. The next carriages drive up.

"Sofya Denisovna, get in!" Voices are heard. "You too, please, Nikolai Mironych! Tprrr! Don't worry, ladies, there will be seats for all! Take care!"

"Listen, Makar!" cries the bride's father. "Take another route back from the church! It brings bad luck!"

The carriages clatter along the road – there is noise and shouting... At last everyone has gone, and again it grows quiet. The bride's father returns to the house. In the hall, footmen are clearing the table; in the dark room next door, which everyone in the house calls the "ante-room", musicians are blowing their noses; everywhere there is bustling and running about, but it seems to him that the house is empty. The members of the military band potter around in their dark little room. In no way can they find room for their unwieldy music stands and instruments. They arrived not long before, but already the air in the "ante-room" has become palpably thick, making it hard to breathe. Their "elder", Osipov, who from old age has a moustache and side whiskers spreading in tufts, stands before a music stand, seriously examining a score.

"You've worn well, Osipov," says the colonel. "How many years have I known you? About twenty!"

"More, Your Honour. Kindly remember that I played at your wedding."

"Yes, yes." The colonel sighs and grows thoughtful. "It's history, brother... I married off my sons, praise God, and now I'm giving away my daughter, and the old woman and I are now orphans... Now we have no children. We are quite clear of obligations."

"Who knows? Perhaps, Yefim Petrovich, God will send more, Your Honour..."

Yefim Petrovich looks with amazement at Osipov and laughs up his sleeve.

"More?" he asks. "What did you say? God will send more children? You mean to me?"

He chokes with laughter, and tears appear in his eyes; out of politeness the musicians also laugh. Yefim Petrovich looks around for his wife, in order to tell her what Osipov said, but she herself is already rushing straight towards him, swiftly, angrily, with tear-filled eyes.

"Have you no shame, Yefim Petrovich!" she says, throwing up her hands. "We keep looking and looking for the rum, we're run off our feet, and you're standing here! Where's the rum? Nikolai Mironych needs rum, but you couldn't care less! Go and ask Ignat where he put the rum!"

Yefim Petrovich goes to the basement, where the kitchen is located. Women and footmen are dashing about on the muddy staircase. A young soldier, having thrown his dress coat over one shoulder, is kneeling on a step and twirling the ice-cream mould; sweat is flowing from his red face. In the dark and crowded kitchen, amid clouds of smoke, work the cooks who were hired from the club. One is cleaning a capon, another is fashioning little stars from a carrot, a third, as red as beetroot, is thrusting a roasting pan into the oven. Knives are clinking, plates clattering, fat sizzling. Finding himself in this bedlam, Yefim Petrovich forgets what the old woman told him to do.

"Is it not too crowded in here for you, my friends?" he asks.

"We're all right, Yefim Petrovich. Rest assured, we don't mind a crowded space."

"You really work hard, lads."

In a dark corner appears the figure of Ignat, the snack-bar assistant from the club.

"Rest assured, Yefim Petrovich," he says. "We'll leave everything in the best state. What do you want the ice cream to be made with? Rum, Sauternes or nothing?"

Returning upstairs, Yefim Petrovich wanders for a long time through the rooms, then stops at the door of the "ante-room" and again strikes up a conversation with Osipov.

"So then, brother..." he says. "We remain orphans. While the new house is drying out, the newly-weds will live with us, and then goodbye! That's the last we'll see of them..."

They both sigh... Out of politeness the musicians also sigh, making the air even stuffier.

"Yes, brother," Yefim Petrovich continues dully, "she was our only daughter, and we've given even her away. He's an educated man, speaks French... It's just that he drinks, but who doesn't drink nowadays? Everybody drinks."

"It doesn't matter that he drinks," says Osipov. "The main thing is, Yefim Petrovich, that he knows his business. And, even if he drinks, why shouldn't he? It's all right to drink."

"Of course it's all right."

Sobbing is heard.

"Can he really appreciate what we've done for him?" Darya Danilovna is complaining to an old woman. "You see, my dear, we gave him ten thousand roubles, down to the last copeck, signed over the house to Lyubochka with three hundred hectares of land... Is it easy to say? Can he really appreciate it? Nowadays they are not such as to appreciate!"

The table with fruit is already prepared. Wineglasses stand packed together on two trays, bottles of champagne are wrapped in napkins, samovars hiss in the dining room. A footman without a moustache, but with side whiskers, is noting on a piece of paper the names of those to whose health he will propose a toast at supper, and is reading them as if memorizing them. Someone's dog is chased from the rooms. There is a tense air of expectation... And now anxious voices are heard:

"They are coming! They are coming! Master, Yefim Petrovich, they are coming!"

The old lady, stupefied, with an expression of extreme bewilderment, seizes the bread and salt. Yefim Petrovich puffs out his cheeks, and together they hasten to the entrance hall. The musicians, discreetly but hurriedly, tune their instruments. From outside comes the noise of the carriages. The dog again enters from the yard. They chase it away, and it gives a yelp. One more minute of waiting – and from the "ante-room" bursts out the sound of a deafening, wild, furious march. The air is filled with exclamations, kisses, the popping of corks. The footmen wear stern expressions...

Lyubochka and her husband, a staid gentleman in gold-rimmed glasses, look stunned. The deafening music, bright light, universal attention, crowds of unknown faces, dispirit them... They look around vacantly, see nothing, understand nothing.

Tea and champagne are drunk – everything proceeds decorously and with clockwork precision. A multitude of relations, some strange old men and women whom no one had ever seen before, clergymen, retired military men with flat heads, representatives of the groom's father and mother, godparents, stand around the table, carefully sipping tea and talking about the political situation in Bulgaria. Young ladies huddle against the walls like flies. Even the ushers have lost their anxious look and stand quietly by the door.

An hour or so later, the whole house is shaking with music and dancing. The ushers again look as though they have broken loose from chains. In the dining room, where there is a table of *zakuski*,* crowd old men and non-dancing youths. Yefim Petrovich, who has already drunk about five glasses of vodka, winks, snaps his fingers and chokes with laughter. The thought has occurred to him that it would be good to marry off the ushers, and this delights him – it seems so clever and amusing, and he is happy, so happy, that he cannot get the words out, but only guffaw... His wife, who has eaten nothing since morning and is tipsy from the champagne, smiles blissfully and says to everyone:

"You must not go to the bedroom, ladies and gentlemen! It's indiscreet to go to the bedroom. Don't look in the bedroom!"

This means: be so good as to look in the bedroom! All her maternal vanity and all her talent has gone into this bedroom. And it was something to be proud of! In the middle of the bedroom stand two beds with high mattresses; lace pillows, silk blankets, quilted, with complicated, incomprehensible monograms. On

Lyubochka's bed lies a bonnet with pink ribbons, and on her husband's bed a mouse-coloured dressing gown with pale-blue tassels. All the guests, after looking at the beds, consider it their duty to wink meaningfully and say "Y-y-yes-s-s". The old woman beams and says in a whisper:

"This bedroom cost three hundred roubles, my friends. I'm not joking! Well, let's go, it's indelicate for men to come in here."

Dinner is served after two o'clock. The footman with side whiskers proposes the toasts and the musicians play a fanfare. Yefim Petrovich is completely drunk, and by now knows no one. It seems to him that he is not in his own house, but on a visit, and that he has been offended. He puts on his coat and hat in the hall and, looking for his galoshes, cries in a hoarse voice:

"I don't wish to stay here any longer! You are all scoundrels! Villains! I shall expose you for what you are!"

His wife is standing nearby and says to him:

"Calm down, you godless soul! Calm down, wretch, devil! What have I done to deserve this?"

The Fool

(A Bachelor's Tale)

PROKHOR PETROVICH scratched the back of his head, took a pinch of snuff and continued:

"They drank two bottles of sherry at my place. I sit, drink and am aware that they are walking around me, smiling maliciously and congratulating me. Near me sits the host's daughter, but I, a drunken fool, know that I am talking nonsense. I talk about family life, about irons and pots... After each word there is a hot kiss... Tfoo! It's sickening even to remember. I wake up in the morning with a splitting headache, a foul mouth, but I feel and understand that I am no longer a wastrel, not small fry, but a genuine fiancé – with a ring on my finger! I go to my now-deceased father – I say, 'Well, Papa dear, I have something to tell you... I want to marry.' Father, of course, thinks it's a joke... Doesn't believe me.

"'How can you,' he says, 'a raw youth, marry? Good lord, you are not yet even twenty years old!'

"And I certainly was young then. Younger than the first snow... I had light-brown curly hair, a passionate heart in my chest, and instead of this pot belly – a slender, almost feminine waist...

"'Live a bit more and then marry,' says my father.

"I stand my ground... I'm known for my will, I'm spoilt. I refuse to give in.

"'So who do you want to marry?' he asks.

"'Maryashka Kritkina.'

"My father is horrified.

"'To that wretched woman? You're out of your mind! Good lord, her father is a rogue, up to his ears in debt... They're duping you! They want to lure you into their clutches! You fool!'

"Indeed, I was a fool. I was terribly stupid... If you knocked me on the head, it could be heard in the next room. Loudly! Up to the age of thirty I said not a single sensible word. And a fool, as you yourselves know, is eternally in trouble. So too was I... It seems I was never out of trouble: now it was one thing, now another... And it served me right – never be a fool. First they beat me, then they chased me out of the house and tavern... I was expelled from high school seven times... Now I wanted to marry... Well, sir... My father curses, shouts, almost manhandles me, but I stand my ground.

"I wanted to marry, and that's all there was to it! Whose business was it? No father could have stood in my way, if that's what I wanted to do! I wasn't a child!

"My now-deceased mother rushed in. She couldn't believe her ears, and fell down in a faint... I stood my ground. Was it possible, I thought, for me not to marry, if I wanted to have my own family? After all, Maryasha, I thought, was beautiful... She was not beautiful, but seemed so to me. I wanted her to be beautiful, to get that foolish idea into my head... She was slightly hunchbacked, cross-eyed, rather thin... And on top of that, she was a fool... Like some strange, stuffed animal. The Kritkins considered my marriage to her advantageous. They were poor, whereas I had means. My father was a wealthy man. He went to his boss:

"'Kind sir, Your Excellency! Don't let my reprobate son marry! For the love of God! The boy will perish!'

"Unfortunately for me, the boss had strange ideas. Liberal views were just then coming into fashion – these views...

"'I cannot,' he says, 'meddle in the domestic life of my subordinates. And I advise you not to encroach on your son's freedom...'

"'But he's a fool, Your Excellency!'

"The boss banged his fist on the table!

"'Whatever he is, dear sir, he has the right to conduct himself as he wishes! He is a free man, dear sir! When will you barbarians learn to understand life?! Send your son to me!'

"They called me. I did up all my buttons and went.

"'What may I do for you, sir?'

"'This is what, young man! Your parents stand in the way of your acting according to the dictates of your heart. This is cruel and contemptible on their part. Believe me, young man, that the sympathy of decent people will always be on your side. If you're in love, then go where your heart draws you. And if in their ignorance your parents impede you, then tell me. I shall deal with them as I see fit... I... I shall show them!'

"And, in order to show that his views were of the most sincere kind, he added:

"'I shall be at your wedding. I can even stand in as your father. But tomorrow I shall go and meet your fiancée.'

"I bowed and, rejoicing, left. My father was standing right there, almost crying, but I thumbed my nose at him behind his back.

"The next day *he* went to see my fiancée. He liked her.

"'She is thin,' he says, 'but has a kindly face. Kindness,' he says, 'is somehow written on her face. She is full of grace. You are lucky, young man!'

"Three days later he brought my fiancée a present.

"'Accept this,' he says, 'from an old man who wishes you happiness.'

"And he even shed a few tears... Five days later was the betrothal. At the betrothal *he* drank punch and two glasses of champagne. Kind man!

"'She's lovely,' he said, 'your little woman! Thin, cross-eyed, but there is something French about her. What fire!'

"Three days before the wedding, I arrive at my fiancée's. With a bouquet, you know...

"'Where is Maryasha?' – 'Not at home.' – 'But where is she?'

"My father-in-law-to-be falls silent and grins. My mother-in-law sits there drinking coffee with sugar (she always used to drink with a lump of sugar in her mouth).

"'So where is she? Why don't you speak?' – 'Why are you interrogating us like this? Go away, get out of here! Beat it!'

"I look closely and see that my father-in-law is completely drunk, utterly sloshed... what scum...

"'No,' he says, grinning. 'Find yourself another fiancée, but Maryashka... She's gone up in the world! He-he-he! She went to her benefactor!' – 'To what benefactor?' – 'To the same one... To Your pot-bellied Excellency... He-he-he... You shouldn't have introduced them!'

"I gasped!"

Prokhor Petrovich blew his nose loudly, grinned and repeated:

"I gasped, and since then have become wise..."

The Coroner

THE DISTRICT DOCTOR AND CORONER were driving one fine spring morning to an autopsy. The coroner, a man of about thirty-five, looked thoughtfully at the horses and said:

"There are very many mysterious, unexplained things in nature, but even in ordinary life, doctor, one often meets with some incidents that are definitely inexplicable. Thus, I know of several mysterious, strange deaths, the cause of which only spiritualists and mystics will undertake to explain, while people with a clear head just throw up their hands in perplexity. For example, I know one very intelligent lady who foretold her death and died for no apparent reason, having precisely fixed her day of death. She said she would die on a certain day, and she did."

"There is no action without a cause," said the doctor. "If there is a death, there is also a reason. But as for predicting, then surely there is nothing strange about it. All women have the gift of premonition and foreboding."

"That may be so, doctor, but the woman in question was quite different. There was nothing of the feminine in her prediction. She was a young woman, healthy, clever, entirely unprejudiced. She had such perceptive, clear, honest eyes – an open, intelligent face with a pure, typically Russian smile in her look and on her lips. The only characteristic about her that was feminine, if you like, was her beauty. She was shapely, graceful, like this birch tree here, and had wonderful hair! So that you get a full understanding of her, I shall add more: that she was a person full of the most infectious gaiety, insouciance and that imaginative, pleasant light-heartedness that occurs only in thoughtful, simple-hearted, joyful people. Could there be any suggestion of mysticism, spiritualism, the gift of premonition or anything similar? She would have laughed at all that."

The doctor's carriage stopped by a well. The coroner and doctor drank their fill of water, stretched and waited for the coachman to finish watering the horses.

"Well then, what did the lady die of?" asked the doctor when the carriage was again rolling along the road.

"She died strangely. One fine day her husband came to her and said that towards spring it would not be a bad idea to sell the old carriage and instead buy something newer and lighter, and that it would not hurt to change the left trace-horse and to put Bobchinsky (such was the husband's name for the horse) out to pasture.

"His wife heard him out and said:

"'Do what you like – to me now it's all the same. By summer I shall already be in the cemetery.'

"Her husband, of course, just shrugged his shoulders and smiled.

"'I'm not joking at all,' she said. 'I tell you seriously, I shall soon die.'

"'That is, how soon?'

"'Right after giving birth. I shall have my baby and die.'

"Her husband attached no importance to these words. He did not believe in such premonitions, and in addition knew very well that women in a family way tend to be capricious and in general abandon themselves to gloomy thoughts. A day passed, and his wife again told him she would die straight after giving birth, and then each day she said the same thing, but he laughed and called her a simple woman, a fortune-teller, a hysteric. As death approached, it became an *idée fixe** of his wife. When her husband did not listen to her, she went to the kitchen and spoke there about her death with the nanny and cook.

"'I have not much longer to live, dear nanny. As soon as I give birth, I shall immediately die. I don't want to die so young, but it looks as if such is my fate.'

"The nanny and cook of course were in tears. The priest's wife or lady of the manor would arrive to see her, and she would lead them to a corner and start to unburden her soul – always about the same thing, about her approaching death. She would speak seriously, with an unpleasant smile and even an angry face, allowing no protestation. She was a fashionable woman, a woman of style, but now at the approach of death she abandoned all that and grew slovenly. She no longer read, laughed or dreamt aloud… Furthermore, she drove to the cemetery with her aunt and chose a place there for her grave, and about five days before giving birth she wrote her will. And bear in mind, all this was happening at a time when she enjoyed excellent health, without the smallest hint of any illness or injury. Giving birth is a difficult process, sometimes mortal, but in the case of the woman I'm speaking about everything was going well, and there was certainly nothing to worry about. In the end, her husband was exasperated by the whole business. At dinner once he grew angry and asked:

"'Listen, Natasha, when will this foolish business end?'

"'It's not foolish. I'm being serious.'

"'Rubbish! I would advise you to stop being a fool, so that later you'll not be ashamed of yourself.'

"But then the labour started. Her husband brought from town the very best midwife. The birth was his wife's first, but it couldn't have gone better. When it was all over, the new mother asked to look at the baby. She looked and said:

"'Well, now I can die.'

"She said goodbye, closed her eyes and half an hour later yielded up her soul to God. She was conscious until the very last minute. At any rate, when instead of water she was offered milk, she quietly whispered:

"'Why do you give me milk instead of water?'

"So that's the story. She dies just as she had foretold."

The coroner fell silent, sighed and said:

"So do tell me, what did she die of? I assure you, on my word of honour, that I haven't made this up, but it's a fact."

The doctor looked thoughtfully at the sky.

"They should have done a post-mortem on her," he said.

"Why?"

"So as to discover the cause of death. It was not because of her prediction that she died. She probably poisoned herself."

The coroner quickly turned to face the doctor and, screwing up his eyes, asked:

"Why do you conclude that she poisoned herself?"

"I do not conclude, but suggest. Did she get on well with her husband?"

"Hm... not very. A misunderstanding arose soon after the wedding. It was such an unfortunate occurrence. One day the deceased found her husband with another woman... But she soon forgave him."

"But what came first, the betrayal of the husband or the appearance of the idea of death?"

The coroner looked intently at the doctor, as if trying to guess why he had asked such a question.

"Let me..." he replied after a pause. "Let me... try and remember." The coroner took off his hat and rubbed his forehead. "Yes, yes... She began to talk of dying soon after that incident. Yes, yes indeed."

"Well, do you see... She had probably decided to poison herself, but because she didn't want to kill the baby along with herself, she postponed her suicide until the baby was born."

"It's hardly likely, hardly likely... It's impossible. By then she had forgiven him."

"She may have forgiven him, but she continued to think ill of him. Young wives don't easily forgive."

The coroner forced a smile, and in order to conceal his evident emotion, lit a cigarette.

"It's hardly likely, hardly likely..." he repeated. "The thought of such a possibility didn't even enter my head. And besides... he was not really as guilty as it looks... He betrayed her in a very strange way, almost unwillingly: he arrived home one night tipsy, wanting to make love, but his wife was in an interesting condition... Then he happened to meet a woman, the Devil take her, who had come to visit for three days – a frivolous tart, silly, unattractive. It cannot really be considered betrayal. Even the wife herself looked on it like that, and soon… forgave him. After that they didn't even talk about it…"

"People do not die without cause," said the doctor.

"That is so, of course, but all the same… I cannot accept that she poisoned herself. But it's strange how until now the possibility that she died like that didn't even occur to me!… And no one thought about it! Everyone was surprised that her prediction came true, and the thought of the possibility… of such a death was remote… It simply cannot be that she poisoned herself! No!"

The coroner fell to thinking. The thought of the woman who had strangely died did not leave him even during the autopsy. As he made notes about what the doctor was dictating, he gloomily moved his eyebrows and rubbed his forehead.

"But is there really such a poison that kills in a quarter of an hour, little by little and without any pain?" he asked the doctor when the latter was opening the skull.

"Yes, there is. Morphine, for example."

"Hm… It's strange… I remember, she had something like it near her… But it's hardly likely!"

On the return journey the coroner bore a weary look, was nervously biting his whiskers and seemed unwilling to talk.

"Let's continue awhile on foot," he suggested to the doctor. "I'm tired of sitting."

After walking a hundred steps, the coroner seemed to have grown very weak, as if climbing a high mountain. He stopped and, looking strangely at the doctor, as if with drunken eyes, said:

"My God, if your assumption is valid, then really, this is… cruel, inhuman! Poisoned herself, in order to punish her husband! Is there really sin so great! Oh, my God! Why did you put this damned thought into my head, doctor?"

The coroner clutched his head in despair and continued:

"It is about my wife and myself that I told you. Oh, my God! Well, I am to blame – I hurt her, but is it really easier to die than to forgive? That's exactly women's logic – cruel, merciless logic. Oh, but then even in life she was cruel! Now I remember! Now it's all clear to me!"

The coroner talked and now shrugged his shoulders, now clutched his head – now he sat down in the carriage, now he continued on foot. That new thought, conveyed to him by the doctor, seemed to stun him, poison him. He felt lost, weakened in soul and body – and, when he returned to town, said goodbye to the doctor, refusing dinner, even though the day before he had given him his word to dine with him.

A Serious Step

Alexei Borisych, who has only just parted from a post-prandial meeting with Morpheus,* is sitting with his wife, Marfa Afanasyevna, by the window and grumbling. He is displeased that his daughter Lidochka has gone for a stroll in the garden with Fyodor Petrovich, a young man…

"I can't bear it," he mutters, "when young girls so forget themselves that they lose modesty. I see nothing in these ramblings in the garden, along dark paths, besides immorality and depravity. You are her mother, but see nothing… So, you think it's quite all right for a girl to be engaged in foolishness… You think it doesn't matter if they start a love affair there. You yourself would be glad in old age, having abandoned shame, to leap to a rendezvous."

"Why are you irritating me?" asks the old woman angrily. "He's grumbling and doesn't himself know why. Bald scoundrel!"

"So then? You think… let them… let them kiss out there, embrace… Very well… let them… It's not I who'll have to answer before God if a young girl's head is turned… Kiss, my dears! Behave as if you're engaged!"

"Don't be too hasty… Maybe nothing will come of it."

"God grant that nothing will come of it…" sighs Alexei Borisych.

"You have always been the enemy of your own child… You never desired anything but harm for Lisa. Watch out, Alexei, take care that God doesn't punish you for your cruelty! I fear for you! After all, you haven't much longer to live!"

"As you wish, but I can't allow this… He is not a match for her, and there is no need for her to rush… Judging by our circumstances and her beauty, she will have even better fiancés… However, why am I discussing this with you? As if I need to discuss it with you! He needs to be sent packing, and Lidka put under lock and key – that's all… That's just what I'll do."

The old man speaks sluggishly, yawning, as if chewing rubber – evidently he is grumbling because he is feeling anxious and letting his tongue run away with him, but the old woman takes to heart every word of his. She throws up her hands, snaps and clucks like a hen. "Tyrant", "monster", "unbeliever", "idolater" and other swear words well known to her simply jump from her tongue straight into Alexei Borisych's "mug"... The matter would end, as always, with an outpouring of spittle and tears, but now the old people suddenly see something extraordinary: their daughter Lidochka, with dishevelled hair, is rushing along the path towards the house. At the same time, far away at a turn in the path, Fyodor Petrovich's straw hat appears from behind a bush. Just then, the young man himself appears, strikingly pale. He hesitantly takes two steps forward, then waves his hand and quickly steps back. Then Lidochka is heard running into the house, flying through all the corridors and loudly locking herself in her room.

The old couple exchange looks in dull amazement, cast their eyes down and go slightly pale. Both are silent, not knowing what to say. The situation is as clear as daylight for them. Without saying anything, both understand and sense that while just now they were grouching and sparring with each other, their daughter's fate was being decided. Even the most basic human sensitivity, not to mention a parent's heart, will allow them to understand what Lidochka is going through right now, having locked herself in her room, and what significant, fateful part in her life will be played by the receding straw hat...

Alexei Borisych gets up with a groan and starts to pace back and forth in the room... The old woman follows his movements, and with a sinking heart waits for him to begin speaking.

"What strange weather we're having these days," says the old man. "At night it's cold, in the day the heat is unbearable."

The cook brings in the samovar. Marfa Afanasyevna wipes the cups and pours the tea, but neither of them touches it.

"We should call her... Lida... down to tea..." mutters Alexei Borisych. "Otherwise the samovar will have to be put on just for her... I don't like bother!"

Marfa Afanasyevna wants to say something but cannot. Her lips move, her tongue does not obey, and her eyes cloud over as if lurking behind a shroud. A minute later, and she's crying. Alexei Borisych wants very much to caress the woebegone old woman, and himself feels like whimpering, but his pride prevents it: he has to show character.

"All this is good and marvellous," he mutters. "Only, he should have spoken to us first... Yes... He first should have properly asked for our Lidochka's hand... Perhaps we would not even have consented!"

The old woman waves both her hands, loudly sobs and goes to her room.

"It's a serious step..." thinks Alexei Borisych. "One mustn't make a decision thoughtlessly. One has to be serious, look at it from all sides... I shall go and question her, how and what... I shall talk to her and decide... We can't go on like this!"

The old man draws his dressing gown more tightly around himself and minces to Lidochka's door.

"Lidochka!" he says, hesitantly touching the door handle. "You... ah? Are you unwell, or what?"

There is no answer. Alexei Borisych sighs. For want of anything better to do, he shrugs and moves away from the door.

"We can't go on like this!" he thinks, shuffling along the corridor in his slippers. "We have to look at it from all sides... to ponder, to talk, to consider... Marriage is a sacrament that must not be treated lightly... I shall go and discuss the matter with the old woman..."

The old man minces to his wife's room. Marfa Afanasyevna is standing before an open trunk, and with trembling hands is sorting through the linen.

"There are no nightdresses at all..." she mutters. "Good parents, who care, give even children's clothes for a dowry, but we have neither handkerchiefs nor towels... One might think she is not our own daughter, but an orphan..."

"We have a serious matter to talk about, and you talk about rags... It's shameful even to look... A vital question is to be settled, and she stands, like a merchant's wife, in front of a trunk counting rags... We can't go on like this!"

"But what's to be done?"

"We have to think, to consider the matter from all sides... to discuss..."

The old couple hear how Lidochka unlocks her door, sends the maid with a letter to Fyodor Petrovich, and again locks herself in the room...

"She is sending him a firm reply," whispers Alexei Borisych. "How stupid they are, God forgive them! It never occurred to her to discuss it with her elders! Well, that's what young people are like!"

"I have just thought, Alyosha!" The old woman throws up her hands. "We really have to find new lodgings in town! If Lidochka will not be living with us, why do we need eight rooms?"

"This is all idle talk... nonsense... Now we have to talk about serious things..."

Until supper the old couple scurry through the rooms like shadows, beside themselves with worry. Marfa Afanasyevna rummages pointlessly in the linen, whispers to the cook, constantly sobs – and Alexei Borisych grumbles, wants to talk about serious matters and talks nonsense. Lidochka appears towards supper. Her face is pink, and her eyes slightly swollen...

"Ah, good evening!" says the old man without looking at her.

They sit down to eat, and eat the first two courses in silence... On the servants' faces, in their movements, in the way they walk – in everything can be seen a kind of bashful solemnity...

"We should, Lidochka, ah..." the old man begins, "seriously consider... from all sides... Mm-yes... Shall we have some fruit liqueur? Glafira, bring us some fruit liqueur! It wouldn't hurt to have champagne, but if we don't it doesn't matter... Mm-yes... We can't go on like this!"

The fruit liqueur is served. The old man drinks one small glass after another…

"So let's discuss…" he says. "It's a serious matter, vital… We can't go on like this!"

"It's terrible, Papa dear, how you love to talk so much!" sighs Lidochka.

"Well, well…" the old man says in a frightened voice. "I really only do this… for something to say… Don't be angry…"

After supper, mother and daughter whisper together for a long time.

"Most likely they're talking about trifles," thinks the old man, pacing back and forth through the rooms. "They don't understand, the silly ones, that this is serious… important… We can't go on like this, it's impossible!"

Night falls… Lidochka lies in her room and does not sleep… The old couple don't sleep either: they whisper till dawn.

"The flies give us no peace!" mutters Alexei Borisych.

However, the fault lies not with flies, but with human nature.

The Fiancé

A MAN WITH A PURPLISH-GREY NOSE approached the bell and hesitantly rang it. The public, hitherto relaxed, anxiously began to bustle about… Baggage carts began to rumble along the platform. Ropes noisily began to be stretched over the carriages… Whistling, the locomotive began to back up to the carriages. It was coupled to them. Someone, somewhere, fussing around, broke a bottle. Leave-takings, loud sobs, women's voices were heard…

A young man and a young girl were standing near one of the second-class carriages. They were saying goodbye and crying.

"Goodbye, my darling!" said the young man, kissing the girl on her blond head. "Goodbye! I am so unhappy! You are leaving me for a whole week! For a loving heart this is really a whole eternity! Good–bye… Dry your tears… Don't cry…"

Tears flowed from the girl's eyes. One little tear fell onto the young man's lip.

"Goodbye, Varya! Give my regards to everyone… Oh yes! By the way… If you see Mrakov there, then give him these… these… Don't cry, my dear… Give him these twenty-five roubles…"

The young man drew from his pocket a twenty-five-rouble note and gave it to Varya.

"Be so kind as to give… I owe him… Ah, how hard it is!"

"Don't cry, Petya. On Saturday without fail I… shall return… So don't you forget me…"

The blond head pressed against Petya's chest.

"You? Forget you? Is that really possible?"

The second bell rang. Petya hugged Varya, blinked and began to howl like a child. Varya hung on his neck and started to moan. They entered the carriage.

"Goodbye! Darling! Sweetheart! In a week!"

The young man kissed Varya for the last time and left the carriage. He stood by the window and drew from his pocket a handkerchief, in order to wave… Varya fixed her wet eyes on his face…

"Get into the carriage!" commanded the conductor. "The third bell is about to go! I b-e-eg you!"

The third bell rang. Petya waved his handkerchief. But suddenly his face fell… He smacked his forehead and ran like a madman into the carriage.

"Varya!" he said, gasping. "I gave you twenty-five roubles for Mrakov… Darling… Give me a receipt! Quickly! A receipt, my dear! How could I have forgotten?"

"It's too late, Petya! Oh! The train has started!"

The train started. The young man leapt from the carriage, crying bitterly, and began to wave his handkerchief.

"You better send the receipt in the mail!" he cried to the blond head that was nodding at him.

"I really am such a fool!" he thought as the train disappeared from view. "I give money without getting a receipt! Ah? What a blunder, like a child!" He sighs. "She must be approaching the station now… My darling!"

In Autumn

IT WAS NEARLY NIGHT-TIME.

A group of carters and pilgrims were sitting in Uncle Tikhon's tavern. They had been driven into the tavern by an autumn downpour and a furious wind that lashed like a whip any faces exposed to it. The soaked and tired travellers were sitting by the walls on benches, and, listening to the wind, were dozing. Boredom was written on their faces. A wet accordion lay on the knees of one of the carters, a fellow with a scratched, pockmarked face. He had been playing, and absent-mindedly stopped.

Above the door, around a dim, dirty lamp, swirled splashes of rain. The wind howled like a wolf, screamed, and seemed as if it was trying to tear the tavern door from its hinges. From the yard came the sound of horses snorting and splashing in the mud. It was damp and cold.

Behind the counter was sitting Uncle Tikhon himself – a tall, broad-faced man with sleepy, bloated eyes. On the other side of the counter was standing a man of about forty: his clothes were dirty, but not cheap, and had been carefully chosen. He was wearing a loose, muddy summer coat and checked calico trousers, and had rubber galoshes on his bare feet. His head, the hands in his pockets and his thin, sharp elbows shook as if he were running a fever. From time to time, along his whole emaciated body, from his terribly haggard face to his rubber galoshes, ran light spasms.

"Give me, for Christ's sake," he was saying to Tikhon in a broken, shaky tenor voice, "a little glass... this one here is too small. On credit, of course!"

"I don't know... There are a lot of scoundrels like you who loaf around here!"

The scoundrel looked at Tikhon with contempt, with hatred. He would have killed him, if he could.

"You should understand, you are such a fool, such an idiot! It's not I who's asking. Putting it in language you can understand: it's my guts that are craving it! My disease is asking for it! You should understand!"

"There's nothing to understand. Get out..."

"You see, if I don't drink now, you should understand, if I don't satisfy my craving, then I may commit a crime! God knows what I may do! You've seen, you fool, in all your life in the tavern, many drunken people – were you really not able to understand before now what sort of people they are? They are sick! Put them in chains, beat them, torture them, but give them vodka! Come on, I beg you most humbly! Do me a favour! I'm humiliating myself... God, how I'm humiliating myself!"

The scoundrel shook his head and slowly spat.

"Give money, then you'll get vodka!" said Tikhon.

"Where am I to get money? It's all gone on drink! All, completely! This coat is all that's left. I can't give it to you, because I have nothing underneath... Do you want my hat?"

The scoundrel gave Tikhon his thick wool-and-cloth cap, from which in places the wadding showed through. Tikhon took the hat, examined it and shook his head.

"I wouldn't take it if it was free," he said. "It's rubbish..."

"You don't like it? Well, then give me credit if you don't like it. When I come back from town I'll bring you five copecks. Then you can choke on them! Choke!"

"What kind of swindler are you? What kind of man? Why did you come?"

"I want a drink. It's not I who wants it, my disease wants it! Try and understand!"

"Why are you bothering me? There are a lot of you down-and-outs wandering along the road. Go away and ask Christian believers, let them help you, for Christ's sake, if they wish, but for Christ's sake I would only give you bread. Swine!"

"You fleece these paupers, but I... I'm sorry! I can't make them even poorer! I can't!"

The scoundrel suddenly interrupted his speech, reddened and turned to the pilgrims:

"But here's an idea, Christian believers! Donate a little five-copeck coin. My insides are begging! I'm sick!"

"Drink some water," grinned the fellow with the pockmarked face.

The scoundrel was ashamed. He began to cough and fell silent. A minute later he was again begging Tikhon. In the end he began to cry, and offered his wet coat for a little glass of vodka. In the darkness they did not see his tears. The coat was rejected, because some of the pilgrims were women who did not wish to see a naked man.

"What can I do now?" the scoundrel asked quietly, full of despair. "What can I do? I need a drink. Otherwise I shall commit a crime, or decide to kill myself... what can I do?"

He paced back and forth in the tavern.

The postal tarantass arrived with bells ringing. The wet postman entered the tavern, drank a glass of vodka and left. The tarantass went on its way.

"I shall give you some gold," the scoundrel said, turning to Tikhon and suddenly becoming as pale as a sheet. "If you like, I shall give it to you. So be it... It may be despicable, abominable on my part, but take it... I shall do this despicable thing because I'm not myself... And in court I would be acquitted... Take it, but only on one condition: give it back to me when I return. I give it to you in front of witnesses..."

The scoundrel put his wet hand inside his coat and got from there a little gold round case. He opened it and glanced at the portrait that was inside.

"I should take out the portrait, but I have nowhere to put it. I'm all wet. To hell with you – take it with the portrait. Only on one condition... My dear man, dear fellow... I beg you... Don't touch the face with your fingers... I implore you, dear man! Excuse me for having spoken so rudely to you... I am a fool... Don't touch the face with your fingers, and don't look at it..."

Tikhon took the gold case, examined its hallmark and put it in his pocket.

"A stolen watch," he said, filling the glass. "Well, all right... drink..."

The drunkard took the glass in his hands, looked at it with eyes that gleamed as much as drunken, lacklustre eyes could gleam, and drank... He drank with feeling, with frantic deliberation. Having spent on drink the watchcase with the portrait, he lowered his eyes in embarrassment and went to a corner. There he found room for himself on a bench near one of the women pilgrims, huddled up and closed his eyes.

Half an hour passed in stillness and silence. Only the wind made a noise, humming its autumn rhapsody in the chimney. The pilgrims began to say their prayers, and noiselessly settled themselves under the benches for the night. Tikhon opened the watchcase and looked at the woman's head, which was smiling from the golden frame at the tavern, at Tikhon, at the bottles.

The creaking of a cart was heard in the courtyard. A horse snorted, and there was the sound of splashing through mud. Into the tavern ran a little peasant with a sharply pointed beard, wearing a long sheepskin coat. He was wet and covered in mud.

"Come on, then!" he cried, banging a five-copeck piece on the counter. "A glass of the best Madeira! Pour it out!"

Turning on one leg, the dashing fellow glanced around the room.

"Only things made of sugar will melt, you fools! You're afraid of the rain, are you, idiots? Precious people! But who is this here?"

The man rushed to the scoundrel and looked him in the face.

"Are you here? *Barin!*" he said. "Semyon Sergeich! Our master! Well? What are you doing loafing around in this tavern? Is this really the place for you? Eh... Poor soul."

The *barin* looked at the man and covered his face with his sleeve. The man sighed, shook his head, waved his hands despairingly and went to the counter for vodka.

"It's our *barin*," he whispered to Tikhon, nodding towards the scoundrel. "Our landowner, Semyon Sergeich. Look what a state he's in! Do you see what he's like now? Well? That's what it is... that's what drunkenness leads to..."

After downing his vodka, the man wiped his lips with his sleeve and continued:

"I'm from his village – from Akhtilovka, four hundred versts from here... His father owned serfs... It's such a pity, brother! Such a pity! He was such a fine gentleman... That horse there, in the yard. Do you see her? It was he who gave me the money for the horse. Ha-ha! It's destiny!"

Ten minutes later the carters and pilgrims were sitting around the man. In a quiet, nervous tenor voice, to the sounds of the autumn, he told them the story. Semyon Sergeich was sitting in the same corner, muttering with his eyes closed. He was also listening.

"All this resulted from weakness of character," said the man, moving around and gesticulating with his hands. "From having too much... He was a rich gentleman, his generosity was known throughout the province... He had more to eat and drink than anyone could ever want! You yourselves probably saw him... He drove past this very tavern many times in his carriage. He was rich... I remember, about five years ago, he was going across on the Mikishkinsky ferry, and instead of five copecks gave a rouble. His ruin started when he began behaving in a silly way. First, it was to do with a woman. He fell in love, poor man, with someone from town... He loved her more than his life. He fell in love with a crow, not a falcon...* This despicable woman was called Marya Yegorovna, but her surname was so strange you couldn't even pronounce it. He fell in love and asked her to marry him, as God's law demands. And she, of course, agreed, because he was a *barin* and not of humble stock, didn't drink and had money... I remember one evening going past their garden. I look, and see them sitting on a bench kissing. He kisses her once, and she, the snake, kisses him twice. He takes her hand, and she... blushes! Just huddles up to him, the she-devil!... I love you, Senya, she says... And Senya, like an idiot, happily goes everywhere, stupidly boasting... Here he gives a rouble, there he gives two... To me he gave money for a horse... He forgave everyone their debts in celebration. The time came for the wedding... They were properly married. At the very moment when the guests were sitting down to the meal, she upped and escaped in a carriage... In town she ran straight to her lover, a lawyer. Right after the wedding, the bitch! How about that? At that very moment! And then? After that he went mad, took to drink. So now you can see. He goes around like a madman, thinking about her, the bitch. He loves her! He must be going to town now on foot to catch a glimpse of her...

"The second thing, brothers, that brought about his ruin, was to do with his brother-in-law, his sister's husband... He agreed to be a guarantor to the bank for his brother-in-law... for about thirty thousand... The brother-in-law, the scoundrel, knew, of course, where his interests lay and didn't give a damn, and our *barin* lost all thirty thousand... A stupid man suffers torments for his stupidity... The wife had children with her lover, the brother-in-law bought an estate near Poltava, but our *barin* just goes like a fool from tavern to tavern, and complains to us peasants: 'I lost faith, brothers! There is no one I can... trust now!' This is faint-heartedness! Everyone has his own grief... so does it mean everyone should start drinking? Take our village elder, for example. His wife goes around with the teacher in broad daylight, spends her husband's money on booze, but the elder himself walks around with a smile on his face... He only grows a little thin..."

"God gives strength to those who can bear it," sighed Tikhon. "There are different strengths – it's true."

The little peasant spoke for a long time. When he finished, silence fell in the tavern.

"Hey, you... What's your name?... Poor wretch! Come and have a drink!" said Tikhon, turning to the *barin*.

The *barin* came to the counter and gratefully gulped down the charitable offering...

"Give me the watchcase for a minute!" he whispered to Tikhon. "I'll just have a look and... give it back..."

Tikhon frowned and silently gave him back the watchcase. The fellow with the pockmarked face sighed, shook his head and demanded vodka.

"Drink up, *barin*! Come on! Without vodka it's good, but with vodka it's even better! Grief isn't grief with vodka! Carry on!"

After drinking five glasses, the *barin* retired to the corner, opened the watchcase and with drunken, lacklustre eyes looked for the dear face... But the face was no longer there... The virtuous Tikhon had scratched it out of the medallion with his nails.

The lantern blazed up and went out. The female pilgrim in the corner began to mutter rapidly in her sleep. The fellow with the pockmarked face said his prayers aloud and stretched out on the counter. Someone else drove up... And the rain poured and poured. It grew colder and colder, and it seemed as if there would be no end to the dreadful, dark autumn. The *barin* fixed his eyes on the watchcase and kept seeking the woman's face... The light from the candle was growing fainter.

Spring, where are you?

A Slander

THE CALLIGRAPHY TEACHER Sergei Kapitonych Akhineyev was marrying his daughter Natalya to the history and geography teacher Ivan Petrovich Loshadiny. The wedding celebrations were going as smoothly as clockwork. In the hall there was singing, playing, dancing. Footmen in black tailcoats and soiled white ties, who had been hired from the club, were dashing back and forth through the rooms like madmen. There was noise and the sound of conversation. The maths teacher Tarantulov, the Frenchman Pasdequoi and the junior financial auditor Yegor Venediktych Mzda, sitting side by side on a sofa and speaking quickly and interrupting each other, were telling the guests about cases of people who had been buried alive and expressing their opinions about spiritualism. None of the three believed in spiritualism, but all admitted that in this world there are many things the mind of man will never comprehend. In another room the literature teacher Dodonsky was telling the guests about cases in which a sentry has the right to shoot passers-by. The conversations were, as you can see, frightening, but most enjoyable. People who, because of their social position, did not have the right to come in were looking through the windows from outside.

Precisely at midnight the host Akhineyev went to the kitchen to see whether everything was ready for supper. The kitchen was filled to the rafters with smoke from roasting goose and duck, as well as many other smells. On two tables were placed and arranged in tasteful disarray selections of *zakuski* and drinks. The cook Marfa, a red-faced woman with a doubly distended belly, was fussing around the tables.

"Do show me, my dear, the sturgeon!" said Akhineyev, rubbing his hands and smacking his lips. "What a smell, what an aroma! I could eat the whole kitchen! Come on, show me the sturgeon!"

Marfa went to one of the benches and carefully raised a greasy sheet of newspaper. Under this sheet, on a vast plate, lay a big jellied sturgeon adorned with capers, olives and carrots. Akhineyev looked at the sturgeon and sighed. His face shone, his eyes rolled. He bent down and emitted through his lips the sound of an unoiled wheel. After standing for a while he snapped his fingers with delight and once more smacked his lips.

"A-ha! The sound of a passionate kiss… Who are you kissing here, Marfusha?" A voice was heard from the next room, and in the doorway appeared the close-cropped head of assistant class teacher Vankin. "Who are you with? A-a-ah… how delightful! With Sergei Kapitonych! He's quite the old man, I must say! Tête-à-tête with the fair sextet!"

"I am not at all kissing," said Akhineyev in embarrassment. "Who told you that, you fool? I was… ah, smacking my lips because of the… thinking of the pleasure… At the sight of the fish…"

"Tell me another one!"

Vankin grinned broadly and disappeared through the door. Akhineyev reddened.

"The devil knows what he's going to do!" he thought. "He'll go now, the bastard, and gossip. He'll shame me before the whole town, the swine…"

Akhineyev went timidly into the hall and looked around furtively: where was Vankin? Vankin was standing next to the piano and, boldly bending down, was whispering something to the inspector's sister-in-law, who was laughing.

"It's about me!" thought Akhineyev. "About me, the Devil take him. And she believes it too… she believes it! She's laughing! My God! No, I can't leave it there… no… I'll have to do something, so that they don't believe him… I shall have to tell everyone about him, and show him up as the foolish scandalmonger that he is."

Akhineyev scratched his head and, still embarrassed, went up to Pasdequoi.

"I've just been in the kitchen, giving instructions about supper," he said to the Frenchman. "I know you love fish, so I have sturgeon, my friend... amazing! Two *arshins** long! He-he-he... And incidentally... I almost forgot... In the kitchen just now, with this sturgeon, I have quite a story to tell you! I go into the kitchen just now, wanting to inspect the food... I look at the sturgeon, and from pleasure... from the aroma, I smack my lips! And at this moment that fool Vankin suddenly comes in and says... ha-ha-ha... and says: 'A-a-ah... so you're kissing her?' Kissing Marfa, the cook! He really believed it, the stupid man! The woman is nothing to look at – she is just like all others, but he... kissing! The crackpot!"

"Who's a crackpot?" asked Tarantulov, who was walking past.

"That one over there. Vankin! I go, you see, into the kitchen..."

And he related what had happened with Vankin.

"He made me laugh, the crackpot! To me it would be more pleasant to kiss the watchdog than Marfa," added Akhineyev. He glanced around and saw Mzda behind him.

"We are talking about Vankin," he said to Mzda. "The stupid crackpot! He goes into the kitchen, you see, sees me next to Marfa, and suddenly thinks up a joke. 'Why,' he says, 'are you kissing her?' He seemed rather drunk. I tell him I would rather kiss a turkey-cock than Marfa. 'I have a wife,' I say. 'You are such a fool!' He made me laugh!"

"Who made you laugh?" asked the divinity teacher, going up to Akhineyev.

"Vankin. I am standing, you know, in the kitchen and looking at the sturgeon..."

And so on. After some half an hour all the guests already knew the story about the sturgeon and Vankin.

"Let him tell them now," thought Akhineyev, rubbing his hands. "Let him! He will start to tell them, and right away they'll say: 'That's enough nonsense, you fool! We know all about it!'"

Akhineyev was so relieved that in his joy he drank four more small glasses of vodka. After supper he showed the young people to their bedroom and went to his own and fell asleep like an innocent child. The next day he no longer remembered the story of the sturgeon. But alas! Man proposes, but God disposes. An evil tongue did its evil work, and Akhineyev's stratagem did not help him. Exactly a week later, on Wednesday after the third lesson to be precise, when Akhineyev was standing in the middle of the teachers' common room talking about the wayward tendencies of the pupil Visyekin, the director came up to him and took him aside.

"Look here, Sergei Kapitonych," said the director. "Excuse me... It's not my business, but, all the same, I must have you understand... It's my responsibility... Do you see, rumours are going around that you're carrying on with this... with a cook... It isn't my business, but... You are carrying on with her, kissing her... Do what you want – only, please, not so openly! I beg you! Don't forget, you're a teacher!"

Akhineyev froze in stupefaction. He went home as if stung by a swarm of insects and scalded by boiling water. As he walked home, it seemed to him that the whole town was looking at him, as if he had been smeared with pitch... At home, more trouble awaited him.

"So why are you not eating anything?" his wife asked him at dinner. "What are you thinking about? Are you thinking about your little love affairs? Are you pining for Marfushka? I know all about it, you devil! Some kindly people have opened my eyes! O-o-oh... you brute!"

And she smacked him on the cheek... He rose from the table and, not feeling the ground under his feet, trudged without a hat or coat to Vankin's. He found Vankin at home.

"You swine!" Akhineyev said to Vankin. "Why did you throw mud at me before all the world? Why did you set off this slander about me?"

"What slander? What are you imagining?"

"But who started the rumour, telling people I was kissing Marfa? Wasn't it you who told them? Wasn't it you, you scoundrel?"

Vankin started to blink, and he blinked with every fibre of his worn-out face. He raised his eyes to the icon and said:

"I swear to God! Strike me blind and let me die if I said even one word about you! Let me rot in hell! Let me be stricken with cholera!..."

Vankin's sincerity could not be doubted. Clearly it was not he who had started the rumour.

"But who had, then? Who?" thought Akhineyev, recalling all his acquaintances and beating his breast. "So who?"

"So who?" we ask the reader too...

The Pink Stocking

A DULL, RAINY DAY. For a long time the sky has been obscured by storm clouds, and no end to the rain is predicted. Outside there is slush, puddles and wet jackdaws, while inside the rooms are dark, and cold enough to have the stoves lit.

Ivan Petrovich Somov paces back and forth in his study, grumbling about the weather. The drops of rain on the windows and the darkness of the rooms arouse in him melancholy thoughts. He is insufferably bored, but there is no way of killing time... The newspapers have not yet been delivered, there is no chance of going hunting, and it is not yet dinner time...

Somov is not alone in the study. At the writing table sits Mrs Somov, a small, pretty young lady wearing a light smock and pink stockings. She is painstakingly writing a letter. Each time he goes past her, the restless Ivan Petrovich peeps over her shoulder at the writing. He sees large, badly formed letters, narrow and thin, with irritating tails and flourishes. There are a multitude of blots, crossings-out and fingerprints. Mrs Somov does not like to hyphenate words, and each of her lines, on reaching the edge of the page, cascades down, with dreadful contortions, like a waterfall...

"Lidochka, to whom is it that you write so much?" asks Somov, seeing that his wife has started scribbling on the sixth sheet.

"To my sister Varya..."

"Hm... it's a long letter! Let me read it, out of curiosity."

"Take it, read it – only, there's nothing interesting in it..."

Somov takes the written sheets and, as he paces, starts to read. Lidochka rests her elbows on the back of the armchair and watches the expression on his face. After the very first page his face falls and conveys something like fright... On the third page, Somov knits his brow and slowly scratches the back of his head. On the fourth he stops, looks in puzzlement at his wife and falls to thinking. After thinking awhile, he sighs and again gets down to reading… His face expresses perplexity and even fright…

"No, this is impossible!" he mutters on finishing the letter and flinging the sheets on the table. "Absolutely impossible!"

"What's the matter?" asks Lidochka in fright.

"What's the matter! You covered six pages, spent two full hours on the writing and… and you don't know what's the matter! If only there was a single thought! You read and read and you're struck by some kind of amnesia, and the result is like the gibberish on boxes of Chinese tea! Oof!"

"Yes, it's true, Vanya…" says Lidochka, reddening. "I wrote carelessly…"

"What the devil do you mean, 'carelessly'? Even in a carelessly written letter there is meaning and sense, there is substance, but you have… excuse me, I can't even find a name! Complete nonsense! There are words and phrases, but not the slightest substance. Your whole letter is exactly like the conversation of two little boys: 'And we are eating blinis now!' – 'And a soldier came to visit us!' You just go on and on like that! You draw it out, you repeat yourself… Little thoughts jump around like grasshoppers in a sieve: it's impossible to make out where it begins, where it ends… Well, isn't it so?"

"If I wrote with care," says Lidochka, trying to justify herself, "then there wouldn't be any mistakes…"

"Oh, I'm not talking about mistakes! It screams poor grammar! There is hardly a line that is not inaccurate in some way. There are neither commas nor full stops, and as for the spelling… brrr! 'Ground' is written with a 'd' at the end, not a 't'. And the handwriting? It's not handwriting, but a hopeless muddle! I'm not joking, Lida… This letter of yours amazes and stuns me… Don't you be angry, my dear, but I really never thought that when it comes to grammar you are such a cobbler… And besides, by your position in society you belong to the educated, cultivated class. You are the wife of a university man, the daughter of a general! Listen, weren't you educated somewhere?"

"What do you mean? I graduated from Von Mebka's boarding school..."

Somov shrugs and, sighing, continues to pace. Lidochka, conscious of her ignorance and feeling ashamed, also sighs and lowers her eyes. Some ten minutes pass in silence...

"Listen, Lidochka, you know this is really dreadful!" says Somov, suddenly stopping in front of his wife and looking in horror at her face. "Good lord, you're a mother... Understand? A mother! How on earth will you teach your children if you yourself know nothing? You have a good brain, but of what use is it if it didn't acquire even the rudiments of learning? Well, forget about learning... children learn at school, but surely you are even shaky in the sphere of morals! You do sometimes blurt out things that make my ears ache!"

Somov again shrugs, pulls his dressing gown more tightly around himself and continues to pace... He is vexed and hurt, but at that moment feels sorry for Lidochka, who does not protest, but just blinks... It is hard and bitter for them both. Because of their grief, neither of them notices how time is flying and dinner time is approaching.

Sitting down to dine, Somov, who liked to eat calmly and with enjoyment, drinks a big glass of vodka and starts a conversation on another subject. Lidochka listens to him, and assents, but suddenly, during the soup course, her eyes fill with tears and she begins to whimper.

"It's my mother's fault!" she says, wiping her tears with the napkin. "Everyone advised her to send me to high school, and from high school I probably would have gone on a higher-education course!"

"On a course... to high school..." mutters Somov. "That would have been really too much, my dear! What is the good of being a bluestocking? Bluestocking... the devil knows what it is! It's neither a woman nor a man, neither one thing nor another, neither this nor that... I hate bluestockings! I would never have married an educated woman..."

"You are confused," says Lidochka. "You are angry that I am uneducated, but at the same time you hate educated women. You resent my having no ideas in my letter, but are opposed to my having been educated..."

"You're cavilling at words, my dear," yawns Somov, from boredom pouring himself a second glass...

Under the influence of the vodka he has drunk, and the substantial dinner, Somov becomes more cheerful, kinder and gentler... He sees how his pretty wife prepares the salad with an anxious face, and is filled with a surge of fondness for women, with tolerance, forgiveness...

"I upset her unnecessarily today, the poor thing," he thinks. "Why did I say so many vile things to her? In truth, she is a silly one, uncivilized, limited, but... surely a medal has two sides, and *audiatur et altera pars...** Perhaps those who say that a woman's thoughtlessness is founded on their vocation are a thousand times correct... If we assume that she is called upon to love her husband, bear children and cut salad, why the devil does she need education? Of course!"

At this, he remembers how difficult clever women in general can be, how they are demanding, strict and uncompromising, and how, on the contrary, it is easy to live with dear, stupid Lidochka, who does not interfere in the many things she does not understand and does not criticize anybody. It is peaceful to live with Lidochka, and you do not risk being controlled...

"Never mind those clever and educated women! You live better and more peacefully with unpretentious ones," he thinks, taking a plate of chicken from Lidochka...

He recalls how a civilized man sometimes has the desire to have a chat and share thoughts with a clever and educated woman...

"So what?" Somov thinks. "When I want to have a chat about intelligent matters, I shall go to Natalya Andreyevna... or to Marya Frantsevna... It's very simple!"

The Proud Man

(A Story)

THIS INCIDENT HAPPENED at a wedding at merchant Sinerylov's house.

The best man Nedoryezov, a tall young man with goggling eyes and a close-cropped head, wearing a tailcoat with bulging flaps, was standing in a crowd of young ladies and having a discussion.

"Beauty is essential in a woman, but a man will get by even without good looks. What is important for a man is to have intelligence, education – but for him, looks... to hell with it! If you have no education in your head, and no intellectual ability, then you are not worth two copecks, even if you are handsome... Yes indeed... I don't like handsome men! *Fi donc!**

"You say that only because you yourself are not handsome. Over there, look through the door to the other room – there's a man sitting there, a really good-looking man! His eyes alone are capable of bewitching a person! Just look at him! Fascinating! Who is he?"

The best man looked in the other room and smirked contemptuously. There, a handsome, black-eyed, dark-haired man was sitting sprawled in an armchair. Sitting cross-legged and playing with a chain, the dark-haired man was screwing up his eyes and looking loftily at the guests. A disdainful smile was playing on his lips.

"He's nothing special," said the best man. "So-so... One might even say he's ugly. He has a kind of foolish face... The Adam's apple in his throat is two *arshins* long."

"But all the same, he's charming!"

"To your taste, handsome, but to mine... not. And if he's handsome, it means he's stupid, uneducated. Who is he?"

"We don't know... Probably not of the merchant class..."

"Hm... I bet he's stupid... He's shaking his legs... It's disgusting to look at! Now I'll find out what kind of bird he is... what the man's mind is like. Wait."

The best man coughed and bravely went into the other room. Stopping in front of the dark-haired man, he coughed once again, thought for a moment and began:

"How are you, sir?"

The dark-haired man looked at him and smirked.

"Not so bad," he said reluctantly.

"Why only 'not so bad'? One must always be positive."

"But why is it necessary to be positive?"

"This is why. Everything nowadays advances. Electricity, for example, and the telegraph, all sorts of things, telephones. Yes, sir. Consider progress, for example... What does the word mean? Surely it means that everything has to go forward... So you too go forward."

"So where, for example, should I go now?" smirked the dark-haired man.

"What does it matter where you go? Wherever you want... There are many places... Even if you were to go to the buffet, for example... Would you like to do that? A little brandy each, to get acquainted... Well? Just an idea..."

"All right," agreed the dark-haired man...

He and the best man made for the buffet. A close-cropped waiter in tails and a soiled white tie poured two glasses of brandy. The best man and the dark-haired man drank.

"Good brandy," said the best man. "But there is something better... Let's each have a glass of red wine, to get acquainted..."

They each drank a glass of red wine.

"So now that we know ourselves," said the best man, wiping his lips, "and, one may say, have drunk—"

"Not 'ourselves', but 'each other'..." corrected the dark-haired man. "You don't yet know how to speak, but talk about telephones. If I were as ignorant as you are, I would remain silent, not disgrace myself... 'Now that we know ourselves...' Ha!"

"What are you laughing at?" The best man was offended. "I said 'ourselves' for a laugh, as a joke... There is no reason to grin like that! It may be something girls like, but I don't like those teeth... Who are you? Where are you from?"

"None of your business..."

"What's your rank? Your surname?"

"None of your business... I am not such a fool as to tell anyone I meet what my rank is... I am a proud man, and don't mix with the likes of you. I don't care much about people like you..."

"Well, how about that... Hm... So you will not give your surname?"

"I don't want to... If I were to give my name and introduce myself to every nitwit, my tongue would wear out. I am a proud man, and to me you are like the waiter... You are an ignoramus!"

"Well, how about that... What a fine gentleman you are... Well, now I shall discover what kind of impostor you are."

Raising his chin, the best man set off to the bridegroom, who at that moment was sitting with his bride and blinking, red as a lobster...

"Nikisha!" said the best man, turning to the bridegroom and nodding towards the dark-haired guest. "What is the surname of that impostor?"

The bridegroom shook his head.

"I don't know," he said. "He's no acquaintance of mine. I suppose Father invited him. You ask Father."

"But your father is in the study, in a drunken stupor... He's snoring like a wild beast. And do *you* not know him?" the best man asked, turning to the bride.

The bride said that she did not know the dark-haired man. The best man shrugged and began to question the guests. The guests said they were seeing the dark-haired man for the first time in their life.

"It means he's a fraud," decided the best man. "Without an invitation, he comes here and enjoys himself, as with acquaintances. Very well! We shall show him 'ourselves'!"

The best man went up to the dark-haired guest and placed his arms akimbo.

"So, did you have an invitation to come in?" he asked. "Be so good as to show your invitation."

"I am a proud man and will not show my invitation to just any person. Get away from me... Why are you bothering me?"

"That means you do not have an invitation? And if you have no invitation it means you're a cheat. Now it's clear to us where you're from and what your rank is. We ourselves know... that is... we know... what sort of person you are... You're a cheat – that's all."

"If an intelligent man were to talk so rudely to me, I would punch him on the snout, but from a fool like you I expect nothing else."

The best man rushed through the rooms, got together about six male friends and with them went up to the dark-haired guest.

"Be so good, dear sir, as to show your invitation!" he said.

"I don't want to. Go away, before I forget myself..."

"You don't wish to show your invitation? Therefore you came in without one? By what right? It means you are a cheat. Kindly leave here! Be so good, sir! Come on! We are now going to throw you out..."

The best man and his friends took the dark-haired guest by the arms and carried him to the exit. The other guests started to object. The dark-haired man began to talk loudly about rudeness and his self-esteem.

"Please be on your way! Come on, handsome man!" muttered the triumphant best man as he carried him to the door. "We know you handsome men!"

At the door they pulled the dark-haired guest's coat on him, put on his hat and gave him a push on the back. The best man giggled with pleasure and hit him with his ring on the back of the head... The dark-haired man swayed, fell on his back and slid down the stairs.

"Goodbye! Give our regards to those at home!" rejoiced the best man.

The dark-haired man rose, patted his coat a few times and, lifting his head, said:

"Fools always act like fools. I am a proud man and will not demean myself in front of you, but will let my coachman tell you who I am. Come down! Grigory!" he called to the street.

The guests descended. A minute later a coachman entered the vestibule from the courtyard.

"Grigory!" said the dark-haired man, turning to him. "Who am I?"

"My master – Semyon Panteleych..."

"And what is my rank and how did I achieve that rank?"

"Honorary citizen,* and you achieved that rank through your studies."

"Where can I be found, and what is my occupation?"

"You work at the merchant Podshchekin's factory, in the mechanical and technical department, and your salary is three thousand..."

"Now do you understand? And here is my invitation too! I was invited to the wedding by the bridegroom's father, the merchant Sinerylov, who is now completely drunk."

"My dear fellow! My dear man!" cried the best man. "Why did you not say so before?"

"I am a proud man... I have my self-esteem... Goodbye, sir!"

"No, stay... It would be a sin, brother! Come back, Semyon Panteleych! Now it's clear what sort of man you are... Let's go and drink, for your own education... to get some ideas..."

The proud man frowned and went back upstairs. Two minutes later he was already standing at the buffet and drinking brandy.

"Without pride one cannot live in this world," he explained. "No one should ever give in! No one! I understand my own worth. But you, ignoramuses, will never understand!"

Two Letters

I

A Serious Question

MY DEAR AND BELOVED UNCLE, ANISIM PETROVICH!

Your compatriot Kurosheyev has just been at my place, and let drop that your neighbour Murdashevich returned the other day from abroad with his family. I was all the more struck by this news as the rumour earlier was that the Murdasheviches were staying abroad for good.

Beloved and dear uncle! If you love your nephew even a little, then go, my dear, to Murdashevich and find out how his ward Mashenka is getting on. I confess to you the secret of my soul. In you alone can I confide. I love Mashenka, love her passionately, more than life itself! Six years of separation have not diminished my love for her one iota. Is she alive and well? Write and tell me how you find her. Does she remember me, love me as before? Can I write her a letter? Find out everything, my dear, and tell me in detail.

Tell her I am no longer that timid, poor student... I am already a circuit-court lawyer, have a practice, money. In short, for complete happiness the only thing I lack is her... The only thing!

I embrace you in expectation of a prompt reply.

VLADIMIR GRECHNEV

II

The Reply

MY DEAR NEPHEW VOLODYA!

The day after receiving your letter I went to Murdashevich's. He's a lovely man! He's grown old and grey while abroad, but still remembers me, his old friend, so that when I entered he embraced me and, looking me in the face for a long time, timidly and affectionately exclaimed: "I don't recognize you!" But when I mentioned my surname, he embraced me once again and said: "Now I remember." He's a fine man! I drank and ate at his place, and then we played préférence, and each bet ten roubles. With many expressions and in different voices he told me about being abroad, and made me laugh a lot with naughty descriptions of funny German customs. But German science, he says, has advanced a long way. He showed me also a picture he bought on a trip through Italy, which depicts a person of the female sex in strange, indecent clothing. I even saw Mashenka. She was wearing a rich pink dress with expensive jewellery. She remembers you and even shed a few tears when she asked about you. She expects a letter from you and thanks you for the memories and the kind feelings. You write that you have a practice and money! Look after your money, my dear, and exercise moderation and restraint. When I was young I abandoned myself to sensual excess, and though it didn't last long and I was temperate enough, I still repent. Finally, I bless you and wish you all the best.

Your uncle and well-wisher,

ANISIM GRECHNEV

P.S. The way you write is difficult to understand, but very charming and eloquent. I showed your letter to all the neighbours. Having read it, they think you are a writer, and Father Grigory's son, Vladimir, even copied it to send it to the newspaper. I showed it also to Mashenka and her husband, the German Uhrmacher, to whom Mashenka was married last year. The German read and praised it. Now I show and read your letter to everyone. Write more! By the way, Murdashevich's caviar is very tasty.

The Guardian

I OVERCAME MY TIMIDITY and entered General Shmygalov's study. The general was sitting at his table playing patience – "Capricieuse".*

"What do you want, dear boy?" he asked me affectionately, indicating the armchair.

"I have come to you, Your Excellency, on a business matter," I said, sitting down and for some unknown reason buttoning up my frock coat. "I've come to you on business of a private, not official nature. I've come to ask you for the hand of your niece Varvara Maksimovna."

The general slowly turned his face to me, regarded me attentively and dropped his cards on the floor. His lips moved for a long time before he said:

"You... what?... Are you mad, or what? Are you mad, I'm asking you? You... dare?" he hissed, turning crimson. "You dare, you silly boy, you beardless youth?! You dare to joke... sir..."

And, stamping his foot, Shmygalov shouted so loudly that even the windows shook:

"Stand up! You forget who you're talking to! Be so kind as to clear off, and don't let me catch sight of you! Kindly leave! Get out!"

"But I want to get married, Your Excellency!"

"You may marry somewhere else, not here! You are not yet grown up enough for my niece, sir! You are not a match for her! Neither your finances nor your social status gives you the right to make such a... proposal! It is impertinence on your part! I forgive you, silly boy, and ask you not to bother me again!"

"Hm... You have already dismissed five fiancés in this way... Well, you will not succeed in sending away a sixth. I know the reason for these refusals. Look here, Your Excellency... I give you my honest and honourable word that, if I marry Varya, I shall not demand from you a single copeck of the money that you embezzled as Varina's guardian. I give you my honest word!"

"Repeat what you said!" said the general in an unnatural cracking voice, having crouched down and come up to me in a measured tread, like a teased gander. "Repeat it! Repeat it, you scoundrel!"

I repeated it. The general turned crimson and retreated.

"This is the last straw!" he began to bleat, running around and raising his arms. "The last straw, that my subordinates utter terrible, unforgivable insults to me in my very own house! My God, what have I come to! I feel… faint!"

"But I assure you, Your Excellency! Not only shall I not demand money, but I shall not utter even a single word about how, through weakness of character, you embezzled Varina's money. And I shall order Varya to be silent! I give you my word! Why are you getting excited, hitting the chest of drawers. I shall not take you to court!"

"A silly boy, a beardless youth… a pauper… You dare to utter such vile things straight to my face! Kindly leave, young man, and remember that I shall never forget this! You have offended me terribly! However… I forgive you! You uttered this impertinence out of thoughtlessness, out of stupidity… Ah, be so good as not to touch anything on my table, the Devil take you! Don't touch the cards! Go away, I'm busy!"

"I'm not touching anything! What are you imagining? I give my honest word, general! I give my word that I shall not even allude to this matter. And I shall forbid Varya to make demands on you! What more do you want? You are a strange man, really… You embezzled ten thousand, which was left to her by her father… Well? Ten thousand is not a lot of money… It can be forgiven…"

"I embezzled nothing… no sir! I shall now prove it to you! Here now… I shall prove it!"

With trembling hands the general pulled a box out of the table, drew from it a pile of papers and, red as a lobster, began to leaf through them. He leafed through for a long time, slowly and aimlessly. The poor devil was terribly nervous and disconcerted.

Luckily for him, a footman came into the study and announced that dinner was served.

"Very well... After dinner I shall prove it to you," muttered the general, hiding the papers. "Once and for all... in order to avoid scandal... Let's just dine... you shall see! You are, God forgive me... a raw youth, a rogue... wet behind the ears... Come and dine! After dinner I shall... show you..."

We went to dine. During the first and second courses the general was angry and scowling. He frenziedly salted his soup, growled like distant thunder and moved noisily on his chair.

"Why are you so angry today?" Varya asked him. "I don't like you when you are like this... really..."

"How dare you say that you don't like me?" the general snapped at her.

During the third and last course, Shmygalov sighed deeply and blinked his eyes. A cowed and dejected expression spread over his face... He seemed so unfortunate, aggrieved! A heavy sweat appeared on his brow and nose. After dinner the general invited me into his study.

"My dear boy!" he began, not looking at me, and tugging at my frock coat. "Take Varya, I consent... You are a good, kind man... I consent... I give you my blessing... you and her, my angels... Forgive me for scolding you here before dinner... I was angry... I'm really a loving person... fatherly... Only I, ah... wasted not ten thousand, but, ah... sixteen... I even spent what her aunt Natalya left her... gambled it... lost it at cards... Let's celebrate... with champagne... Have you forgiven me?"

The general stared at me with his grey eyes, which seemed at once jubilant and about to cry. I forgave him six thousand more and married Varya.

Good stories always end with a marriage!

Despair

A YOUNG LAD, tow-haired and with high cheekbones, wearing a torn sheepskin coat and big black felt boots, waited until the district doctor, having finished seeing his patients, was returning to his lodgings from the hospital, and timidly approached him.

"Please, Your Worship," he said.

"What do you want?"

The lad rubbed his palm up over his nose, looked at the sky and only then replied:

"Please, Your Worship... You have, Your Honour, under arrest my brother Vaska, a blacksmith from Varvarin..."

"Well, and so what?"

"I happen to be Vaska's brother... Our father had two sons: he, Vaska, and me, Kirila. Besides us, there are three sisters, and Vaska is married and has a child... There are many people, but no one to work... I think the forge has been off for already two years now. I myself work at the cotton factory, and don't know the blacksmith's trade – and what kind of worker is my father? Not only can he not work, he cannot even eat: he is too ill to lift a spoon to his mouth."

"So what do you want from me?"

"Have pity, release Vaska!"

The doctor looked at Kirila with astonishment and walked on without saying a word. The boy ran forward and fell to his knees.

"Doctor, good sir!" he begged, blinking and again rubbing his palm up over his nose. "Show God's mercy, let Vaska come home! I shall pray eternally to God for you! Your Honour, let him go! We are all dying of hunger! Mother wails all day long! Vaska's wife wails... I could just die! Life isn't worth living any more! Have pity, release him, good sir."

"Are you stupid, or out of your mind?" asked the doctor, looking angrily at him. "How can I release him? After all, he's under arrest!"

Kirila began to cry.

"Release him!"

"Tfoo, you crank! What right do I have? Am I the jailer, or what? They brought him to me at the hospital to be treated – I treated him, but I do not have the right to release him any more than I have the right to put you in prison. Dimwit!"

"But you see, he was jailed for no reason! Before the trial it seems he spent a year in jail, but now the question is: why is he still there? It would be different if he killed someone or stole a horse, but to be jailed for no reason!"

"I suppose so, but what does it have to do with me?"

"They jailed a man and themselves don't know why. He was drunk, Your Honour, remembered nothing and even hit his father on the ear, cut his cheek on a branch in his drunken state, and two of our lads – who wanted, you see, Turkish tobacco – persuaded him to get into an Armenian shop to steal the tobacco. He, being drunk, agreed, the fool. They broke, you know, the lock, climbed in and began to binge. Everything was destroyed, glass broken, flour scattered. In short, they were drunk! Well, the village policeman came at once… this and that happened, and it was investigated. They spent a whole year in jail, and last week, on Wednesday, all three were brought to trial in town. A soldier sat behind them with a gun… People swore on oath. Vaska was the least guilty of all, but he was judged to be the ringleader. Both lads went to jail, and Vaska was sent to a convicts' unit for three years. And for what? Be fair!"

"But again, this has nothing to do with me. Go to the authorities."

"I have already been to the authorities! I went to the court, wanted to submit a petition, but they did not accept it. I even went to the district policeman and the investigator, and they both said: 'It's not my business!' So whose business is it? And here in the hospital there is no one senior to you. You can do what you want, Your Honour."

"You fool!" sighed the doctor. "Once the jurors convict, nothing can be done by either the governor or even the minister, much less the district policeman. You meddle in vain!"

"But who judged him?"

"The gentlemen of the jury..."

"And who were those gentlemen? They were our people! It was Andrei Guryev. It was Alyoshka Khuk."

"Well, I'm getting cold talking to you..."

The doctor waved his hand and went quickly to his door. Kirila wanted to follow him, but, seeing how the door slammed, he stopped. For ten minutes he stood motionless in the middle of the hospital yard and, without putting on his hat, looked at the doctor's lodgings. He then sighed deeply, slowly scratched himself and went to the gate.

"So who can I go to?" he muttered, going out to the street. "One says 'It's not my business', another says 'It's not my business'. So whose business is it? No, probably until you bribe someone you'll get nothing done. The doctor himself implied as much, by continually looking at my hand. Would I give him five roubles? 'Well, brother, I shall now go to the governor.'"

Putting one foot before the other, continually and needlessly looking back, he lazily plodded along the road, seemingly considering where to go... It was not cold, and the snow crunched softly under his feet. Before him, not further than half a verst away, on a hill, lay the district town, where not long before his brother had been tried. To the right was dimly outlined the jail with its red roof and sentry boxes at the corners; to the left was a big urban grove, now covered with hoar frost. It was quiet – only an old man in a woman's short fur-trimmed jacket and a vast peaked cap was walking ahead, coughing and shouting at a cow he was driving to town.

"Hello, Grandad!" said Kirila, drawing alongside the old man.

"Hello..."

"Are you driving your cow for sale?"

"No, not so..." lazily replied the old man.

"Are you a smallholder, or what?"

They began to talk. Kirila explained why he had been at the hospital, and what he had spoken to the doctor about.

"Of course the doctor does not know about these things," the old man said to him as they entered the town. "Though he's a *barin,* he was trained to prescribe remedies, but as for giving actual advice, or let's say writing a report – he can't do that. There is a special authority for that. You were at the district court and the commission of rural police. These can't deal with your matters either."

"So where can I go?"

"For your peasant affairs the most important person is an appointed representative in the regional assembly. Go to him. Mr Sineokov."

"Is he in Zolotov?"

"Well, yes, in Zolotov. He is the chief. If it has to do with your affairs, even the district police officer does not have the right to go against him."

"It's a long way to walk, brother!... Probably fifteen versts, maybe more."

"If one has to, one will even walk a hundred versts."

"That's true... to submit a petition, or what?"

"You'll find out there. If you need a petition, the clerk will quickly write it for you. The appointed representative has a clerk."

After parting with the old man, Kirila stood in the middle of the square, thought awhile and left town. He decided to go to Zolotov.

Five days later, returning to his lodgings after seeing patients, the doctor again saw Kirila in his yard. This time the lad was not alone, but was with a gaunt, very pale old man who kept nodding his head like a pendulum and mumbling.

"Your Honour, I've come to see Your Worship again," began Kirila. "I've come with my father. Have mercy, release Vaska! The representative didn't even talk to me. He said, 'Go away!'"

"Your Honour," the old man said, wheezing from his throat and raising his trembling eyebrows, "be merciful! We are poor people, have no way of thanking Your Honour, but if it pleases Your Worship, Kirila or Vaska can work off our debt to you. Let them work."

"We'll work it off," said Kirila, raising his hand as if wanting to take an oath. "Release him! The family is dying of hunger! They are crying, Your Honour!"

The young man quickly looked at his father and pulled him by the arm. They both, as if by command, fell at the feet of the doctor. The doctor waved his hand and, without looking back, quickly went to his door.

The Thief

THE CLOCK STRUCK TWELVE. Fyodor Stepanych threw on his fur coat and went outside. The night-time dampness enveloped him... A damp cold wind was blowing, a fine rain was drizzling from the dark sky. Fyodor Stepanych stepped over the half-destroyed fence and walked quietly along the street. The street was wide, just like a square – such streets are rare in European Russia. There was neither lighting, nor a pavement... nor even any hint of those luxuries.

Near the fences and walls flashed dark silhouettes of people hurrying to church. Two figures were splashing through the mud in front of Fyodor Stepanych. In one, who was small and hunchbacked, he recognized the local doctor, the only "educated man" in all the region. The old doctor was not particular about his acquaintances, and always amicably sighed when he saw Fyodor. On this occasion the old man was wearing a formal, old-fashioned cocked hat, and his head resembled two ducks' heads with their backs glued to him. From under the skirt of his light fur coat dangled a sword. Next to him walked a tall, thin man, also in a cocked hat.

"Christ is risen, Gury Ivanych!" said Fyodor Stepanych, stopping the doctor.

The doctor silently shook his hand and drew aside the lapel of his coat in order to display proudly to the exile the buttonhole from which hung the "Stanislav".

"I would like to join you in your home after matins, doctor," said Fyodor Stepanych. "You might allow me to break my fast with you... Please... Back there on this night I always used to break my fast with a family. It will bring back memories..."

"That would hardly be convenient..." The doctor was embarrassed. "I have a family, you know... a wife... Although you are, ah… but not really… there's still prejudice! However, it doesn't matter… Hm… I have a cough…"

"And Barabayev?" said Fyodor Stepanych, twisting his mouth and smirking maliciously. "Barabayev was convicted along with me, we were exiled together, but he nevertheless dines and has tea with you every day. He stole more, that's the truth!…"

Fyodor Stepanych stopped and leant against the wet fence. He let the others continue on their way. Far ahead of him, lights were twinkling. Dying out and then flaring up, they were moving in the same direction.

"They are processing with the cross," thought the exile. "Just as they used to do there…"

A ringing sound was coming from the lights. Tenor bells were filling the air with all kinds of sounds, which quickly subsided, as if hurrying somewhere.

"The first Easter here, in this cold," thought Fyodor Stepanych, "and… not the last. How dreadful! And now, probably, there…"

And he began to think about "there"… There, now, they do not have muddy snow under the feet, or cold puddles, but new growth. There the wind does not lash against the face like a wet rag, but carries the breath of spring… The sky there is dark, but starry, with a white streak in the east… Instead of this muddy fence there is a green garden and a little house with three windows. Behind the windows are light, warm rooms. In one of the rooms is a table, covered with a white tablecloth, with *kulich*,* *zakuski*, vodka…

"How good it would be now to knock back some of that vodka! The vodka here is horrible, impossible to drink…"

The next morning there would be a good, deep sleep. After sleep, visits, drinking bouts… He also remembered, of course, Olya, with her cat-like, pathetic, pretty little face. Now she was probably asleep, but was not dreaming about him. These women soon find consolation. Had it not been for Olya, he would not be here. She wronged him, the stupid woman. She needed money, needed it terribly, to the point of infirmity, like every fashionable woman! Without money she could neither live, nor love, nor suffer…

"And if they banish me to Siberia?" he asked her. "Will you go with me?"

"Of course! Even to the end of the world."

He stole, was caught and sent to Siberia, but Olya lost heart and did not go, of course. Now her stupid little head is sinking into a soft lace pillow, and her feet are a long way from muddy snow.

"She appeared in court all dressed up in her finery, and did not look at me even once. She laughed at the defence lawyer's witticisms... To kill her would not be good enough..."

These recollections greatly wearied Fyodor Stepanych. He grew tired and felt achy, as if he had been thinking with his whole body. His legs became weak, gave way, and he had not the strength to go to church, to matins... He returned home and, without taking off his fur coat and boots, collapsed on the bed.

Over his bed was hanging a cage with a bird. They both belonged to the landlord. It was some kind of strange bird, with a long beak, emaciated, of a species unknown to him. Its wings were clipped; some of the feathers had been plucked from its head. It was fed with something sour, of which the whole room reeked. The bird was fluttering anxiously in the cage, pecking against the tin of water and singing, now like a starling, now like an oriole...

"It won't let me sleep!" thought Fyodor Stepanych. "The dev-vil..."

He rose and shook the cage with his hand. The bird fell silent. The exile lay down and pulled off his boots against the edge of the bed. A minute later the bird again began to flutter. A little piece of the sour food fell on his head and hung from his hair.

"Will you not stop? Not keep silent? You are the last straw!"

Fyodor Stepanych leapt up, tugged frenziedly at the cage and flung it into a corner. The bird fell silent.

But ten minutes later the exile saw it come out from the corner to the middle of the room and begin to bore into the clay floor... Its beak was like a gimlet... It bored and bored, but seemed to have lost its tip. Its wings began to beat, and it seemed to the exile that he was lying on the floor and the wings were beating him on the temple… Finally the beak broke and the base burrowed into the bird's feathers… The exile dozed off…

"Why did you kill this little creature, you murderer?" he heard in the morning.

Fyodor Stepanych opened his eyes and saw before him his landlord – a holy fool and elder of the dissenting Church. The landlord's face was shaking with anger and covered in tears.

"Why, cursed one, did you kill my little bird? Why did you kill that songster of mine, you Satan's devil? Well? What kind of man are you? Why did you do it? There's no shame in your eyes, you cruel dog! Get out of my house and never let me see you again! Leave, this minute! Now!"

Fyodor Stepanych put on his fur coat and went outside. The morning was grey, dull… Looking at the leaden sky, it was hard to believe that high above it the sun was shining. It still continued to drizzle with rain…

"Bong-djour! Greetings of the season, mon-sher!" the exile heard as he went through the gate.

Past the gate on a new droshky came rolling his fellow countryman Barabayev. His countryman was in a top hat and under an umbrella.

"He's making visits!" thought Fyodor Stepanych. "The swine has been able to insinuate himself even here… He has acquaintances… I should have stolen a lot more!"

Approaching the church, Fyodor Stepanych heard another voice, this time a woman's. Driving towards him was the postal tarantass, laden with cases. From behind the cases peeped out a woman's head.

"Where is… good gracious, Fyodor Stepanych! Is it you?" squeaked the little head.

The exile ran up to the tarantass, focused his eyes on the head, recognized it and grabbed the woman's hand…

"Am I really not dreaming?! What's this? You've come to me?! You decided to, Olya?"

"Where does Barabayev live here?"

"What is Barabayev to you?"

"He wrote to me... Imagine, he sent two thousand roubles... Besides that, I shall receive three hundred a month. Are there theatres here?..."

Until evening the exile roamed through town looking for lodgings. It poured with rain all day, and the sun never appeared.

"Can these brutes live without sun?" he thought, kneading the slush with his feet. "They are happy and contented without the sun! But to each his own."

On the Approach of the Wedding Season

(From the Notebook of an Agent)

KUCHKIN, Ivan Savvich, provincial secretary, 42 years old. Ugly, pockmarked, nasal, but very imposing. Accepted into good houses and has an aunt who is the wife of a colonel. Lives on interest from lending his money. A crook, but basically a decent man. Seeks a girl of about 18 or 20 who would be from a good home and speak French. She has to be nice-looking and have a dowry of about 15–20,000.

FYESHKIN, a retired officer. Drinks and suffers from rheumatism. Wants a wife who would look after him. Would agree to take even a widow, if only she is not more than 25 and has capital.

PRUDONOV, photographic retoucher, seeks a bride with a photographer's studio, which would not be mortgaged and bring in not less than 2,000 a year. Drinks, but not all the time, though heavily. Dark-haired and has black eyes.

GNUSINA, a widow. Has two houses and about a hundred thousand in cash. Is looking for a general, even if retired. Has a barely visible squint in the left eye and speaks with a lisp. She claims that though she passes for a widow, she is actually a maiden, as her late husband fell ill with the shakes in all his limbs on their wedding day.

ZHENSKY, Difterit Alexeich, an actor, 35 years old, unknown rank. He says his father has a distillery, but is probably lying. Always wears a frock coat and white tie, because he has no other clothes. Left the theatre because he lost his voice. Wishes to have a merchant's widow of any build, if only she has money.

BUTUZOV, former staff captain, condemned to exile in Tomsk Province for embezzlement and forgery. Wishes to bring happiness to an orphan who would go with him to Siberia! Has to be of noble birth.

Lethargy

A SESSION IS IN PROGRESS in a chamber of the circuit court. On the defendant's bench sits a middle-aged gentleman with a haggard face, accused of embezzlement and forgery. A gaunt, narrow-chested secretary is reading a bill of indictment in a quiet tenor voice. He does not pay attention to either full stops or commas, and his monotone voice is like the droning of bees or the babbling of a brook. During such a reading it is good to dream, to reminisce, to sleep... The judges, the jurors and the public are restless from the tedium... It is quiet. Now and then only the measured tread of someone in the judge's corridor or a discreet cough into the fist of a yawning juror can be heard.

The counsel for the defence has propped up his curly head on his fist and is quietly dozing. Under the influence of the droning secretary his thoughts lose all order and start to wander.

"What a long nose that bailiff has," he thinks, blinking his heavy eyelids. "Nature really had to make a mess of a clever face! If people had longer noses, say of two or three *sazhen*,* perhaps the world would become too crowded and houses would have to be built much bigger..."

The defence counsellor shakes his head, like a horse that has been bitten by a fly, and continues to think:

"What's going on now at home? Everyone is usually at home at this time: my wife, my mother-in-law, the children... My children Kolka and Zinka are probably now in my study... Kolka is standing on the armchair, leaning with his chest against the edge of the table and drawing something on my papers. He has already drawn a horse with a pointed muzzle and a dot instead of an eye, a man with an extended arm, a crooked little house; and Zina is standing right there, near the table, stretching out her neck as she tries to see what her brother is drawing... 'Draw Papa!' she says.

Kolka gets down to doing me. He has already drawn a man, and only has to add a black beard – and Papa is finished. Kolka starts looking in the code of laws for little pictures while Zina tidies the table. Their eyes are caught by the servants' bell – they ring it; they see the inkpot – fingers must be dipped in it; if the box on the table is not locked, then it means they have to rummage in it. In the end, the thought dawns on them that they are Red Indians, and that they can hide very well from enemies under my table. They both crawl under the table, screaming and squealing, and play there until the lamp or the little vase falls from the table... Oh! And in the sitting room now the wet nurse is probably strolling sedately with the third child... The child wails and wails... wails without cease!"

"In the current accounts of Kopyelov," drones the secretary, "Achkasov, Zimakovsky and Chikina, no interest was given, so the sum of 1,425 roubles, 41 copecks was added to the balance for 1883..."

"Perhaps at home they are already having dinner!" drift the defence counsellor's thoughts. "Sitting at the table are my mother-in-law, my wife Nadya, my wife's brother Vasya, the children... As usual, there is a look of dull anxiety and dignity on my mother-in-law's face. Nadya, thin and already fading, but still with perfectly white, clear facial skin, is sitting at the table looking as if she is being forced to be there; she is not eating, and gives the impression of being unwell. Her face, like her mother-in-law's, is filled with anxiety. And no wonder! She is busy with the children, the kitchen, her husband's linen, guests, moths in the fur coats, greeting visitors, playing the piano! How much responsibility and how little work! Nadya and her mother do nothing very much. If from boredom they water the flowers or quarrel with the cook, then for two days they groan wearily and talk about slaving away... My wife's brother, Vasya, chews quietly and stays gloomily silent, because he received a 'one'* today in Latin. The lad is quiet, obliging, grateful, but wears out such a mass of boots, trousers and books that it is simply a disaster... The children, of course, play up. They demand vinegar and pepper, complain about each other, continually drop spoons. The head spins even to think about it! My wife and mother-in-law are vigilant in maintaining good manners... God forbid if anyone places an elbow on the table, holds the knife in their fist or eats with it – or, when offering food, passes the dish from the right and not the left. All the food, even the ham and peas, smell of powder and boiled-fruit sweets. Everything is unpalatable, sickly sweet, meagre. There is not a trace of good cabbage soup and *kasha*,* which I ate when I was a bachelor. My mother-in-law and my wife speak French all the time, but when the talk is about me, then my mother-in-law starts to speak Russian, because such an insensitive, callous, shameless, coarse man as I am is unworthy of being spoken about in the tender French language... 'Poor Michel is probably hungry,' my wife is saying. 'This morning he drank a glass of tea without bread and just ran off to court...' – 'Don't worry, my dear!' gloats my mother-in-law. 'A man like him will not go hungry! He's probably already been five times to the buffet. They've made for themselves a buffet in court, and every five minutes ask the chairman if it's not possible to have a break.' After dinner my mother-in-law and my wife talk about reducing expenses... They calculate the amounts, make notes and in the end find that expenses are disgracefully large. The cook is summoned, and they start to review the matter with her; they reproach her, and a quarrel arises over five copecks... There are tears, venomous words... Then comes the tidying of the rooms, the rearrangement of the furniture – and all because they have nothing to do."

"Collegiate Assessor Cheryepkov showed," drones the secretary, "that though he was sent the receipt number 811, nonetheless he did not receive forty-six roubles and two copecks that was owed to him, which even then he declared..."

"When you think, and judge, and consider all the circumstances," the defence counsel continues to reflect, "and, quite rightly, give it all up as a bad job and send everyone to the Devil... When you exhaust yourself, go crazy, go mad all day, befuddled with boredom and banality, then against your will you wish to give your soul even one bright moment of rest. You go to Natasha or, when you have money, to the Gypsies – and you forget everything… honestly, you forget everything! The devil only knows where, far from town, in a private room, lounging on a sofa, the Gypsies are singing, jumping, making a racket – and you feel how the voice of the charming, terrifying, wild Gypsy Glasha is transforming your whole soul… Glasha! Dear, delightful, wonderful Glasha! What teeth, eyes… what a back!"

But the secretary drones on and on and on… In the defence counsel's eyes everything starts to blend and jump. The judges and jurors vanish into their shells, the public ripples, now the ceiling sinks, now it rises… Thoughts also jump and finally break off. Nadya, his mother-in-law, the long nose of the court bailiff, the defendant, Glasha – all these leap about, whirl and go far, far away…

"It's good…" quietly whispers the defence counsel, falling asleep. "It's good… You lie on a sofa, and around you it is cosy… warm… Glasha is singing…"

"Mr Counsel!" A stern voice is heard.

"It's good… it's warm… There is neither his mother-in-law nor the wet nurse… nor is there soup smelling of powder… Glasha is kind, good…"

"Mr Counsel!" The same stern voice is heard.

The defence counsellor shudders and opens his eyes. The black eyes of the Gypsy Glasha are looking straight at him, full lips are smiling, a dark-complexioned, beautiful face is beaming. Stunned, still not quite having woken up, thinking that this is a dream or a spectre, he slowly rises and, mouth gaping, looks at the Gypsy.

"Mr Counsel, do you wish to ask something of the witness?" asks the chairman.

"Ah… yes! This is the witness… No, I… I don't. I have nothing to ask."

The defence counsellor shakes his head and finally wakes up. He now understands that it is indeed the Gypsy Glasha who is standing before him, that she had been summoned here as a witness.

"But, forgive me, I do have something to ask," he says loudly. "Witness," he says, turning to Glasha. "You sing in Kuzmichov's Gypsy choir. Tell me, how often in your restaurant did the defendant go on a binge? Well then... And do you remember whether he paid for himself every time, or did it happen that others paid for him? Thank you... That's all."

He drinks two glasses of water, and his lethargy completely vanishes...

The Willow

Has anyone driven along the postal road between B— and T—?

Whoever has, of course, also knows Andreyevsky's mill, which stands by itself on the bank of the Kozyavka River. The mill is small, with two millstones. It is more than a hundred years old, and stopped working already long ago, and so it is no wonder that it resembles a small, hunchbacked, wizened little old woman ready to collapse any minute. And this little old woman would have collapsed long ago if she had not been leaning against a wide, old willow tree. The willow is so wide that even two people could not embrace it. Its shining leaves descend to the roof, to the dam; the lower branches touch the water and spread along the ground. It is also old and hunchbacked. Its bent trunk is disfigured by a big, dark hollow. Push your hand into the hollow and your hand will get stuck in black honey. Wild bees will start to buzz around your head and sting you. How old is it? Arkhip, its companion, says it was already old when he worked for the master in the grand house and then for the mistress doing menial jobs – and this was some time ago.

The willow supports another ruin too – the old man Arkhip, who sits by its roots all day long, fishing. He is old, hunchbacked like the willow, and his toothless mouth resembles the hollow. By day he fishes, and at night he sits by the roots and thinks. Day and night, both the old willow and Arkhip whisper. Both have seen much in their day. Listen to their tale…

About thirty years ago, on Willow Sunday,* the old willow's name day, the old man was sitting in his place, looking at the spring day and fishing… As always, it was quiet all around. All that could be heard was the whispering between the old man and the tree, and from time to time the splashing of the frolicking fish. The old man was fishing and waiting for midday. At midday he began to cook fish soup. Midday arrived, when the willow's shadow began to leave the bank.

Arkhip knew the time also from the postal bell. Exactly at midday, the T— post drove across the dam.

Even on this Sunday Arkhip heard the bell. He put down his fishing rod and directed his gaze at the dam. The troika crossed the knoll, descended the slope and approached the dam at a walking pace. The postman was asleep. Drawing up to the dam, for some reason the troika stopped. Until now, Arkhip had not been surprised, but at last his interest was aroused. Something unusual happened. The coachman looked around, uneasily slid off his seat, pulled the handkerchief from the postman's face and struck him with a flail. The postman did not stir. A crimson patch began to spread on his fair-haired head. The coachman leapt from the cart and, swinging his arm, delivered another blow. A minute later, Arkhip heard steps near him: the coachman was descending the bank and walking straight towards him... His sunburnt face was pale, his eyes were staring vacantly into the distance. His whole body trembling, he ran up to the willow, and, without noticing Arkhip, thrust the post bag into the hollow; then he ran back up, jumped on the cart and, strange as it appeared to Arkhip, gave himself a blow on the temple. His face stained with blood, he whipped the horses.

"Help! Murder!" he cried.

The sound echoed, and for a long time Arkhip heard this shout of help.

Some six days later investigators arrived at the mill. They made a map of the mill and dam, measured the depth of the river for some reason and, after dining under the willow, went away. All during the investigation, Arkhip was sitting under the mill wheel, shaking as he looked in the bag. There he saw envelopes with five stamps. Day and night he looked at these stamps and thought. The old willow was silent by day and cried at night. "You fool!" thought Arkhip, listening to the weeping of the tree. A week later, Arkhip was already going with the bag to town.

"Where is the office?" he asked, entering the border post.

They indicated a big yellow house with a striped sentry box by the door. He went in and in the entrance hall saw a *barin* with shining buttons. The *barin* was smoking a pipe and scolding a guard about something. Arkhip went up to him and, shaking all over, told him about the incident with the old willow. The official took the bag from him, unfastened the strap, went pale and then reddened.

"Just a moment," he said, and ran to the office.

There, officials surrounded him... They came running, began to bustle about and whisper... Ten minutes later, the official brought out the bag to Arkhip and said: "You've come to the wrong place, brother. Go to Nizhnaya Street: there they will tell you what to do, but this is the Treasury, my good man. Go to the police."

Arkhip took the bag and left.

"The bag has become lighter!" he thought. "It's become lighter by half!"

On Nizhnaya Street he was directed to another yellow house, with two sentry boxes. Arkhip went in. There was no entrance hall, and the office started right at the stairs. The old man went up to one of the desks and told the clerks the story of the bag. They snatched the bag from his hands, shouted at him and sent for their supervisor. A fat man with a moustache appeared. After a short interrogation he took the bag and locked himself with it in another room.

"So where is the money?" a voice was heard a minute later from the room. "The bag is empty! But tell the old man that he can go! Or arrest him! Take him to Ivan Markovich! No, rather let him go!"

Arkhip bowed and left. A day later, the crucians and perch were already seeing his grey beard...

It was late autumn. The old man was sitting and fishing. His face was just as dark as the leaves of the willow, which had turned yellow: he did not like autumn. His face became even gloomier when he saw the coachman near him. Without noticing him, the coachman approached the willow and thrust his hand into the hollow. The bees, wet and lazy, began to crawl up his sleeve. After feeling around for a while, he went pale, and an hour later was sitting by the river, staring vacantly into the water.

"Where *is* it?" he asked Arkhip.

Arkhip was silent at first, and sullenly ignored the killer, but soon took pity on him.

"I took it to the authorities," he said. "But don't be afraid, you fool... I said I found it there, under the willow..."

The coachman leapt up, let out a roar and went for Arkhip. He beat him for a long time. He mercilessly beat his old face, knocked him to the ground, stamped on him with his feet. After beating the old man, he did not leave him, but stayed to live at the mill with Arkhip.

By day he slept and was silent, and at night he walked along the dam. The shadow of the postman was walking along the dam, and he talked to it. Spring came, but the coachman still continued to wander silently. Once, at night, the old man went up to him.

"Enough loitering around here, you fool," he said to him, giving the postman a sidelong look. "Go away."

And the postman said the same... And the willow whispered the same...

"I cannot," said the coachman. "I would go, but my legs are sore and my soul is hurting!"

The old man took the coachman by the arm and brought him to town. He took him to Nizhnaya Street, to the same office where he had handed in the bag. The coachman fell on his knees before the supervisor and confessed. The moustached man was amazed.

"Why do you slander yourself, you fool?" he said. "Are you drunk? Do you want me to lock you up in the cold? You've gone completely mad, you swine! You're just getting confused... The criminal was not found – that's all there is to it! What more do you want? Clear off!"

When the old man reminded him about the bag, the moustached man burst out laughing, but the clerks were puzzled. Evidently, their memory was poor... The coachman did not find redemption at Nizhnaya Street. He had to return to the willow...

And he had to run from his conscience into the water, to disturb that very place where Arkhip's floats were bobbing. The coachman drowned himself. On the dam, the old man and the old willow now see two shadows... Do they not whisper to them?

The Fiancée

I

It was ten o'clock in the evening and a full moon was shining over the garden. In the Shumin's house, vespers – which had been arranged by Granny Marfa Mikhaylovna – had only just finished. Now Nadya, who had gone out to the garden for a moment, could see how in the hall they were laying the table for *zakuski*, how Granny was bustling around in her splendid silk dress. Father Andrei, the cathedral archpriest, was talking to Nadya's mother, Nina Ivanovna, who in the evening light through the window somehow seemed very young. Father Andrei's son, Andrei Andreyich, was standing nearby, listening attentively.

The garden was quiet, cool and dark, with faint shadows lying on the ground. From somewhere far, far away, probably outside town, came the sound of frogs croaking. It was May, the merry month of May! Nadya breathed deeply and wanted to think that not here, but somewhere else, beneath the sky, above the trees, far beyond town, in the fields and woods, spring life was now unfolding – mysterious, beautiful, rich and sacred, inaccessible to the understanding of weak, sinful man. And for some reason she wanted to cry.

She, Nadya, was already twenty-three years old. From the age of sixteen she had dreamt longingly of marriage, and now at last she was engaged to Andrei Andreyich, the very man who was standing at the window. She liked him, and the wedding was already set for the 7th of July, yet she felt no joy, slept badly and had lost her gaiety… From the kitchen in the basement, through an open window, came the sound of people rushing about, the clattering of knives, the slamming of the door to the lift shaft. There was a smell of roast turkey and marinated cherries. Somehow, she felt that life would go on like this for ever, without change, without end.

Now someone came out of the house and stopped on the porch: it was Alexander Timofeyich, or just Sasha, a guest who had arrived from Moscow ten days before. Once, long ago, Granny had been supporting out of charity an impoverished widowed gentlewoman, Marya Petrovna, a small, thin, sickly distant relative. Sasha was her son. For some reason he was said to have artistic talent, and when his mother died, Granny, for the salvation of her soul, sent him to Moscow, to the Komissarovsky school. Two years later he transferred to the school of art, where he stayed for almost fifteen years, just barely managing to finish an architectural course. He did not practise as an architect, though, but worked for a Moscow lithographer. Usually very ill, he came to stay with Granny almost every summer, to rest and recover his health.

Now he was wearing a buttoned-up frock coat and shabby canvas trousers, ragged around the ankles. His shirt was unironed, and his appearance in general was one of neglect. He was very thin, with big eyes, long, slender fingers and a dark bearded face. All the same, he was handsome. He was like a relative of the Shumins, and felt at home at their place. The room in which he stayed while there had long been called "Sasha's room".

Standing on the porch, he saw Nadya and went up to her.

"It's lovely here at your place," he said.

"Of course it's lovely. You should stay till autumn."

"Yes, I might have to. Perhaps I'll stay till September."

He began to laugh for no reason and sat down next to her.

"I'm sitting here looking at Mama," said Nadya. "She looks so young from here!" After a pause she added: "My mama has, of course, her weaknesses, but all the same she is an remarkable woman."

"Yes, she's a good woman..." agreed Sasha. "Your mama is – in her own way – of course a very kind and dear woman, but... how can I put it? Early this morning I went to the kitchen, where four servants were sleeping right on the floor. There were no beds. Instead of bedding, just rags, stench, bedbugs, cockroaches... It's the same as twenty years ago, no change at all. Well, Granny, God bless her, Granny doesn't know any different. But your mother speaks French, doesn't she? And acts in plays. I'd have thought she would understand."

When Sasha spoke, he extended before the listener two long, thin fingers.

"Everything here seems to me somehow chaotic and disorganized," he continued. "The devil knows what anyone does. Mama just wanders around all day, like some duchess – Granny also doesn't do anything, and you are the same. Your fiancé Andrei Andreyich also does nothing."

Nadya had heard all this the previous year and, it seemed, the year before that, and knew that it was impossible to discuss some things with Sasha. This used to make her laugh, but now for some reason she found it irritating.

"This is all very trite and is becoming tedious," she said, rising. "You should think up something new."

He laughed and also rose, and they walked together to the house. She – tall, beautiful, shapely – now next to him looked very healthy and elegant. Sensing this, she experienced a surge of pity for him, and felt somehow uncomfortable.

"You talk a lot of nonsense," she said. "You've just mentioned my Andrei, but you really don't know him."

"'My Andrei'... Never mind about your Andrei! I feel sorry for your youth."

When they entered the downstairs room, the others were already sitting down to supper. Granny – or, as she was known in the house, Gran – very fat, ugly, with thick eyebrows and little whiskers, was talking loudly, and by her voice and manner of speaking it was clear that she was the head of the house. She owned the trade stalls in the market and the old house with its columns and garden, yet each morning would pray for God to save her from ruin; then she would start crying. There was her daughter-in-law, Nadya's mother, Nina Ivanovna, fair-haired, tightly laced up, in pince-nez and with diamonds on her fingers; and Father Andrei, an old man, thin, toothless, always wearing an expression as if he were preparing to say something very funny; and his son Andrei Andreyich, Nadya's fiancé, stout and handsome, with curly hair, looking like an actor or artist – all three were discussing hypnotism.

"You will put on weight in a week if you stay here," said Granny, turning to Sasha. "Just eat more. What do you look like!" She sighed. "You look dreadful! You are really like the Prodigal Son."

"Having wasted his substance with riotous living," Father Andrei said slowly, with smiling eyes. "He would fain have filled his belly with the husks that the swine did eat…"*

"I do love my dear father," said Andrei Andreyich, touching his father's shoulder. "He's a delightful old man. A kind old man."

Everyone fell silent. Sasha suddenly started to laugh and pressed his napkin to his mouth.

"So then, do you believe in hypnotism?" Father Andrei asked Nina Ivanovna.

"I cannot, of course, say that I believe in it," replied Nina Ivanovna, assuming a very serious, even severe expression, "but one has to admit there is much in nature that is mysterious and incomprehensible."

"I agree with you completely, but I feel it's necessary to add that faith significantly restricts for us the realm of mystery."

A big, very succulent turkey was served. Father Andrei and Nina Ivanovna continued their conversation. Nina Ivanovna's diamonds glittered on her fingers; then tears glistened in her eyes and she grew agitated.

"Though I wouldn't dare to argue with you," she said, "still, you must agree, there are many insoluble mysteries in life!"

"More than one, I dare to assure you."

After supper Andrei Andreyich played the violin, and Nina Ivanovna accompanied him on the piano. He had graduated in philology at the university ten years before, but had never worked and had no definite occupation: he just took part in charity concerts now and again. In town he was known as an artist.

Andrei Andreyich played on; all listened in silence. The samovar quietly simmered on the table, but only Sasha drank tea. Then, when the clock struck twelve, a string on the violin suddenly snapped. Everyone burst out laughing, began to bustle around and take their leave.

After seeing off her fiancé Nadya went upstairs to the room where she lived with her mother (Granny occupied the lower floor). Downstairs in the main room they started to put out the lights, but Sasha kept sitting and drinking tea. He always spent a long time drinking tea, as is customary in Moscow – up to seven cups at a time. Nadya, after she had undressed and got into bed, for a long time still heard how the servants downstairs were clearing up, how Granny was angrily scolding them. Finally, all was quiet; all that could be heard, from time to time, was the sound of Sasha's deep cough in the room below.

II

When Nadya awoke, it must have been around two o'clock and starting to get light. Somewhere far away she heard the sound of a watchman tapping. She was not tired, and found the bed too soft and uncomfortable. Nadya, as she always did on May nights, sat up in bed and began to think. And her thoughts were the same as those on the previous night: repetitive, pointless, obsessive thoughts about how Andrei Andreyich had begun to pay court to her and make her a proposal, how she had agreed and then little by little came to appreciate that kind, clever man. But now, for some reason, with the wedding just a month away, she had grown fearful and anxious, as if expecting some vague, oppressive outcome.

"Tik-tok, tik-tok..." came the sound of the lazy tapping of the watchman. "Tik-tok..."

Through the big old window she could see the garden and distant bushes of densely blossoming lilac, drooping and faded from the cold, and a thick white mist, quietly stealing up to the lilac, wanting to envelop it. In the distant trees sleepy rooks were cawing.

"My God, why is my heart so heavy?"

Perhaps it was the fear felt by every bride before her wedding. Who knows? Or was it now the influence of Sasha? But hadn't Sasha been saying the same thing for several years now? He always spoke eloquently, but seemed naive and rather strange. Yet, all the same, why could she not get Sasha out of her head? Why?

The watchman had now long stopped tapping. Beneath the window and in the garden birds started singing, and the mist began to dissipate. Everything was lit up with spring sunshine, as if with a smile. Soon the whole garden, warmed and caressed by the sun, was revived. Drops of dew began to sparkle like diamonds on the leaves, and the old, long-neglected garden seemed on this morning so young and beautiful.

Granny had already awoken. Sasha's deep cough could be heard. There was the sound downstairs of the samovar being prepared, chairs being moved.

The time seemed to pass slowly. Nadya had already long ago risen and taken her stroll in the garden, yet still the morning seemed to drag.

Then her mother came down, tear-stained, holding a glass of mineral water. She dabbled in spiritualism and homeopathy; she read a lot and loved to talk about the doubts to which she was prone. And all this, it seemed to Nadya, contained a deep, ominous meaning. Now Nadya kissed her mother and walked beside her.

"Why were you crying, Mama?" she asked.

"Last night I started to read a story about an old man and his daughter. The old man worked somewhere, and the boss fell in love with his daughter. I didn't read to the end, but there was one place where it was hard not to cry." Nina Ivanovna took a sip from the glass and continued: "This morning I remembered the story and started to cry again."

"For me, all these days are so joyless," said Nadya after a brief silence. "Why can't I sleep at night?"

"I don't know, my dear. But when I can't sleep, I shut my eyes very tight, like this, and picture to myself Anna Karenina – the way she walks and talks – or visualize something from history, from the ancient world…"

Nadya felt that her mother did not, and could not, understand her. She felt this for the first time in her life, and the feeling frightened her. She wanted to hide away, and went to her room.

At two o'clock they sat down to lunch. It was a Wednesday, a fast day, which was why Granny was served meatless borscht* and bream with *kasha*.

In order to annoy Granny, Sasha ate some soup with meat, as well as the borscht. While eating he joked constantly, but his jokes came out heavily, unfailingly with the intention of conveying a moral, and were not at all funny. When he, trying to be witty, extended his very long, emaciated, corpse-like fingers, it occurred to the others that he was very sick and perhaps not long for the world, and they pitied him to the point of tears.

After dinner, Granny went to her room to rest. Nina Ivanovna played the piano for a while and then also left.

"Oh, dear Nadya," Sasha began, launching into their usual after-dinner conversation. "If only you would listen to me! If only!"

She had sunk into an old armchair and closed her eyes, while he quietly paced back and forth in the room.

"If only you would go away and study!" he said. "Only educated and enlightened people are interesting, only they are needed. Because the more such people there are, the sooner the kingdom of heaven on earth will be ushered in. Little by little your town will then be razed to the ground – everything will collapse, all will change, as if by magic. And here there will then be huge, magnificent houses, wonderful gardens, extraordinary fountains, remarkable people… But that is not the main thing. The main thing is that the multitude, in our sense of the word, as it is now – that evil will no longer exist, because everybody will believe and will know what they live for, and none will seek support in the multitude. My dear, dearest girl, go away! Show everyone that you find this stale, drab, sinful life repulsive. Show it, if only to yourself!"

"Don't go on like that, Sasha. I'm going to be married."

"Oh, enough of that! Who has to get married?"

They went out into the garden and walked around for a while.

"However that may be, my dear, you have to reflect, have to understand, how dishonourable, how immoral this idle life of yours is," continued Sasha. "Do understand, you see... if, for example, you and your mother and grandmother do nothing, then it means that someone else has to work for you. You are making someone else's life a misery, but is that really honourable? Is it not a disgusting thing to do?"

Nadya wanted to say "Yes, that's true", wanted to say she understood, but her eyes filled with tears and she suddenly fell silent, shrank inwardly and went to her room.

Andrei Andreyich arrived towards evening and, as usual, played the violin for a long time. He was in general a taciturn man, and loved his violin, perhaps because he did not have to talk while playing. Before eleven o'clock, when leaving for home, already in his coat, he embraced Nadya and greedily began to kiss her face, shoulders, arms.

"My dear, my darling, beautiful one!..." he muttered. "Oh, how happy I am! I am mad with happiness!"

It seemed to her that she had heard this long ago, very long ago, or read it somewhere... in an old, ragged, already long-forgotten novel.

In the large downstairs room, Sasha sat at the table and drank tea, holding the saucer on the long fingers of one hand; Granny was playing patience; Nina Ivanovna was reading. The little flame in the icon lamp was flickering, and everything seemed serene and peaceful. Nadya said goodnight and went upstairs to her room, lay down and immediately fell asleep. But, as on the previous night, it had barely started to get light when she awoke. She was not tired, and her heart felt heavy, restless. She sat with her head on her knees, thinking about her fiancé, about the wedding... For some reason she recalled that her mother had not loved her late husband; now she had nothing, and lived fully dependent on her mother-in-law, Granny. And Nadya, however much she thought, could not understand why until now she had seen her mother as someone special, unusual. Why had she not seen her for the simple, ordinary, unhappy woman that she was?

Downstairs, Sasha was not sleeping either – she could hear him coughing. He was a strange, naive man, thought Nadya, and in his dreams, in all those wonderful gardens, extraordinary fountains, she sensed something absurd. But for some reason there seemed in his naivety, even in the absurdity, so much beauty that she barely had time to think about whether she should go and study when a chill came over her and her heart was flooded with a feeling of rapturous joy.

"But it's better not to think about it, better not to think…" she whispered. "I don't have to think about that."

"Tik-tok…" The watchman's tapping was heard far away. "Tik-tok… tik-tok…"

III

In the middle of June Sasha suddenly grew bored and prepared to leave for Moscow.

"I can't live in this town," he said gloomily. "There's no water supply, no drains! It makes me feel sick to eat dinner: the filth in the kitchen is intolerable…"

"Stay a while longer, prodigal son," entreated Granny, for some reason in a whisper. "The wedding's on the seventh!"

"I don't want to."

"But you said you were going to stay till September."

"Well, now I don't want to. I have to work."

The summer turned out damp and cold. The trees were wet; everything in the garden looked bleak and cheerless; it was indeed a good time to want to work. In the rooms upstairs and down, unfamiliar women's voices could be heard – Granny's sewing machine was clattering as they rushed to prepare the trousseau. Of fur coats alone, Nadya had been given six, the cheapest of which, according to Granny, had cost three hundred roubles. All this activity irritated Sasha. He sat seething in his room, but they nevertheless persuaded him to stay, and he gave his word that he would not leave before the first of July.

The time passed quickly. On St Peter's Day* after lunch Andrei Andreyich went with Nadya to Moskovskaya Street to view once again the house that had been rented and had already long been prepared for the young couple. It was a two-storey house, of which just the upper floor had been made ready for their use. The reception-room floor, which had been painted to look like parquet, shone. There were Viennese chairs, a piano and a music stand for the violin. The smell of paint was pervasive. On the wall in a golden frame hung a big oil painting of a naked lady next to a violet vase with a broken handle.

"Wonderful picture," said Andrei Andreyich with a sigh of respect. "It's by the artist Shishmachevsky."

Further on was the sitting room with a round table, sofa and armchairs upholstered in bright blue. Over the sofa was a big photographic portrait of Father Andrei wearing a *kamilavka** and his medals. They went into the dining room, with its sideboard, then into the bedroom; there, in the semi-darkness, stood two beds, side by side, and it seemed that when the bedroom had been furnished it was with the belief that what went on in there would always be very satisfactory and could not be otherwise. Andrei Andreyich took Nadya through the rooms, all the time with his arm around her waist, but she felt weak and guilty, and hated all those rooms, beds and armchairs. The naked lady made her feel sick. It was clear to her by now that she had stopped loving Andrei Andreyich, or perhaps had never loved him – but she did not understand, and could not understand, how to say it, to whom to say it and why, though she thought about it all day, all night... He held her by the waist, spoke so tenderly, modestly, and was so happy walking through this flat of his, but she saw in everything only vulgarity – foolish, naive, unbearable vulgarity – and his hand around her waist felt hard and cold, like a metal hoop. At each moment she was ready to run away, to burst into tears, to throw herself out the window. Andrei Andreyich took her to the bathroom – there he turned a tap that had been fitted into the wall and water suddenly began to flow.

"What do you think of that?" he said, and burst out laughing. "I arranged to have a one-hundred *vedro** tank in the loft, so you and I will now have water."

They walked through the courtyard, then out to the street, where they took a cab. Dust was blowing in thick clouds, and it seemed there would very soon be rain.

"Are you cold?" asked Andrei Andreyich, screwing up his eyes from the dust.

She remained silent.

"You remember that yesterday Sasha reproached me for doing nothing," he said after a pause. "Well, he's right! Entirely right! I do nothing and can't do otherwise. Why is this, my dear? Why is it so disgusting even to think about some day putting a cockade on my hat* and going to work? Why am I so repulsed when I see a lawyer or a Latin teacher or a member of the council? Oh, Mother Russia! Mother Russia, how many idle, useless people you still have to bear! How many such as I, long-suffering country!"

And then he made some generalizations about his doing nothing, seeing in it a sign of the times.

"When we are married," he continued, "we'll go together to the country, my dear, and work there. We'll buy ourselves a little plot of land with a garden and a river running through it, and shall work, observe life... Oh, how good that will be!"

He took off his hat and let his hair blow about in the wind. She listened and thought: "My God, I want to go home! God!" As they approached the house, they overtook Father Andrei, who was walking.

"There goes my father!" joyfully exclaimed Andrei Andreyich, waving his hat. "I really love my dear father," he said, paying off the driver. "He's a delightful old man. A kind old man."

Nadya went into the house feeling angry and unwell, thinking about how all evening there would be guests, and how it would be necessary to entertain them, to smile, to listen to the violin, to listen to all sorts of nonsense and talk only about the wedding. Granny, an imposing presence, resplendent in her silk dress, haughty as she always seemed to be with guests, was sitting by the samovar. Father Andrei came in with his cunning smile.

"I have the pleasure and inestimable consolation of seeing you in good health," he said to Granny, and it was hard to tell whether he was joking or speaking seriously.

IV

The wind beat on the windows and roof. There was a whistling sound, and in the stove the house sprite mournfully, sullenly hummed its song. It was after midnight. Everyone in the house had already gone to bed, but no one was asleep, and Nadya imagined she could still hear the playing of the violin downstairs. There was a loud bang, probably the sound of a shutter coming off its hinges. A minute later Nina Ivanovna came in wearing just a nightdress and carrying a candle.

"What was that bang, Nadya?" she asked.

Nadya's mother, smiling timidly, with her hair plaited in a single braid, on this wild night seemed older, uglier, more shrunken. Nadya recalled how not long ago she had considered her mother to be a remarkable woman, and had proudly taken in her every word, but now she could in no way remember those words: everything that she remembered was so weak and superficial.

The sound of several bass voices seemed to come from the stove, and even the words, "Ah-h, my... God!" could be heard. Nadya sat up in bed and, clutching her hair, burst into tears.

"Mama, Mama," she said, "my dear, if you only knew what's happening to me! I beg you, implore you, let me go away! I beg you!"

"Where to?" asked Nina Ivanovna, not understanding, as she sat down on the bed. "Go away where?"

Nadya cried for a long time and could not say a word.

"Let me leave this town!" she said at last. "You must understand, there must be no wedding, and will not be! I don't love that man. I can't even talk about him."

"No, my darling, no," Nina Ivanovna said quickly, having taken fright. "Calm yourself. It's just that you're upset. It will pass. This happens. You probably quarrelled with Andrei. But lovers' quarrels don't mean a thing."

"Please go away, Mama, go away!" sobbed Nadya.

"Yes," said Nina Ivanovna, after a short silence. "How long ago was it that you were a child, a girl, and now you are already going to be married... In nature, everything keeps changing. And you will not notice how you yourself mature and grow old, and will have such an obstinate daughter as I."

"My dear, my kind mother, you are so intelligent, but unhappy," said Nadya. "You are very unhappy. But why do you talk nonsense? For God's sake, why?"

Nina Ivanovna wanted to say something, but could not utter a word. She sobbed and went to her room. Bass voices again began to drone in the stove, and it suddenly grew frightening. Nadya leapt out of bed and went quickly to her mother's room. Nina Ivanovna, her face tear-stained, was lying in bed under a blue blanket holding a book in her hands.

"Mama, listen to me!" Nadya said. "I entreat you, think about it and understand – just understand how shallow and degrading our life is! My eyes have been opened – I now see everything. What is your Andrei Andreyich? He really is so ignorant, Mama! My God! Understand, Mama, he is stupid!"

Nina Ivanovna sat up with a start.

"You and your granny torment me!" she said, sobbing. "I want to live! To live!" she repeated, striking her chest twice with her fist. "Give me my freedom! I'm still young, I want to live, but you have made an old woman of me!..."

She began to cry bitterly, lay down and curled up under the blanket. She seemed so small, so pathetic and foolish. Nadya went to her room, dressed and, having sat down by the window, began to wait for morning. All night she sat and thought, while someone outside kept banging the shutter and whistling.

In the morning Granny complained that during the night the wind had brought down all the apples in the garden and broken an old plum tree. It was so grey, dull and cheerless a day that a fire even had to be lit. Everyone complained about the cold, and the rain beat against the windows. After tea Nadya went to Sasha's room and, without saying a word, knelt in the corner by the armchair and covered her face with her hands.

"What's the matter?" asked Sasha.

"I can't..." she began. "I don't know, don't understand how I was able to live here before! I despise my fiancé, despise myself, despise this whole idle, meaningless life..."

"Well, well..." said Sasha, still not understanding what the outburst was about. "That's all right... That's good."

"This life is hateful to me," Nadya continued. "I can't bear it for even one more day. So tomorrow I'm leaving. Take me with you, for God's sake!"

Sasha looked at her for a moment in astonishment, then he rose and rejoiced, like a child. He waved his arms and began to stamp his feet, as if dancing with joy.

"Wonderful!" he said, rubbing his hands. "God, how good this is!"

She looked steadily at him with big, loving eyes, as if fascinated, straight away expecting him to say something meaningful to her, something boundless in its significance. He still said nothing, but already she sensed that before her eyes new, wide vistas were opening, vistas whose existence she had not previously been aware of, and already she was looking at him full of expectation, ready for anything, even death.

"I shall leave tomorrow," he said after a moment's thought, "and you drive to the station to see me off... I shall take your bag in my suitcase and get you a ticket. At the third bell, you get into the carriage – and we'll go. You'll go with me to Moscow, and from there go on alone to St Petersburg. Do you have a passport?"

"Yes."

"I swear to you, you'll not be sorry and regret it," Sasha said enthusiastically. "You will go, will study, and there find your destiny. When you change your life, everything will change. The main thing is to change your life: nothing else matters. So then, do we leave tomorrow?"

"Oh, yes! For God's sake!"

Nadya felt very excited, weighed down as never before at the thought that until her departure she would have to suffer and be prey to agonizing thoughts. But she had barely gone up to her room and lain on the bed when she fell asleep, and slept soundly, with a tear-stained face and a smile, until the evening.

V

They sent for a cab. Nadya, already in her hat and coat, went upstairs to see her mother and all her things once again. She stood awhile in her room next to the still-warm bed, looking around, and then went to her mother's room. Her mother was asleep, and it was quiet in the room. Nadya kissed her mother, smoothed her hair and stood motionless for a couple of minutes... Then, without hurrying, she returned downstairs.

Outside, it was raining heavily. The cab, with its covered top all wet, was standing by the entrance.

"There won't be room for you to go with him, Nadya," said Granny as the servants began to load the suitcases. "What an idea to see someone off in such weather! You should stay at home. Just look at the rain!"

Nadya wanted to say something but could not. Sasha helped her settle in the cab, covering her legs with a travelling rug. Then he himself found room next to her.

"Good luck! God bless you!" Granny cried from the porch. "Do make sure, Sasha, that you write to us from Moscow!"

"All right. Goodbye, Granny!"

"May the Queen of Heaven be with you!"

"Good lord, what weather!" said Sasha.

Only now did Nadya begin to cry. To her now it was clear that she was undeniably leaving, something she still did not believe when she was saying goodbye to Granny and looking at her mother. Goodbye, town! And she suddenly remembered everything: Andrei, his father, the new flat and the naked lady with the vase – and none of it was any longer frightening, oppressive: it was all trivial, petty, and kept being pushed further and further back into her consciousness. And when she was in the carriage and the train was setting off, then it was all in the past. Such big, serious concerns shrank into a little ball, and there opened up a vast, wide future, which until now she had barely noticed. The rain beat against the carriage windows. All that could be seen was a green field, telegraph poles flashing past, birds sitting on the wires – and suddenly Nadya caught her breath with joy: she remembered that she was going to freedom, going to study, doing what long ago used to be called "going to the Cossacks". She laughed, and cried, and prayed.

"It's going to be a-ll right," Sasha said, grinning. "A-ll right!"

VI

Autumn passed, and then winter. Nadya suffered bouts of deep melancholy and every day thought about her mother and Granny, thought about Sasha. The letters from home were sympathetic and kind, and it seemed as if everything had already been forgiven and forgotten. In May, after the exams, feeling happy and well, she went home, stopping in Moscow on the way in order to see Sasha. He was just the same as the summer before: bearded, with dishevelled hair, still in the same frock coat and canvas trousers, still with the same big beautiful eyes, but he looked unhealthy, exhausted. He had aged and lost weight, and still coughed from time to time. And he seemed to Nadya somehow colourless and unsophisticated.

"My God, Nadya has come!" he said, bursting into joyous laughter. "My dear, darling girl!"

They sat for a while in the lithography office, where the air was smoky and stuffy and smelt strongly of Indian ink and dye, then they went to his room, which was untidy and also smelt of smoke. On the table near the samovar, which had gone cold, lay a broken plate with a dark scrap of paper. There were many dead flies on the table and the floor. By all appearances it was evident that Sasha's private life was chaotic, and that he lived as well as he could, with complete disdain for comfort, and that if anyone were to speak to him about his personal happiness, his private life and their love for him, he would not understand and would only burst out laughing.

"It's all right, everything turned out all right," Nadya said hurriedly. "Mama came to St Petersburg to see me in the autumn, and said that Granny is not angry, but keeps going to my room to make the sign of the cross at the walls."

Sasha looked happy, but coughed from time to time and spoke in a cracked voice. Nadya kept peering at him without understanding whether he was in fact seriously ill or only seemed so to her.

"Sasha, my dear," she said, "you're unwell, aren't you?"

"No, it's all right. I'm ill, but it's nothing serious..."

"Oh, my God," Nadya said in agitation, "why aren't you being treated, why aren't you looking after your health? My dear, darling Sasha," she said, tears streaming from her eyes, and for some reason there appeared in her mind Andrei Andreyevich and the naked lady with the vase, and all her past, which now seemed as distant as her childhood. She began to cry, because Sasha no longer seemed to her as fresh, intelligent and interesting as he was the year before. "Dear Sasha, you are very, very unwell. I wish I knew what to do to stop you looking so pale and thin. I owe you so much! You cannot even imagine how much you did for me, my good Sasha! You are now really the closest and dearest person to me."

They sat awhile, talked awhile. Nadya told him how she had spent the winter in St Petersburg. She sensed in his words, in his smiles and his whole appearance something obsolete and old-fashioned which had long ago decayed and perhaps had already gone to the grave.

"I'm going to the Volga the day after tomorrow," said Sasha, "and then for treatment with koumiss.* I want to try koumiss. A friend and his wife are going with me. His wife is a wonderful woman. I keep pestering her, trying to persuade her to go away and study. I want her to transform her life."

After talking, they went to the station. Sasha treated her to tea and apples. When the train set off and he, smiling, waved his handkerchief, it was clear even from his stance that he was very unwell, and unlikely to live long.

Nadya arrived at her home town at noon. As she drove home from the station the streets seemed very wide, but the houses small and low. No people were about, and she met only the German piano tuner in a red coat. All the houses seemed covered in dust. Granny, now quite old and as stout and ugly as ever, embraced Nadya and cried for a long time with her face pressed to Nadya's shoulder, and could not be pulled away. Nina Ivanovna, also greatly aged and grown plain, had somehow become thin, but as before was still tightly laced and had diamonds glittering on her fingers.

"My dear girl!" she said, trembling all over. "My dear girl!"

Then they sat down and silently cried. It was clear that Granny and Mother sensed that the past was gone irrevocably and for good: they now had neither a place in society nor their former prestige, nor the right to invite people to come and visit them. It was like what happens when, in the midst of a light-hearted, care-free life, the police suddenly appear unexpectedly at night, make a search and the head of the house turns out to be an embezzler and forger – and goodbye for ever to the light-hearted, carefree life!

Nadya went upstairs and saw the same bed, the same windows with simple white curtains and, through the windows, the same garden flooded with sunshine and gaily filled with birdsong. She ran her hand over her table and sat down and thought for a while. Later she dined well and drank tea with delicious, rich cream, but something was no longer right – the rooms felt empty and the ceilings low. At night she went to bed and, covering herself, felt somehow strange to be lying in that warm, very soft bed.

Nina Ivanovna came in for a moment and sat down the way the guilty sit – shyly and cautiously.

"Well then, Nadya?" she asked after a short silence. "Are you happy? Very happy?"

"Yes, Mama."

Nina Ivanovna rose and made the sign of the cross over Nadya and the windows.

"As you see, I've become religious," she said. "You know, I now study philosophy and keep thinking, thinking... And to me now much has become as clear as day. Above all, it seems to me that life must be seen as if through a prism."

"Tell me, Mama, how is Granny's health?"

"It seems to be all right... When you went away then with Sasha and a telegram arrived from you, Granny collapsed reading it. For three days she lay without moving. After that, she kept praying and crying. But now she's all right."

She rose and paced back and forth in the room.

"Tik-tok..." tapped the watchman. "Tik-tok, tik-tok..."

"Above all, life must be seen as if through a prism," she said. "In other words, life must be consciously separated into its simplest elements, as if into the seven primary colours, with each element studied separately."

What else Nina Ivanovna said, and when she left, Nadya did not know, as she soon fell asleep.

May passed, and June set in. Nadya had by now grown accustomed to the house. Granny busied herself over the samovar, sighing deeply. Nina Ivanovna talked in the evenings about her philosophy. As before, she lived in the house like a sponger, and had to appeal to Granny for every twenty-copeck piece. There were a lot of flies in the house, and the ceilings of the rooms seemed to be getting lower and lower. Granny and Nina Ivanovna did not go out, from fear that they would meet Father Andrei and Andrei Andreyich. Nadya walked in the garden, and on the street, looking at the houses, at the grey fences, and it seemed to her that everything in the town had already long ago grown old, become obsolete and was still waiting either for its end or the beginning of something young and fresh. Oh, if only that new, bright life would come quickly, when it would be possible to look bravely and straight into the eyes of one's destiny and become aware of one's rights – to be joyous, free! And sooner or later such a life would come! Surely the time would come when things would be so arranged that four servants would not have to live in one room, in the basement, in filth – the time would come when not even a trace of this house would remain, and it would be forgotten, to be remembered by no one. Nadya's only distraction came from the little boys in the neighbouring yard: when she was walking in the garden they knocked on the fence and teased her, laughing:

"The bride! The bride!"

A letter from Sasha arrived from Saratov. In his irregular, wiggly handwriting he wrote that his trip along the Volga was entirely successful, but that in Saratov he was a little unwell, had lost his voice and had already been in hospital for two weeks. She knew what this meant, and was seized by a premonition amounting to certainty. It was unpleasant to her that this premonition, along with thoughts about Sasha, did not upset her as much as they would have before. She passionately wanted to live, to be in St Petersburg, and although her acquaintance with Sasha was still dear to her, it was far, far in the past! She did not sleep at all that night, and in the morning sat by the window listening. And indeed, voices were heard down below – Granny was anxiously and insistently asking about something. Then someone burst into tears... When Nadya arrived downstairs, Granny was standing in the corner and praying, and her face was tear-stained. On the table lay a telegram.

Nadya paced back and forth for a long time in the room, listening to Granny cry, then picked up the telegram and read. It communicated the news that the day before, in Saratov, Alexander Timofeyevich, or Sasha for short, had died of consumption.

Granny and Nina Ivanovna went to church to arrange for a *panikhida*, while Nadya long continued to pace the rooms, thinking. She clearly recognized that her life was now transformed, as Sasha had wanted, that she was now alone, something alien, superfluous, and that she did not need anything here, that everything from her past had been torn away from her and had vanished, as if burnt down, and the ashes scattered to the wind. She went to Sasha's room and stood there.

"Goodbye, dear Sasha!" she thought, while before her appeared a new life, wide and spacious – and this life, still unclear, full of mystery, captivated and lured her.

She went upstairs to her room to pack, and the next morning bid farewell to her family and, feeling joyous and full of life, left town – as she thought, for ever.

The Conundrum

THE STRONGEST MEASURES were taken to ensure that the Uskovs' family secret did not somehow leak out of the house. Half the servants were sent to the theatre and the circus, the other half were sitting confined in the kitchen. The order was given to admit no one. The wife of the uncle, who was a colonel, her sister and the governess, even though they were privy to the secret, behaved as if they knew nothing: they sat in the dining room and did not appear either in the sitting room or in the hall.

Sasha Uskov, a young man of twenty-five, whose behaviour had precipitated the crisis, has already been there for a long time, and, as advised by his defender – a maternal uncle, the kind-hearted Ivan Markovich – is sitting penitently in the hall near the door, preparing to enter the study and offer a candid, sincere explanation of his behaviour.

A family council is taking place behind the door in the study. The discussion concerns a very unpleasant, delicate subject. It is about the fact that Sasha Uskov has given the bank a forged promissory note, whose term expired three days before, and now two paternal uncles and Ivan Markovich – a maternal uncle – are deciding whether to pay the required sum and save the family honour, or wash their hands of the matter and leave it to the judicial authorities.

To those uninvolved and uninterested, such questions appear trivial, but for those unlucky enough to have to deal with them in earnest, they are extremely complex. The uncles have been talking for a long time, but are not a step closer to finding a solution.

"Gentlemen!" says the colonel-uncle in a voice that conveys fatigue and bitterness. "Gentlemen, who says that family honour is prejudice? I don't say that at all. I only warn you about a false view, and suggest the possibility of an inexcusable error. How can you not understand this? I'm not speaking Chinese, you know, but Russian!"

"My dear man, we understand," declares Ivan Markovich gently.

"How can you understand, if you say that I am renouncing family honour? I repeat once again: fam-il-y honour false-ly un-der-stood, is prejudice. Falsely understood! That's what I'm saying! From whatever motive, to conceal and protect an unpunished crook, whoever he may be – is unlawful and unworthy of an honest man: it is… not the salvation of family honour, but civic cowardice! Take the army for example… The honour of the army is for us dearer than any other honour – however, we do not protect any of its members who are criminals, but prosecute them. And why? Does the honour of the army really suffer in this way? On the contrary!"

The other paternal uncle, an official in the Treasury department, a taciturn, dull-witted and rheumatic man, either stays silent or just speaks about the possibility of the initiation of the Uskov family's legal proceedings being reported in the newspapers. In his opinion the matter should be hushed up at the very start, and not be made public, but apart from the reference to newspapers, he says nothing else to support this opinion.

The maternal uncle, the kind-hearted Ivan Markovich, talks smoothly, softly and with a tremor in his voice. He starts by saying that youth has its rights and its characteristic passions. Who among us has not been young and been carried away? Not just ordinary mortals, but even great minds have succumbed to enthusiasm and error. Take, for example, the life stories of great writers. Who among them, when young, did not lose at cards, did not squander money on drink, did not incur the anger of sensible people? Even if Sasha's enthusiasm bordered on the criminal, one must take into account the fact that he, Sasha, received almost no education: he was expelled in the fifth year of high school. He lost his parents in early childhood and thus in his most formative years lacked supervision and a good, wholesome influence. He is a nervous man, easily excited, with an unstable background, but – most importantly – fortune has not favoured him. Even if he is guilty, he still deserves leniency and the sympathy of all compassionate souls. He should of course be punished, but as it is he has already been punished by his conscience and the torments he suffers now, waiting for the decision of his relatives. The comparison to the army, which the colonel made, does much credit to his high mind. His appeal to civic responsibility reflects the nobility of his soul, but we must not forget that the citizen in each individual is closely connected to the Christian...

"Would we be neglecting our civic duty," exclaims Ivan Markovich passionately, "if instead of punishing the erring boy we extend to him a helping hand?"

Ivan Markovich speaks further about family honour. He himself does not have the honour of belonging to the Uskov family, but he knows very well that this famous family goes back to about the thirteenth century, and he does not forget for a minute that his never-forgotten, deeply beloved sister was the wife of a member of this family. In short, this family is dear to him for so many reasons, and he cannot contemplate at all, because of some fifteen hundred roubles, having a shadow fall on the worthy heraldic tree. If all accounts of motives are insufficiently convincing, then he, Ivan Markovich, suggests in conclusion that his listeners understand this: what exactly was the crime? Crime is immoral activity, having evil will at its root. But is human will not free? On this question science still has not given a definite answer. Scholars hold differing views. For example, the newest Lombroso* school does not recognize free will and maintains that every crime is the product purely of the anatomical peculiarities of the individual.

"Ivan Markovich!" the colonel says imploringly. "We are talking in earnest, about an important matter, and you talk about Lombroso! You are a clever man. Think – why are you saying all this? Do you really think that all these digressions and your rhetoric will give us a reply to the question?"

Sasha Uskov sits by the door and listens. He feels neither fear nor shame nor boredom, but only weariness and an empty soul.

It seems to him that it makes absolutely no difference whether they forgive him or not: if he came here to wait for the verdict and explain himself, it is only because the kind-hearted Ivan Markovich implored him to come. He is not afraid of the future. It is all the same to him wherever he is: here in the hall, in prison or in Siberia.

"If it's to be Siberia, let it be Siberia – the Devil take it!"

Life had become unbearably wearisome, and he was sick of it. He was up to his ears in debt and had not a *grosh** in his pocket; his relatives had become repulsive, and sooner or later he would have to part with friends and women because they were starting to view his freeloading life with scorn. The future looked bleak.

Sasha felt indifferent, and only one thing upset him, namely: behind the door they were calling him a scoundrel and a criminal. At every moment he was ready to burst into the study and cry in reply to the unpleasant metallic voice of the colonel:

"You're a liar!"

Criminal – what a terrible word! Thus are called murderers, thieves, robbers and in general people who are morally depraved. But Sasha was far from all that... True, he owed a lot and did not pay his debts. But surely debt was not a crime, and it was a rare man who was not in debt. The colonel and Ivan Markovich were both in debt...

"So what have I done wrong?" thinks Sasha.

He had forged a promissory note. But didn't all young people of his acquaintance do that? For example, didn't Khandrikov and Von Burst, whenever they needed money, forge a promissory note from family or acquaintances and then, on receiving the money from home, honour it by the requisite date? Sasha did just the same, but did not honour the promissory note because he had not received the money that Khandrikov had promised to lend him. It was not his fault, but due to circumstances. True, the use of another's signature is considered reprehensible – all the same, it's not a crime, but a generally accepted practice, not offensive or harmful to anyone. By forging the signature of the colonel, Sasha did not have the intention of causing harm or loss to anyone.

"No, it doesn't mean I'm a criminal," thinks Sasha. "And my character is not such as to be inclined towards crime. I am gentle, sensitive... When I have money, I help the poor..."

Sasha thinks things to this effect, while behind the door they continue to talk.

"Gentlemen, this is really going on for ever!" the colonel says heatedly. "Imagine that we forgive him and pay the debt. But surely after this he will not stop leading a dissolute life, squandering money, going into debt, going to our tailor and ordering himself a suit in our name! Can you guarantee that this stunt of his will be the last? I seem to have profound doubts as to his improvement!"

In reply to him, the Treasury official mutters something, and after him Ivan Markovich smoothly and softly begins to speak. The colonel moves his chair impatiently and drowns the other's words with his grating metallic voice. At last the door opens and Ivan Markovich comes out of the study. Red patches have come out on his gaunt, clean-shaven face.

"Let's go!" he says, taking Sasha by the arm. "Go and give an honest explanation. Without pride, dear boy, but humbly and from the heart."

Sasha enters the study. The Treasury official is sitting; the colonel is standing in front of the table with his hands in his pockets and one knee on a chair. It is smoky and stuffy in the room. Sasha does not look at the official, nor at the colonel. He suddenly feels ashamed and terrified. He looks uneasily at Ivan Markovich and mutters:

"I shall pay... I shall give back..."

"What did you hope for when you forged the note?" he hears the metallic voice say.

"I... Khandrikov promised to lend me the money in time."

Sasha could say no more. He leaves the study and again sits down on the chair by the door. He would gladly leave altogether, but he's choking with hatred, and he wants terribly to stay, in order to interrupt the colonel, to say something cheeky to him. He sits and thinks about what he could say to his hated uncle that would be strong and weighty, but at that moment, in the doors of the sitting room, shrouded in dim light, appears a woman's figure. It is the colonel's wife. She beckons Sasha to come to her and, wringing her hands and crying, says:

"*Alexandre*,* I know you don't like me, but... listen to me, listen, I beg you... My friend, how could this have happened? It really is so terrible, terrible! For God's sake, beg them, explain yourself, entreat them."

Sasha looks at her shaking shoulders, at the huge tears flowing down her cheeks, hears behind him the muffled voices of weary, exhausted people, and shrugs his shoulders. In no way did he expect that his aristocratic relatives would raise a storm because of some fifteen hundred roubles! He can understand neither the tears nor the trembling voices.

An hour later he hears how the colonel's will dominates: the uncles at last agree to hand over the matter to the judicial authorities.

"It's settled!" says the colonel, sighing. "Enough!"

After this decision all the uncles, even the insistent colonel, grow noticeably dispirited. Silence sets in.

"My God, my God!" sighs Ivan Markovich. "The poor woman!"

And he begins to talk quietly about someone who, he says, is probably present in the study in spirit – his sister, Sasha's mother. He feels in his heart how that unhappy, saintly woman would weep, suffer and entreat for the boy. For the sake of her peace beyond the grave, it would be necessary to show mercy to Sasha.

Sobbing is heard. Ivan Markovich is crying and muttering something that cannot be made out through the door. The colonel gets up and paces back and forth in the room. A long conversation begins again.

Now the clock in the sitting room strikes two. The family conference is over. The colonel, so as not to see the man who has caused him so much trouble, goes from the study not into the hall, but to the front entrance... Ivan Markovich goes into the hall... He is excited, and joyfully rubs his hands. His tear-filled eyes look happy, and his mouth twists into a smile.

"Excellent!" he says to Sasha. "God be praised! You, my friend, may go home and sleep soundly. We decided to honour the debt, but on condition that you repent and tomorrow go with me to the country and get a job."

A minute later Ivan Markovich and Sasha, in coat and hat, go down the stairs. The uncle is muttering something edifying. Sasha is not listening, but feels how something heavy and terrifying is gradually being lifted from his shoulders. They have forgiven him – he is free! Joy, like the wind, flows into his chest and fills his heart with sweet coolness. He wants to breathe, to move quickly, to live! Looking at the street lights and the black sky, he remembers that today Von Burst will be celebrating his name day at the Medved,* and joy again seizes his soul...

"I shall go!" he decides.

But then he remembers that he does not have a single copeck, that the comrades to whom he will now go despise him for being penniless. He has to get some money, no matter what!

"Uncle, lend me a hundred roubles!" he says to Ivan Markovich.

His uncle looks him in the face with astonishment and moves backwards to the lamp-post.

"Give it to me!" says Sasha, impatiently shifting from foot to foot and starting to pant. "Uncle, I beg you! Give me a hundred roubles!"

His face is distorted – he is shaking, and he moves aggressively towards his uncle...

"Will you not give it to me?" he asks, seeing that the other is still stunned and uncomprehending. "Listen, if you do not give it to me, then tomorrow I shall renege on my word. I shall not give you the money for the debt. Tomorrow I shall forge a new promissory note."

The stunned Ivan Markovich, in horror, muttering something incoherent, draws from his wallet a one-hundred-rouble banknote and hands it to Sasha. The other takes it and quickly walks away...

After hailing a cab, Sasha calms down and again feels how joy flows into his heart. The rights of youth, which the very kind Ivan

Markovich spoke about at the family conference, are awakened and begin to cast their spell. Sasha imagines the forthcoming binge, and between visions of bottles, women and friends, the thought flashes through his mind:

"Now I see that I am a criminal. Yes, I am a criminal."

A Father

"I CONFESS, I'VE HAD A DRINK... Excuse me, I called in at a beer shop on the way and because of the heat drank two small bottles. It's hot, my boy!"

Old man Musatov drew a rag from his pocket and wiped his clean-shaven, haggard face.

"I've come to you for a moment, Boryenka my angel," he continued without looking at his son, "on a very important matter. Sorry if I'm disturbing you. Do you have ten roubles till Tuesday, my dear? You know, yesterday I had to pay the rent, but money, you know... oof! I need some urgently."

Young Musatov went out without a word and began to whisper behind the door to his landlady and the colleagues who were renting the dacha jointly with him. Three minutes later he returned and silently handed his father a ten-rouble banknote. The other, without looking at it, casually thrust it into his pocket and said:

"*Merci.** Well, how are you? We haven't seen each other for a long time."

"No, not for a long time. Since Holy Week."*

"Five times I planned to come and see you, but I never had time. First it was one thing, then another... It's been hell! But no, I'm lying... All that is a lie. Don't believe me, Boryenka. I said I'd pay back the ten roubles on Tuesday, but don't believe that either. Don't believe a single word of mine. I've nothing to do but lie around lazily, drunkenly and feel shame at appearing in the street in these clothes. You will excuse me, Boryenka. Three times I sent a girl to you for money, and wrote you begging letters. I thank you for the money, but don't believe the letters: I lied. I'm ashamed to rob you like this, my angel; I know you yourself barely make ends meet, and live on locusts,* but with my impudence it can't be helped. Such a cheeky fellow, who turns up only for money!...

Do excuse me, Boryenka. I'm telling you the whole truth because I can't look with indifference on your angelic face."

A minute passed in silence. The old man sighed deeply and said:

"Could you offer me some beer, perhaps?"

His son went out silently, and again whispers were heard behind the door. When he returned a little later with beer, the old man brightened up at the sight of the bottles and abruptly changed his tone.

"I was at the races the other day, my boy," he said with a guilty look. "There were three of us, and in the tote we took a three-rouble ticket on Shustri. And thanks a lot to that Shustri! We each got thirty-two roubles on the one bet. I can't live without the races, my boy. It's a noble pleasure. My wench always scolds me about the races, but I go. I love it, can't help myself!"

Boris, a fair-haired young man with a melancholy, expressionless face, walked slowly back and forth in the room, silently listening. When the old man paused to clear his throat, his son went up to him and said:

"The other day, Papa, I bought some boots for myself, but they seem too tight. Would you like to have them? I'll let you have them cheap."

"Maybe," agreed the old man, grimacing. "Only, for the same price, without reduction."

"Very well. I shall lend you the money."

The son crawled under the bed and drew out the new boots. The father took off his heavy, brown, obviously second-hand boots and tried on the new pair.

"A perfect fit!" he said. "All right, let me have them. But on Tuesday, when I get my pension, I shall send you the money for them. No, I'm lying," he continued, suddenly again lapsing into his previous tearful tone. "I lied about the tote, and I lied about the pension. You are deceiving me, Boryenka… I am really aware of your generous nature. I see through you! You found the boots too small because your soul is big. Ah, Borya, Borya! I understand everything and feel everything!"

"Have you moved to a new flat?" his son broke in to change the subject.

"Yes, my boy, to a new one. I move every month. My wench, with her character, can't stay long in one place."

"I was at your old flat, wanted to invite you to stay at my dacha. With your health it would not hurt to take some fresh air."

"No!" The old man waved his hand. "My woman wouldn't let me, and I myself don't want to. You've tried a hundred times to drag me out of my hole, and I myself have tried, but it's been no damned use. Forget it! I shall die like a dog in the ditch. I sit here now with you, looking at your angelic face, and myself so long to go home to my hole. That seems to be my fate. You can't drag a dung beetle to a rose. No. However, it's time I was going, my boy. It's getting dark."

"But wait, I'll go with you. I myself have to be in town today."

The old man and the young put on their coats and left. When a little later they were driving in a cab, it was already dark and lights were glimmering in the windows.

"I robbed you, Boryenka!" muttered his father. "Poor, poor children! It must be a great grief to have such a father! Boryenka, my angel, I can't lie when I see your face. Forgive me. Dear God – to what length my shamelessness will go! Now I've just cleaned you out, embarrassed you by turning up drunk. Your brothers I also rob and embarrass, but you should have seen me yesterday! I shall not hide the truth, Boryenka. Yesterday some neighbours and all sorts of layabouts came to visit my woman, and I drank with them too and began to abuse you, my children, for all it was worth. I cursed you and complained that it was as if you had abandoned me. I wanted, do you see, to move the drunken women to pity and to play the part of the unfortunate father. That's my style: when I want to hide my defects, I shift all my troubles onto my innocent children. I can't lie to you, Boryenka, or hide. I came to you arrogantly, but when I saw your gentleness and charity I was speechless, and my conscience was turned upside down."

"Enough, Papa. Let's talk about something else."

"Mother of God, what children I have!" continued the old man, ignoring his son. "What a lavish gift God sent me! Such children should not have been given to me, a good-for-nothing, but to a real man, with a soul and feelings! I am unworthy!"

The old man took off his little peak cap with the button and crossed himself several times.

"Praise to you, God!" he sighed, glancing around as if looking for an icon. "Wonderful, rare children! I have three sons, and they are all the same: sober, reliable, hard-working – and what minds! Cabby, what minds! One of them, Gregory, has a mind that would do for ten men. He speaks French and German, and talks as well as any of your lawyers – so you listen carefully to him… Children, my children, I can't believe you are mine! I can't believe it! You are a martyr, Boryenka. I am ruining you and will go on ruining you… You'll keep giving me money, though you know it doesn't go on necessities. The other day I sent you a begging letter, describing my illness, but I really lied: I wanted money from you for rum. And you gave it to me because you were afraid I would be offended by a refusal. All this I know and feel. Grisha is also a martyr. On Thursday, my boy, I went to see him when I was drunk, filthy, dressed in rags… I smelt of vodka like a tavern. I went straight up to him, quite a sight, went to talk to him about something stupid, in the presence of his colleagues, boss and clients. I shamed him for life. But like you he wasn't a bit embarrassed, just turned a little pale. He smiled and came up to me as if it was nothing at all, and even introduced me to his comrades. Then he came home with me, and gave me not a word of reproach! I rob him more than I do you. Take now your brother Sasha – now, there's a martyr! He married, you know, a colonel's daughter from aristocratic circles, received a dowry… You'd think he had no time for me. No, my boy, as soon as he married, after the wedding, he came to visit me with his young wife… in my hole… He really did!"

The old man sobbed and suddenly began to laugh.

"At the time, to make matters worse, we were eating grated radishes with kvass, and frying fish, and the stench in the flat was enough to make the Devil sick. I lay drunk, and my wench leapt up with a red face to meet the young people… It was disgraceful, in a word. But Sasha rose to the occasion."

"Yes, our Sasha is a good man," said Boris.

"The very greatest! All you children of mine are made of gold: you, and Grisha, and Sasha, and Sonya. I torment you, torture you, shame you, rob you, but in my whole life I have not heard from you a single word of reproach, not seen a single scowl. It would be understandable if I'd been a respectable father, but… tfoo! You have seen nothing of me but evil. I am a bad, dissolute man… Now, praise God, I have become less wild, and have lost my spark, but certainly before, when you were small, I had much drive and character. Whatever I did or said, it all seemed to me to be right. I used to return home from the club drunk and quarrelsome and start to reproach your deceased mother about her spending. All night I would make her life a misery, and think she deserved it. Often, you would get up in the morning and go to school and I would still be showing her my true character. Lord above, how I tormented her, the martyr! And when you returned from school and I was asleep, you didn't dare eat before I got up. After dinner it would start all over again. You probably remember. God forbid that anyone should have such a father. God sent me to you as a trial. Really, a trial! You children will see it through to the end. Honour your father, that you may enjoy long years of life.* For the trials you've had, may God send you a long life. Cabby, stop!"

The old man jumped down from the droshky and ran into a tavern. Half an hour later he returned, grunted drunkenly and sat down next to his son.

"So where is Sonya now?" he asked. "Still at boarding school?"

"No, she finished in May and now lives with Sasha's mother-in-law."

"Well, well!" exclaimed the old man in amazement. "She's a fine girl – must have followed the example of her brothers. Ah,

Boryenka, she has no mother to console her. Listen, Boryenka, she... does she know how I live? Does she?"

Boris did not reply. Five minutes passed in deep silence. The old man sobbed, wiped his face with his rag and said:

"I love her, Boryenka! You know she is my only daughter, and in old age there is no greater consolation than a daughter. Could I meet up with her? Is it possible, Boryenka?"

"Of course, whenever you want."

"Really? And she wouldn't mind?"

"Come, come! She herself has been looking for you, hoping to meet."

"Really? What children! What do you think, cabby? Arrange it, Boryenka, dear boy! She's a young lady now, refined, drinks consommé and other things like that, in the manner of the nobility, and I don't want to appear before her looking so scruffy. We'll do this, Boryenka. I shall give up alcohol for three days, so that my foul drunken mug arrives looking as it should – then I shall come to you, and you will lend me one of your suits. I shall shave, have a haircut, and you will go and bring her to your place. Agreed?"

"All right."

"Cabby, stop!"

The old man again leapt from the droshky and ran into a tavern. Before they reached his flat he jumped down twice more, and each time his son quietly and patiently waited for him. When they had dismissed the cab and were creeping through the long, dirty courtyard to "the woman's" flat, the old man assumed a profoundly embarrassed and guilty look, and timidly began to groan and smack his lips.

"Boryenka," he said ingratiatingly, "if my old baggage starts telling you something, pay no attention to it and... you know, be evasive, though as polite as possible. She's ignorant and impudent, but all the same a good woman. A kind, warm heart beats in her breast!"

The long courtyard came to an end, and Boris entered a dark vestibule. The door creaked on a pulley, and there was a smell of cooking and samovar steam and a sound of sharp voices. Passing from the vestibule through the kitchen, Boris saw only dark smoke, a cord hung with linen and the samovar chimney, through a crack of which were pouring golden sparks.

"And here is my cell," said the old man, stooping and entering a small room with a low ceiling and an atmosphere unbearably stuffy from its proximity to the kitchen.

There, three women were sitting at a table enjoying a social visit. Seeing the visitor, they exchanged looks and stopped eating.

"Well, did you get it?" sharply asked one of them, who was evidently "the woman" herself.

"I got it, I got it," muttered the old man. "Well, Boris, you are welcome, have a seat! We are plain people, young man… We lead a simple life."

He began to bustle about aimlessly. He felt ashamed in front of his son, yet at the same time evidently wanted to strut in front of the women and as usual play the unfortunate, rejected father.

"Yes, my boy, young man, we live simply, unpretentiously," he muttered. "We are simple people, young man… We are not like you, we don't like to try and impress. No, sir. Would you perhaps like some vodka?"

One of the women (who was ashamed to drink in front of a stranger) sighed and said:

"I'll have another drink because of the mushrooms… Mushrooms like these make you drink even when you don't want to. Ivan Gerasimych, if you offer him some mushrooms maybe he'll drink!"

She pronounced the last word like this: dreenk.

"Have a drink, young man!" said the old man, not looking at his son. "We have no wines or liqueurs, my boy – we are simple people."

"He doesn't like it here!" sighed "the woman".

"It's all right, it's all right, he'll drink."

So as not to offend his father by refusing, Boris took a small glass and drank without saying a word. When the samovar was brought, he silently, with a melancholy expression, drank two cups of disgusting tea to please the old man. He listened quietly while "the woman" dropped hints about how in this world there are cruel and godless children who abandon their parents.

"I know what you are thinking now!" said the old man, becoming tipsy and entering his usual drunken, excited state. "You think I've lowered myself, got stuck in the mire, that I'm a pitiful figure, but in my opinion this simple life is much more normal than your life, young man. I don't need anyone and… and I don't intend to demean myself. I can't bear it if some boy looks pityingly at me."

After tea he cleaned a herring and sprinkled onion on it with such feeling that tears of emotion appeared in his eyes. He began to talk again about the tote, about his winnings, about some straw panama hat for which he had paid sixteen roubles the day before. He lied with the same gusto with which he drank and ate the herring. His son sat for an hour in silence before saying goodbye.

"I don't dare detain you!" the old man said haughtily. "Forgive me, young man, for not living as you would wish!"

He swaggered, chuckled self-satisfiedly and winked at the woman.

"Goodbye, sir, young man!" he said, accompanying his son to the vestibule. "*Attendez!*"*

But in the vestibule, where it was dark, he suddenly pressed his face to his son's sleeve and sobbed.

"I would like to see Sonyushka!" he whispered. "Arrange it, Boryenka, my angel! I shall shave, put on your suit… make a serious face… I shall be quiet in her presence. Really, I shall be quiet!"

He looked timidly at the door, behind which could be heard the voices of the women, stopped sobbing and said loudly:

"Goodbye, young man! *Attendez!*"

The Unwanted

IT IS AFTER SIX O'CLOCK on a June evening. A crowd of people that have just alighted from the dacha train are trudging to the dacha settlement from the little station of Khilkoye. They are mostly family men, laden with bags, briefcases and women's hat boxes. They all look weary, hungry and irritable, as if it is not for them that the sun is shining and the grass greening up.

Among others trudges Pavel Matveyevich Zaykin, an official of the regional court, a tall, stooping man in a cheap linen coat and with a cockade on a faded peak cap. He is sweating and red-faced, and looks morose.

"Do you come out to the dacha every day?" a fellow visitor in ginger-coloured trousers asks him.

"No, not every day," Zaykin replies gloomily. "My wife and son live here all the time, but I just come twice a week. I'm too busy to come every day – and besides, it's expensive."

"That's true, it's expensive," the man in the ginger trousers says with a sigh. "In town you can't get to the station on foot: you need a cab... then a ticket costs forty-two copecks... you buy an expensive newspaper, drink a small glass of vodka to give you strength. All these are trifling expenses, but if you're not careful they'll add up to about two hundred roubles over the summer. Of course the beauties of nature are worth more than that, I won't argue about it, sir... the idyllic life, and so on, but surely on our civil-service pay, as you yourself know, every copeck counts. You carelessly waste a copeck, and then you don't sleep all night... Yes, sir... I, dear sir (I don't have the honour of knowing your name and patronymic), I earn almost two thousand a year, sir, and hold the rank of state councillor, but smoke second-rate tobacco and don't have a rouble to spare to buy myself the Vichy mineral water that was prescribed for my liver stones."

"It's utterly abominable," says Zaykin after a pause. "I, sir, am of the opinion that dacha life was invented by the Devil and women. The Devil in this case is responsible for its nastiness, and women for its extreme frivolity. For Heaven's sake, it's not life, but penal servitude, hell! It's stifling here, hot, hard to breathe, and you wander around from place to place like a lost soul and in no way find refuge for yourself. There, in town, there is neither furniture nor servants... everything's been taken to the dacha... you eat the devil knows what, don't drink tea because there's no one to put on the samovar... you don't wash, then you arrive here, you're surrounded by nature and are pleased to trudge on foot through the dust, the heat... Tfoo! Are you married?"

"Yes, sir... Three children," the man in the ginger trousers says with a sigh.

"It's utterly abominable... It's simply amazing that we're still alive."

At last the dacha visitors reach the settlement. Zaykin says goodbye to the man in the ginger trousers and goes to his cottage. He finds the place deathly quiet. The only sounds are the droning of mosquitoes and the cry for help from a fly, which is about to become a spider's dinner. Through the window, which was partially covered by little muslin curtains, could be seen the red hues of faded geraniums. Flies doze on the unpainted wooden walls, around the oleographs. There is not a soul in the vestibule, in the kitchen, in the dining room. In the room which at one and the same time serves as the sitting and reception room, Zaykin finds his son Petya, a small six-year-old boy. Petya is sitting at the table and, with his lower lip pushed out, is breathing heavily and noisily through his nose as he cuts out with scissors from a playing card the jack of diamonds.

"Ah, it's you, Papa!" he says, not turning around. "Hello!"

"Hello... Where is your mother?"

"Mama? She went with Olga Kirillovna to rehearse at the theatre. The day after tomorrow is their performance. They're taking me too... Are you going?"

"Hm!... So when does she return?"

"She said she'll be back in the evening."

"And where's Natalya?"

"Mama took Natalya with her, to help her dress in time for the performance, and Akulina has gone to the forest for mushrooms. Papa, why is it that when mosquitoes bite their stomachs get red?"

"I don't know... Because they suck blood. So no one's at home?"

"No one. I'm here alone."

Zaykin sits down in an armchair and stares vacantly out of the window for a minute.

"So who's going to give us dinner?" he asks.

"They're not doing dinner tonight, Papa! Mama thought you weren't coming today and didn't arrange dinner. She and Olga Kirillovna are eating at the theatre."

"Thank you kindly for informing me, but what did you eat?"

"I've had some milk. They bought six copecks of milk for me. Papa, so why do mosquitoes suck blood?"

Zaykin suddenly feels something heavy ascend to his liver and start to gnaw at it. It becomes so irritating, annoying and unpleasant that he starts to breathe heavily and shiver. He feels that he would like to jump up, throw something heavy on the floor and break out swearing, but then, remembering that the doctors strictly forbade him to get agitated, he rises and, restraining himself, starts to whistle an air from *Les Huguenots*.*

"Papa, do you know how to act in the theatre?" He hears the voice of Petya.

"Oh, don't pester me with your stupid questions!" Zaykin says angrily. "You stick like a bath mat! You're now six years old, but you're just as stupid as you were three years ago... You're a stupid, spoilt boy! Why, for example, are you ruining these cards? How do you dare ruin them?"

"These cards aren't yours," says Petya, turning to him. "Natalya gave them to me."

"You're lying! You're lying, you worthless boy!" Zaykin gets more and more angry. "You always lie! You should be beaten, you're such a little pig! I shall box your ears!"

Petya jumps up, stretches out his neck and looks straight into the red, angry face of his father. His big eyes start to blink, then cloud over with moisture, and the boy's face creases up.

"Why do you swear at me?" wails Petya. "Why do you bother me, you fool? I'm not disturbing anyone, I'm not naughty, I'm obedient, but you... get angry! So why are you scolding me?"

The boy speaks persuasively, and cries so bitterly that Zaykin becomes ashamed of himself.

"Yes, it's true, why am I laying into him?" he thinks.

"Well, it's all right... it's all right," he says, touching the boy on the shoulder. "It's my fault, Petyukha... forgive me. You are a good boy, a fine lad, I love you."

Petya wipes his eyes with his sleeve, sits down with a sigh at the same place as before and starts to cut out a queen. Zaykin goes to his study. He stretches out on the sofa and, putting his hands behind his head, falls to thinking. The recent tears of the boy have eased his anger, and he feels less liverish. He feels only exhaustion and hunger.

"Papa!" Zaykin hears from behind the door. "Shall I show you my insect collection?"

"Show it to me."

Petya enters the study and hands his father a long green box. Before even taking hold of the box, Zaykin hears a desperate buzzing and scratching of legs against the sides of the box. Lifting the lid, he sees many butterflies, beetles, grasshoppers and flies secured to the bottom of the box with pins. All, with the exception of two or three butterflies, are still alive and moving.

"And one of the grasshoppers is still alive!" Petya says in amazement. "We caught it yesterday morning and it still hasn't died!"

"Who was it who taught you to pin them?" asks Zaykin.

"Olga Kirillovna."

"Olga Kirillovna herself should be pinned like this!" says Zaykin in disgust. "Take them away from here! It's shameful to torture animals!"

"God, how abominably he's being brought up," he thinks as Petya goes out.

Pavel Matveyevich has already forgotten about his exhaustion and hunger, and thinks only about the fate of his boy. Meanwhile, through the windows, daylight is gradually fading... Sounds can be heard of the dacha residents returning in groups from their evening bathe. A man stops outside the open window of the dining room and cries: "Do you want any mushrooms?" He shouts and, not receiving an answer, shuffles further along in his bare feet... And now, as dusk deepens to the point that the geraniums behind the muslin curtain lose their outline and the cool of the evening sets in outside the window, the door to the vestibule opens noisily and there is the sound of rapid steps, talk, laughter...

"Mama!" squeals Petya.

Zaykin peeps out from the study and sees his wife Nadezhda Stepanovna, looking healthy and rosy-cheeked as always... With her is Olga Kirillovna, a skinny blond woman with large freckles, and two unfamiliar men: one young and tall, with curly red hair and a big Adam's apple, the other short and stocky, with an actor's clean-shaven face and a crooked, blue-grey chin.

"Natalya, put on the samovar!" cries Nadezhda Stepanovna, her dress audibly rustling. "Did I hear that Pavel Matveyevich has arrived? Pavel, where are you? Hello, Pavel!" she says, running to the study and breathing heavily. "Have you come? I'm very glad... Two of our amateurs have come with me... come along, I shall introduce you... This one here, the taller one, is Koromyslov – he sings beautifully – and the other, this short one... a certain Smerkalov, is a real actor... he reads wonderfully. Oof, I'm exhausted! We've just now had our rehearsal... It's going splendidly! We're putting on *The Tenant with the Trombone*,* and *She Waits for Him...** The show is the day after tomorrow..."

"Why did you bring them here?" asks Zaykin.

"I had to, silly! After tea we have to read through our parts and practise our singing... Koromyslov and I are doing a duet... Oh, I nearly forgot! Send Natalya, my dear, to get sardines, vodka, cheese and something else. They'll probably have supper too... Oh, I'm exhausted!"

"Hm!... I don't have any money!"

"This is really impossible, silly. It's embarrassing! Don't make me blush!"

Half an hour later Natalya is sent to fetch vodka and some food. Zaykin, after drinking his tea and eating a whole loaf of French bread, goes to the bedroom and lies down on the bed, while Nadezhda Stepanovna and her guests, with noise and laughter, get down to rehearsing their parts. For a long time Pavel Matveyevich hears Koromyslov's nasal recitation and Smerkalov's theatrical exclamations. After the reading there follows a long conversation, punctuated by the shrill laughter of Olga Kirillovna. Smerkalov, in his capacity as a real actor, explains the roles with assurance and intensity...

There follows the duet, and after the duet the tinkling of crockery... In his sleep, Zaykin hears how the others persuade Smerkalov to read *The Sinful Woman*,* and how that one, after assuming a pose, begins to recite. He rasps, beats his chest, weeps, guffaws in a hoarse bass... Zaykin winces and buries his head under the blanket.

"It's a long way for you to go in the dark," he hears Nadezhda Stepanovna say an hour later. "Why don't you spend the night with us? Koromyslov can sleep here in the dining room, on the sofa, and you, Smerkalov, on Petya's bed... Petya can sleep in my husband's study... Really, stay!"

At last, when the clock strikes two, all falls silent... The bedroom door opens and Nadezhda Stepanovna appears.

"Pavel, are you asleep?" she whispers.

"No, what is it?"

"Go to your study, my dear, and sleep on the sofa, so I can put Olga Kirillovna on your bed. Go, my dear! I would put her in the study, but she's afraid to sleep alone... Do get up!"

Zaykin rises, puts on his dressing gown and, taking a pillow, trudges to the study... Feeling his way towards his sofa, he strikes a match and sees that Petya is lying on the sofa. The boy is not asleep, and is staring wide-eyed at the match.

"Papa, why is it that mosquitoes don't sleep at night?" he asks.

"Because... because," Zaykin mutters, "because you and I are not wanted here. There's nowhere even to sleep!"

"Papa, and why does Olga Kirillovna have freckles on her face?"

"Oh, stop it! I'm sick of your questions!"

After a little thought, Zaykin dresses and goes outside for a breath of air... He looks at the grey morning sky, at the motionless clouds, listens to the lazy cry of a sleepy corncrake and thinks longingly about the next day when, having gone to town and returned home from court, he'll collapse into bed... Suddenly, from around a corner, appears a male figure.

"Probably the nightwatchman," thinks Zaykin.

But, having looked and approached closer, he recognizes in the figure the dacha resident in ginger trousers of the day before.

"Can't you sleep?" he asks.

"No, I can't sleep, for some reason..." sighs the man in the ginger trousers. "I'm enjoying nature... A dear visitor arrived at my place on the night train, you know... my wife's mother. With her came my nieces... lovely girls. I'm very glad, though... it's a damp night! And are you also glad to be enjoying nature?"

"Yes," mumbles Zaykin. "I too... nature... Do you know if somewhere near here there isn't a tavern or inn?"

The man in the ginger trousers raises his eyes to heaven and falls to thinking...

An Incident in Court

THIS INCIDENT TOOK PLACE at a recent session of the district court in the town of N—.

In the dock was sitting a citizen of N—, Sidor Shelmetsov, a fellow of thirty with lively, Gypsy-like features and cunning little eyes. He was accused of burglary, fraud and false impersonation. The latter offence was compounded by his having assumed a title. The charge was being brought by an assistant to the public prosecutor. This assistant's name was Legion.* Of special characteristics and qualities that might have given him popularity and substantial fees he possessed none: he was like so many others of his kind. He spoke with a nasal twang, did not articulate the letter "k" and was incessantly blowing his nose.

The defence, on the other hand, was being conducted by the most celebrated and popular lawyer of the time. Everyone knew about this attorney. His wonderful speeches were quoted, his name was pronounced with reverence…

In bad novels, which end with the full acquittal of the hero and applause from the public, he plays a major role. In such novels he is usually given a name derived from thunder, lightning and other no less impressive elemental forces.

After the assistant prosecutor had been able to prove that Shelmetsov was guilty and did not deserve leniency, when he had summed up, had convinced the jury and said: "I have finished", the counsel for the defence rose. All those present pricked up their ears. Silence reigned. The lawyer began to speak and… the nerves of the town of N—'s public began to tingle! He extended his swarthy neck and inclined his head to one side; his eyes began to sparkle; he raised his hand, and ineffable sweetness began to flow into ears that strained to hear. His words played on the nerves of the people as on a balalaika. After his first two or three sentences, there was a loud sigh among the public, and a pale lady was taken out of the courtroom. Just three minutes later the chairman was already forced to reach for the bell and call for order by ringing it three times. A bailiff with a red nose turned around on his chair and looked menacingly at the enthusiastic public. All eyes widened, faces went pale in ardent expectation of what the defence counsel would say next. The people strained forward… And what was going on in their hearts?

"We, gentlemen of the jury, are people, and will be judging as human beings!" the counsel for the defence said, among other things. "Before appearing before you, this man suffered six months' detention on remand. In the course of those six months his wife felt deeply the lack of a beloved husband; the children's tears did not dry from the thought that their dear father was not there with them! Oh, if only you could see those children! They are hungry, because there is no one to provide for them, they are crying because they are deeply unhappy… Yes, just look at them! They are stretching out their tiny hands to you, begging you to give them back their father! They are not here, but you can imagine them." He paused. "Imprisonment… Well… He was put with thieves and murderers… Him!" He paused. "You just have to imagine the mental torments caused by that imprisonment, far from his wife and children, in order to… But what can I say?!"

Sobbing was heard among the public… A girl with a big brooch on her chest began to cry. A little old lady who was sitting next to her began to whimper.

The defence counsel spoke and spoke… He disregarded the facts, and dealt more with psychology.

"To know his soul is to know a special, unique world, a world full of impulses. I have studied that world… Studying it, I confess I first came to know 'Man'. I understood Man… Every impulse of his soul tells me that in my client I have the honour of seeing an ideal human being…"

The bailiff stopped looking menacingly and reached into his pocket for a handkerchief. Two more ladies were carried out of the courtroom. The chairman stopped ringing the bell and put on his glasses so that people would not notice the tear welling up in his right eye. Everyone began to reach for their handkerchief. The prosecutor – that slab of stone, that block of ice, that most unfeeling of all living things – shifted uneasily on his chair, reddened and directed his gaze under the table… Tears could be seen glistening through his glasses.

"If only I could abandon this case!" he thought. "Good lord, what a fiasco this is turning into!"

"Just look at his eyes," continued the defence council. His chin was trembling, his voice was shaking, and in his eyes could be seen the agony of his soul. "Is it possible that those meek, tender eyes can look indifferently on crime? Oh, no! They, those eyes, are crying! Refined nerves lie hidden behind those Kalmyck* cheekbones! In that rough, crude chest beats a heart that is far from criminal! And you, you people, how do you dare to say that he is guilty?!"

Now even the defendant himself could not bear it. He too started to cry. He blinked, started to cry and began to fidget restlessly…

"I am guilty!" he said, interrupting the defence counsel. "I am guilty! I confess my guilt! I'm a thief and swindler! I'm a despicable man! I took the money from the box and got my sister-in-law to hide the fur coat I stole… I confess! I'm guilty of everything!"

And the defendant gave an account of what he had done. He was convicted.

A Confession

IT WAS A BRIGHT, FROSTY DAY. I felt good and light-hearted inside, like a cabman who by mistake has been given a gold coin instead of a twenty-copeck piece. I wanted to cry and laugh and pray. I felt as if in sixteenth heaven: I, an ordinary man, had been made a cashier! I rejoiced not because I could now steal – I was not a thief at the time, and would have fought anyone who said I would become one in due course... I rejoiced for another reason: it was a promotion and a paltry increase in salary – that was all.

But I rejoiced for another reason too. Having become a cashier, I immediately sensed something like rose-tinted glasses on my nose. It suddenly seemed to me that people had changed. I give you my honest word! Everyone seemed to have become better. The ugly became good-looking, the evil kind, the proud humble, misanthropes philanthropes. My view of life seemed brighter. I saw in man such wonderful qualities as earlier I had not even suspected. "It's strange," I said, looking at people and rubbing my eyes. "Either something has happened to them or I had not noticed all these qualities before. What charming people!"

On the day of my appointment I noticed a change even in Z.N. Kazusov, a member of our board of directors, a proud, arrogant man who ignored small fry. He came up to me and (what had got into him?), smiling affectionately, slapped me on the shoulder.

"You are too proud for your years, my friend," he said to me. "It's not good! Why do you never call in on us? It's a sin, sir! Young people get together at our place, and it's all very jolly. My daughters keep asking: 'Why is it, Papa, that you don't invite Grigory Kuzmich? He really is such a dear!' But how can one get him to come? However, I say I'll try, I'll invite him... So don't put on airs, my friend, just come!"

Amazing! What had happened to him? Had he gone out of his mind? He was a man-eating ogre and suddenly… what a change!

Arriving at home that day, I was staggered. My mama served for dinner not two courses, as usual, but four. In the evening she served jam and sweet bread for tea. The next day again there were four courses, and again jam. Guests came and drank hot chocolate. On the third day it was the same.

"Mama," I said, "what's wrong with you? Why are you having such a fit of generosity, my dear? Good lord, my salary hasn't doubled. The rise was trivial."

Mama looked at me with astonishment.

"Well, so what are you going to do with your money?" she asked. "Will you hoard it or what?"

What the devil was happening to them? Papa ordered himself a fur coat, bought a new hat and undertook a cure with mineral water and grapes (in winter?!). And five days later I received a letter from my brother. This brother couldn't stand me. We had disagreements about our beliefs – he thought I was an egoist and parasite, incapable of self-sacrifice, and he hated me for that. In his letter he wrote as follows: "Dear brother! I love you, and you can't imagine what hellish torture our quarrel has caused me. Let's make peace! Let's reach out our hands to each other and celebrate our reconciliation! I implore you! In expectation of a reply, I remain with love, a kiss and an embrace, Yevlampy." Oh, dear brother! I replied that I kiss him and rejoice. A week later I received a telegram from him: "Thanks, happy. Short a hundred roubles. Great need. Embrace. Y." I sent him a hundred roubles…

Even *she* changed! She did not love me. When I once dared to hint to her about the longing in my heart, she called me a cheeky fellow and laughed in my face. But meeting me a week after my promotion, she smiled, showing her dimples, and looked embarrassed…

"What's happened to you?" she asked, looking at me. "You've become so good-looking. How did you manage that? Let's go dancing…"

What a dear! A month later her mama was already my mother-in-law. That's how much better-looking I had become! Money was needed for the wedding, so I took three hundred roubles from the cash box. Why not take it, if you know you'll put it back when you get your salary? At the same time I also took a hundred roubles for Kazusov... He asked for a loan... I couldn't possibly refuse him. He was a bigwig and could fire anyone at a moment's notice...*

A week before my arrest I threw a party for them at their request. What the devil, let them swill and guzzle if they so want to! I didn't count the number of people who were at that party of mine, but I remember they filled to overflowing all of my nine rooms. There were old and young... There were even some before whom Kazusov himself cowered. Kazusov's daughters (the eldest was the most beautiful) were dazzling in their attire... The flowers alone that were adorning them cost me more than a thousand roubles! It was all very jolly... Music blared, chandeliers glittered, champagne flowed... Long speeches and short toasts were delivered... One journalist presented me with an ode he had written, another with a ballad...

"We don't know how to value such people as Grigory Kuzmich in our Russia!" Kazusov shouted after supper. "It's a great shame! A shame for Russia!"

And all those who were yelling, making speeches and kissing were whispering and cocking a snook at me behind my back... I saw their smiles, sensed their disdain, heard their sighs...

"He stole the money, the scoundrel!" they whispered with gloating smiles.

But neither the disdain nor the sighs stopped them from eating, drinking and having a good time...

Neither wolves nor diabetics eat the way they ate... My wife, who was glittering with diamonds and gold, came up to me and whispered:

"They are saying over there that you... stole. If it's true, then... be warned! I can't live with a thief! I shall leave you!"

She said this and adjusted her five-thousand-rouble dress... Let them go to the Devil! That same evening Kazusov took five thousand roubles from me... Yevlampy borrowed the same sum...

"If what they're whispering over there is true," said my high-principled brother, putting the money in his pocket, "then... watch out! I can't be the brother of a thief!"

After the ball I took them all for rides out of town in troikas...

It was after five o'clock in the morning when we ended the revels... Exhausted by the wine and women, they lay in the sleighs as we drove back... As the sleighs set off to take them home, they cried to me in farewell:

"Tomorrow is the audit... *Merci!*"

* * *

My dear ladies and gentlemen! I was caught... I was caught – or, to express myself more fully: yesterday evening I was a decent, honourable man, loved by everyone, but today I'm a swindler, a crook, a thief... Shout at me now, curse me, spread the news, show your amazement, judge me, exile me, dash off editorials, throw stones, but only... please, not everyone! Not everyone!

Champagne

(The Tale of a Rogue)

In the year in which my story begins, I was working as the stationmaster of a small stop on one of our south-western railways. Whether I was pleased to be at the station or bored, you may decide from the fact that for twenty versts around there was neither a single human habitation nor a single woman, nor a single decent tavern – and at that time I was young, strong, ardent, unstable and foolish. The only entertainment was the sight of the windows of the passenger trains and the vile vodka which the Jews adulterated with thorn apple. Sometimes I would catch a glimpse of a woman's head in the window of a carriage and stand there like a statue, not breathing, watching until the train appeared like a dot in the distance, or I would drink the disgusting vodka to my heart's content, become objectionable and be unaware of the passing of the long hours and days. The steppe affects me, a native of the north, like the sight of a neglected Tatar cemetery. In summer, its solemn peacefulness – the monotonous chirruping of grasshoppers, the pale moonlight from which I had nowhere to hide – put me into a mood of sadness and melancholy, and in winter the immaculate whiteness of the steppe, its cold prospect, long nights and the howling of wolves gave me troubling nightmares.

Several people lived at the station: my wife and I, a deaf and scrofulous telegraphist and three watchmen. My assistant, a consumptive young man, often went to receive medical treatment in town, where he lived for months on end, leaving me with his duties, along with the right to draw his salary. I had no children, and nothing usually could tempt guests to visit, and I myself was able to visit only fellow employees on the line, and even that not more than once a month. In general, it was a most boring life.

I remember ushering in the New Year with my wife. We were sitting at the table, lazily eating, while in the next room the deaf telegraphist tapped monotonously on his apparatus. I had already drunk five small glasses of vodka with thorn apple and, with my heavy head supported on my fist, was thinking about the invincible boredom that I could not free myself of – and my wife was sitting next to me, looking intently at my face. She was looking at me as only a wife can who has nothing in this world but a handsome husband. She loved me madly, submissively, and not only for my good looks or my soul, but for my sins, my malice and boredom, and even for the cruelty I showed when, in a drunken rage, not knowing on whom to vent my malice, I tormented her with reproaches.

Despite the boredom that was eating away at me, we had prepared a special celebration to greet the new year, and were awaiting midnight with some impatience. This was because we had been keeping two bottles of champagne, the real thing, bearing the label of the Widow Clicquot.* I had won this treasure on a bet in autumn with the regional supervisor, playing cards with him at a christening. Sometimes, during a maths lesson, when the very air is heavy with boredom, a butterfly will flutter into the class from outside. The pupils rouse themselves and with curiosity start to follow its flight with their eyes, as if they are seeing not a butterfly, but something new, strange. In exactly the same way did the ordinary champagne, which had come by chance to our boring station, keep us entertained. We were silent, and just looked from time to time now at the clock, now at the bottle.

When the hands of the clock showed five minutes to twelve, I began slowly to uncork the bottle. I don't know whether I was feeling weak from the vodka or whether the bottle itself was too wet, but I only remember that when the cork flew to the ceiling with a pop, the bottle slipped from my hands and fell to the floor. Not more than a glassful of the wine was spilled, as I was able to pick up the bottle and plug the fizzing top with a finger.

"Well, happy New Year, and all the best!" I said, filling two glasses. "Drink up!"

My wife took her glass and stared at me with frightened eyes. Her face had gone pale and was expressing horror.

"Did you drop the bottle?" she asked.

"Yes, I dropped it. What of it?"

"It's not good," she said, putting down her glass and growing even more pale. "It's not a good omen. It means that this year something bad will happen to us."

"What a peasant you are," I sighed. "You're a clever woman, but you get as flustered as an old nanny. Drink."

"God knows I get flustered, but... something will surely happen! You'll see!"

She did not take even a sip from her glass, but moved aside and fell to thinking. I expressed several old thoughts about superstitions, drank half a bottle, paced back and forth for a while and went out.

Outside, in all its cold, unsociable glory, a still, frosty night had set in. The moon and two white, fluffy clouds around it hung high up, as if glued to the sky above the station, awaiting something. From them came a faint, clear light, a light that was delicate, as if fearing to offend the modesty of the whole world as it lit up everything: snowdrifts, the embankment... The air was very still.

I walked along the embankment.

"Silly woman!" I thought, looking at the sky, which was strewn with bright stars. "Even assuming that omens are sometimes proved right, what bad things can possibly happen to us? Those misfortunes that have already happened, and that are now still with us, are so great that it is hard to imagine anything worse. What greater misfortunes can befall fish that are already caught, fried and served up on the table with sauce?"

A tall poplar, covered with hoar frost, looked in the bluish mist like a giant dressed in a shroud. It looked at me austerely and despondently, as if like me it was aware of its loneliness. I looked at it for a long time.

"My youth is finished for good, and is now like a discarded cigarette end," I continued to think. "My parents died when I was still a child, and I was expelled from school. I was born into a family of the nobility, but received neither an upbringing nor an education, and my accomplishments were no greater than those of any ragamuffin. I had neither protection nor anyone close, nor friends, nor anything I loved doing. I was able to do nothing, and in my prime was suited only to be given this job as a stationmaster. Apart from failure and misfortune, I knew nothing else in life. What further misfortune could befall me?"

Red lights appeared in the distance. A train was coming towards me. The noise it made spread over the sleeping steppe. My thoughts were so bitter that it seemed I was thinking aloud, that the moaning of the telegraph wires and the noise of the train communicated my thoughts.

"What further misfortune could befall me? The loss of my wife?" I asked myself. "Even that was not terrible. I could not hide the fact from my conscience: I did not love my wife. I married her when I was still a boy. Now I was a young man, strong, while she had grown thin – and old, and stupid, packed from head to toe with superstitions. What good was there in her cloying love and sunken chest, in her dull look? I tolerated her, but did not love her. So what could happen? My youth has been lost, as is said, for a pinch of snuff. Women flash by before me only in the windows of carriages, like falling stars. There is no love in my life. My courage, boldness and warmth have all been lost… All has been lost, like waste matter, and my wealth here in the steppe is not worth a copper *grosh*."

The train rushed noisily past me, displaying to my indifferent stare its lighted windows. I saw how it stopped at the green light of the station, how it stood for a moment and set off on its way again. I walked a further two versts before retracing my steps. Gloomy thoughts did not leave me. However bitter it was to me, it seemed that I was growing old, so that my thoughts were sadder and gloomier. You know, limited and proud people have moments when awareness that they are unhappy gives them some pleasure, and they even flaunt their sufferings. Much in my thoughts was true, but much was also absurd and boastful, and something childish and defiant lay in my question: "What further misfortune can happen?"

"Indeed, what can happen?" I asked myself as I returned. "It seems that everything that can happen has already happened. I've been ill, lost money, am reprimanded every day by my boss, have starved... And a mad wolf once ran into the station yard. What else can happen? I've been offended, humiliated... And I've offended others in my lifetime. The only thing I've never been is a criminal, but I seem to be incapable of crime, and so do not fear the courts."

The two clouds had already drifted away from the moon and stood some distance apart, looking as if whispering about something they wanted to keep secret from the moon. A light breeze wafted over the steppe, carrying the muffled sound of the departing train.

At the door of the house I was met by my wife. Her eyes were laughing gaily, and her whole face was exuding happiness.

"I have some news!" she whispered. "Go quickly to your room and put on your new frock coat: we have a visitor!"

"What visitor?"

"My aunt Natalya Petrovna has arrived just now on the train."

"Who is Natalya Petrovna?"

"The wife of my uncle Semyon Fyodorych. You don't know her. She is a very kind, nice woman..."

I probably frowned, because my wife made a serious face and quickly whispered:

"Of course, it's strange that she should have come, but don't be angry, Nikolai, be tolerant. She is really unhappy. Uncle Semyon Fyodorych is a nasty and domineering man, and difficult to live with. She says she'll stay only three days with us, until she gets a letter from her brother."

For a long time my wife whispered more gossip to me about her despotic uncle, about human weakness in general and young wives in particular, about our duty to give succour to everyone, even great sinners, and so on. Understanding absolutely nothing, I put on my new frock coat and went to meet my "aunt".

At the table was sitting a little woman with large dark eyes. The table, the grey walls, the shabby sofa... everything, to the least speck of dust, seemed to grow young and cheer up in the presence of this new young being, who possessed some strange aura, beautiful and wanton. And that the guest was wanton I understood from her smile, her scent, her special way of looking and fluttering her eyelashes, by the tone in which she was speaking to my wife – a virtuous woman... She did not have to tell me that she had run away from her husband, that her husband was old and tyrannical, that she was kind and high-spirited. I understood everything from the first look, and there is hardly a man in Europe who cannot distinguish from the first look a woman of a certain nature.

"I didn't know I had such a big nephew!" said the aunt, offering me her hand and smiling.

"And I didn't know I had such a good-looking aunt!" I replied.

We resumed supper. The cork flew from the second bottle with a pop, and my aunt drained half a glass at one gulp, but when my wife left the room for a moment my aunt no longer stood on ceremony but drank down a whole glass. I got drunk on both the wine and the presence of the woman. Do you know the song?

> Dark eyes, passionate eyes,
> Eyes burning hot and beautiful,
> How I love you,
> How I fear you!*

I do not know what happened then. For those who would like to know how love begins, let them read novels and stories, but I shall just say a little, and with the words of that silly romance:

> It seems that when I saw you
> It was an evil hour...

My whole world turned upside down, and went to the Devil. I remember a terrible, furious maelstrom, which whirled me about like a feather. It whirled for a long time and wiped from the face of the earth my wife, my aunt herself and my strength. From the little station on the steppe it flung me, as you see, on this dark street.

Now tell me: what further misfortune can befall me?

Notes

p. v, *'In Autumn'*: A one-act play that Chekhov wrote in 1885, entitled *On the High Road*, is a dramatic reworking of this story.

p. 3, *in flagrante delicto*: Literally, "in the act of committing a crime" (Latin).

p. 5, *Niobe*: In Greek mythology, the daughter of the Lydian King Tantalus and Dione. Her twelve children were killed when she insulted the goddess Leto.

p. 5, *Tula*: A town noted for its metalworks.

p. 6, *Sakhalin*: The penal colony on Sakhalin, an island located four miles off the south-eastern coast of Khabarovsk Krai in Russia. Chekhov travelled to the island in 1890 and published a book of travel notes, *Sakhalin Island*, an indictment of the Tsarist prison system, in 1891–93.

p. 9, *the Nikolayevsky railway station*: A rail terminal in Moscow.

p. 9, *fleur d'orange*: "Orange blossom" (French).

p. 9, *Herostratus*: The arsonist who in 356 BC burned the temple of Artemis at Ephesus to immortalize his name.

p. 9, *Ephialtes*: The traitor who led the Persian forces of Xerxes along a mountain path to the rear of the Greek army and victory at the Battle of Thermopylae in 480 BC.

p. 13, *jeune premier*: "Romantic lead" (French).

p. 14, *Kostroma*: A historic city around 210 miles north-east of Moscow.

p. 14, *Mac Mahon*: The French general and politician Patrice de Mac Mahon (1808–93), who served as president of France from 1875 to 1879. The sentence "the end justifies the means" is usually associated with the Florentine diplomat and historian Niccolò Machiavelli (1469–1527), author of *The Prince* (1532).

p. 17, *The cat will cry for the mouse's tears*: A Russian proverb meaning "the mischief we do will rebound on ourselves".

p. 18, *pirog*: Also *pirozhok* (pl. *piroshki*), a pie, usually of meat or cabbage.

p. 18, *préférence*: A hugely popular card game in nineteenth-century Russia, often called "Russian preference" in English.

p. 20, *Duma*: A representative regional assembly.

p. 26, *pood*: A unit of weight equal to about 16.38 kg.

p. 27, *Verzhbolovo*: A village on the frontier with Prussia (now the Lithuanian town of Virbalis).

p. 27, *Herodias*: The wife of Herod in the Bible. Since the middle ages she had a reputation for being the supernatural leader of a cult of witches, and her name is often used as a synonym for "termagant".

p. 27, *Xanthippe*: The wife of Socrates. She was known for her allegedly bad-tempered behaviour towards her husband.

p. 28, *Eidkuhnen*: A settlement in Nesterovsky District in the eastern part of Kaliningrad Oblast, Russia (now called Chernyshevskoye in Russian and Eydtkuhnen in German) where trains were changed to a different gauge.

p. 28, *kalatches*: Bread rolls baked in the form of padlocks.

p. 45, *Petrovna*: Both men and women were sometimes addressed by their patronymic rather than their given name.

p. 45, *Nekrasov*: The Russian poet Nikolai Nekrasov (1821–78).

p. 46, *Be fruitful... multiply... replenish the earth*: A reference to God's exhortation to Noah and his sons (Genesis 9:1).

p. 47, *Lazhechnikov*: The Russian historical novelist Ivan Lazhechnikov (1792–1869).

p. 49, *barin*: A landowner or gentleman, a man deserving of respect.

p. 54, *And I shall be whiter... rejoicing*: Psalm 50: 9–10.

p. 54, *It would confound the ignorant... eyes and ears*: From Act II, Sc. 2 of Shakespeare's *Hamlet*.

p. 55, *ingénue*: A French word denoting an actress who plays the part of an innocent or unsophisticated young woman.

p. 55, *Sic transit*: From "*sic transit gloria mundi*" – "thus passes the glory of the world" (Latin).

p. 55, *panikhida*: Funeral service, or requiem mass.

p. 57, *Homo sum*: The beginning of the Latin saying: "*Homo sum, humani nihil a me alienum puto*" ("I am a man, and nothing human is alien to me) – a line from Terence's comedy *Heauton Timorumenos* (*The Self-Tormentor*), written in 163 BC.

p. 59, *bread and salt*: Traditional symbols of hospitality.

p. 64, *zakuski*: Little snacks or hors d'oeuvres (sing. *zakuska*).

p. 72, *idée fixe*: "Obsession" (French).

p. 77, *a postprandial meeting with Morpheus*: That is, a postprandial nap. Morpheus is the god of sleep in Greco-Roman mythology.

p. 89, *fell in love with a crow, not a falcon*: A Russian proverb.

p. 95, *arshins*: The *arshin* is a unit of length equivalent to about 71 cm.

p. 102, *audiatur et altera pars*: "You have to hear out the other side" (Latin).

p. 103, *Fi donc!*: "Foo!" (French).

p. 107, *Honorary citizen*: A title bestowed by the tsar on those who have distinguished themselves in some way but are not thought to merit noble status.

p. 111, *"Capricieuse"*: An old English patience played using two packs of playing cards.

p. 122, *kulich*: Sweet bread or cake, eaten at Easter.

p. 129, *sazhen*: An old Russian unit of length, equal to 3 *arshins*, around 2.13 m.

p. 130, *'one'*: The lowest mark awarded.

p. 131, *kasha*: A kind of gruel or porridge, made from buckwheat.

p. 135, *Willow Sunday*: Palm Sunday. In the Orthodox tradition, the willow is a substitute for palm branches.

p. 144, *Having wasted… swine did eat*: See Luke 15:13–16.

p. 147, *borscht*: A soup made predominantly of beetroot, served with sour cream.

p. 150, *St Peter's Day*: 29th June.

p. 150, *kamilavka*: The tall headgear of an Orthodox priest.

p. 151, *vedro*: An old measure of volume equal to around 12 litres.

p. 151, *a cockade on my hat*: A symbol of being in state service.

p. 158, *koumiss*: A fermented liquor prepared from mare's milk.

p. 165, *Lombroso*: The Italian criminologist Cesare Lombroso (1836–1909).

p. 166, *grosh*: A half-copeck piece, the smallest legal tender.

p. 168, *Alexandre*: The Russian upper classes, especially women, often addressed others in the French form of their name.

p. 169, *the Medved*: A St Petersburg restaurant (literally, "the Bear").

p. 171, *Merci*: "Thank you" (French).

p. 171, *Holy Week*: The week before Easter.

p. 171, *live on locusts*: A reference to John the Baptist, who lived in the wilderness and ate locusts and wild honey (Mark 1:6).

p. 175, *Honour your father... long years of life*: A paraphrase of the biblical injunction "Honour thy father and thy mother: that thy days may be long upon the land which the Lord thy God giveth thee" (Exodus 20:12).

p. 178, *Attendez!*: A term used in certain card games meaning that more stakes are not being accepted (literally, in French, "Wait!").

p. 181, *Les Huguenots*: An opera composed in 1836 by Giacomo Meyerbeer (1791–1864).

p. 183, *The Tenant with the Trombone*: A comedy by Sergei Boykov (1828–77).

p. 183, *She Waits for Him*: A comedy by Vladimir Rodislavsky (1828–85).

p. 184, *The Sinful Woman*: An 1858 narrative poem by Alexei Tolstoy (1817–75).

p. 187, *This assistant's name was Legion*: A biblical reference to Mark 5:9: "My name is Legion: for we are many."

p. 189, *Kalmyck*: Buddhist people of Mongol origin from the area east of the Caucasus.

p. 193, *at a moment's notice...*: The editor of the original version cut eighty-three lines at this point, for an unknown reason.

p. 196, *Widow Clicquot*: *Veuve Clicquot*, a famous brand of champagne.

p. 200, *Dark eyes... I fear you*: A popular romance from 1884 by Sergei Gerdal (Sofus Herdahl), to words by Evgeny Grebyonka (1812–48), based on the music of Florian Hermann's (1822–92) *Valse Hommage*.

Extra Material

on

Anton Chekhov's

The Willow and Other Stories

Anton Chekhov's Life

Birth and Background

Anton Pavlovich Chekhov was born in Taganrog, on the Sea of Azov in southern Russia, on 29th January 1860. He was the third child of Pavel Yegorovich Chekhov and his wife Yevgenia Yakovlevna. He had four brothers – Alexander (born in 1855), Nikolai (1858), Ivan (1861) and Mikhail (1865) – and one sister, Marya, who was born in 1863. Anton's father, the owner of a small shop, was a devout Christian who administered brutal floggings to his children almost on a daily basis. Anton remembered these with bitterness throughout his life, and possibly as a result was always sceptical of organized religion. The shop – a grocery and general-supplies store which sold such goods as lamp oil, tea, coffee, seeds, flour and sugar – was kept by the children during their father's absence. The father also required his children to go with him to church at least once a day. He set up a liturgical choir which practised in his shop, and demanded that his children – whether they had school work to do or not, or whether they had been in the shop all day – should join the rehearsals to provide the higher voice parts.

Education and Childhood

Chekhov described his home town as filthy and tedious, and the people as drunk, idle, lazy and illiterate. At first, Pavel tried to provide his children with an education by enrolling the two he considered the brightest, Nikolai and Anton, in one of the schools for the descendants of the Greek merchants who had once settled in Taganrog. These provided a more "classical" education than their Russian equivalents, and their standard of teaching was held in high regard. However, the experience was not a successful one, since most of the other pupils spoke Greek among themselves, of which the Chekhovs did not know a single word. Eventually, in 1868, Anton was enrolled in one of the town's Russian high schools. The courses at the Russian school included Church Slavonic, Latin and Greek, and if the entire curriculum was successfully completed, entry to a university was guaranteed. Unfortunately, as the shop was making less and less money, the school fees were often unpaid and lessons were missed. The teaching was generally mediocre, but the religious education teacher, Father Pokrovsky, encouraged his pupils to read the Russian classics and such foreign authors as Shakespeare, Swift and Goethe. Pavel also paid for private French and music lessons for his children.

Every summer the family would travel through the steppe by cart some fifty miles to an estate where their paternal grandfather was chief steward. The impressions gathered on these journeys, and the people encountered, had a profound impact on the young Anton, and later provided material for one of his greatest stories, 'The Steppe'.

At the age of thirteen, Anton went to the theatre for the first time, to see Offenbach's operetta *La Belle Hélène* at the Taganrog theatre. He was enchanted by the spectacle, and went as often as time and money allowed, seeing not only the Russian classics, but also foreign pieces such as *Hamlet* in Russian translation. In his early teens, he even created his own theatrical company with his school friends to act out the Russian classics.

Adversity

In 1875 Anton was severely ill with peritonitis. The high-school doctor tended him with great care, and he resolved to join the medical profession one day. That same year, his brothers Alexander and Nikolai, fed up with the beatings they received at home, decided to move to Moscow to work and study, ignoring their father's admonitions and threats. Anton now bore the entire brunt of Pavel's brutality. To complicate things further, the family shop ran into severe financial difficulties, and was eventually declared bankrupt. The children were withdrawn from school, and Pavel fled to Moscow, leaving his wife and family to face the creditors. In the end, everybody abandoned the old residence, with the exception of Anton, who remained behind with the new owner.

Although he was now free of his father's bullying and the hardship of having to go to church and work in the shop, Anton had to find other employment in order to pay his rent and bills, and to resume his school studies. Accordingly, at the age of fifteen, he took up tutoring, continuing voraciously to read books of Russian and foreign literature, philosophy and science, in the town library.

In 1877, during a summer holiday, he undertook the seven-hundred-mile journey to Moscow to see his family, and found them all living in one room and sleeping on a single mattress on the floor. His father was not at all abashed by his failures: he continued to be dogmatically religious and to beat the younger children regularly. On his return to Taganrog, Anton attempted to earn a little additional income by sending sketches and anecdotes to several of Moscow's humorous magazines, but they were all turned down.

Studies in Moscow and Early Publications

The young Chekhov unabatedly pursued his studies, and in June 1879 he passed the Taganrog High School exams with distinction, and in the autumn he moved to Moscow to study medicine. The family still lived in one room, and Alexander and Nikolai were well on the way to becoming alcoholics. Anton, instead of finding his own lodgings, decided to support not only himself, but his entire family, and try to re-educate them. After a hard day spent in lectures, tutorials and in the laboratories, he would write more sketches for humorous and satirical magazines, and an increasing number of these were now accepted: by the early 1880s, over a hundred had been printed. Anton used a series of pseudonyms (the most usual being "Antosha Chekhonte") for these productions, which he later called "rubbish". He also visited the Moscow theatres and concert halls on numerous occasions, and in 1880 sent the renowned Maly Theatre a play he had recently written. Only a rough draft of the piece – which was rejected by the Maly and published for the first time in 1920, under the title *Platonov* – has survived. Unless Chekhov had polished and pruned his lost final version considerably, the play would have lasted around seven hours. Despite its poor construction and verbosity, *Platonov* already shows some of the themes and characters present in Chekhov's mature works, such as rural boredom and weak-willed, supine intellectuals dreaming of a better future while not doing anything to bring it about.

As well as humorous sketches and stories, Chekhov wrote brief résumés of legal court proceedings and gossip from the artistic world for various Moscow journals. With the money made from these pieces he moved his family into a larger flat, and regularly invited friends to visit and talk and drink till late at night.

In 1882, encouraged by his success with the Moscow papers, he started contributing to the journals of the capital St Petersburg, since payment there was better than in Moscow. He was eventually commissioned to contribute a regular column to the best-selling journal *Oskolki* ("Splinters"), providing a highly coloured picture of Moscow life with its court cases and bohemian atmosphere. He was now making over 150 roubles a month from his writing – about three times as much as his student stipend – although he managed to save very little because of the needs of his family. In 1884 Chekhov published, at his own expense, a booklet of six of his short stories, entitled *Tales of Melpomene*, which sold quite poorly.

Start of Medical Career

There was compensation for this relative literary failure: in June of that year Anton passed all his final exams in medicine and became a medical practitioner. That summer, he began to receive patients at a village outside Moscow, and even stepped in for the director of a local hospital when the latter went on his summer vacation. He was soon receiving thirty to forty patients a day, and was struck by the peasants' ill health, filth and drunkenness. He planned a major treatise entitled *A History of Medicine in Russia* but, after reading and annotating over a hundred works on the subject, he gave the subject up and returned to Moscow to set up his own medical practice.

First Signs of Tuberculosis

Suddenly, in December 1884, when he was approaching the achievement of all his ambitions, Chekhov developed a dry cough and began to spit blood. He tried to pretend that these were not early symptoms of tuberculosis but, as a doctor, he must have had an inkling of the truth. He made no attempt to cut down his commitments in the light of his illness, but kept up the same punishing schedule of activity. By this time, Chekhov had published over three hundred items, including some of his first recognized mature works, such as 'The Daughter of Albion' and 'The Death of an Official'. Most of the stories were already, in a very understated way, depicting life's "losers" – such as the idle gentry, shopkeepers striving unsuccessfully to make a living and ignorant peasants. Now that his income had increased, Chekhov rented a summer house a few miles outside Moscow. However, although he intended to use his holiday exclusively for writing, he was inundated all day with locals who had heard he was a doctor and required medical attention.

Trip to St Petersburg and Meeting with Suvorin

Chekhov made a crucial step in his literary career, when in December 1885 he visited the imperial capital St Petersburg for the first time, as a guest of the editor of the renowned *St Petersburg Journal*. His stories were beginning to gain him a reputation, and he was introduced at numerous soirées to famous members of the St Petersburg literary world. He was agreeably surprised to find they knew his work and valued it highly. Here for the first time he met Alexei Suvorin, the press mogul and editor of the most influential daily of the period, *Novoye Vremya* (*New Times*). Suvorin asked Chekhov to contribute stories regularly to his paper at a far higher rate of pay than he had been receiving from other journals. Now Chekhov, while busy treating numerous patients in Moscow and helping to stem the constant typhus epidemics that broke out in the city, also began to churn out for Suvorin such embryonic masterpieces as 'The Requiem' and 'Grief' – although all were still published pseudonymously. Distinguished writers advised him to start publishing under his own name and, although his current collection *Motley Stories* had already gone to press under the Chekhonte pseudonym, Anton resolved from now on to shed his anonymity. The collection received tepid reviews, but Chekhov now had sufficient income to rent a whole house on Sadova-Kudrinskaya Street (now maintained as a museum of this early period of Chekhov's life), in an elegant district of Moscow.

Literary Recognition

Chekhov's reputation as a writer was further enhanced when Suvorin published a collection of sixteen of Chekhov's short stories in 1887 – under the title *In the Twilight* – to great critical acclaim. However, Chekhov's health was deteriorating and his blood-spitting was growing worse by the day. Anton appears more and more by now to have come to regard life as a parade of "the vanity of human wishes". He channelled some of this ennui and his previous life experiences into a slightly melodramatic and overlong play, *Ivanov*, in which the eponymous hero – a typical "superfluous man" who indulges in pointless speculation while his estate goes to ruin and his capital dwindles – ends up shooting himself. *Ivanov* was premiered in November 1887 by the respected Korsh Private Theatre under Chekhov's real name – a sign of Anton's growing confidence as a writer – although it received very mixed reviews.

However, in the spring of 1888, Chekhov's story 'The Steppe' – an impressionistic, poetical recounting of the experiences of a young boy travelling through the steppe on a cart – was published in *The Northern Herald*, again under his real name, enabling him to reach another milestone in his literary career, and prompting reviewers for the first time to talk of his genius. Although Chekhov began to travel to the Crimea for vacations, in the hope that the warm climate might aid his health, the symptoms of tuberculosis simply reappeared whenever he returned to Moscow. In October of the same year, Chekhov was awarded the prestigious Pushkin Prize for Literature for *In the Twilight*. He was now recognized as a major Russian writer, and began to state his belief to reporters that a writer's job is not to peddle any political or philosophical point of view, but to depict human life with its associated problems as objectively as possible.

Death of his Brother

A few months later, in January 1889, a revised version of *Ivanov* was staged at the Alexandrinsky Theatre in St Petersburg, arguably the most important drama theatre in Russia at the time. The new production was a huge success and received excellent reviews. However, around that time it also emerged that Anton's alcoholic brother, Nikolai, was suffering from advanced tuberculosis. When Nikolai died in June of that year, at the age of thirty, Anton must have seen this as a harbinger of his own early demise.

Chekhov was now working on a new play, *The Wood Demon*, in which, for the first time, psychological nuance replaced stage action, and the effect on the audience was achieved by atmosphere rather than by drama or the portrayal of events. However, precisely for these reasons, it was rejected by the Alexandrinsky Theatre in October of that year. Undeterred, Chekhov decided to revise it, and a new version of *The Wood Demon* was put on in Moscow in December 1889. Lambasted by the critics, it was swiftly withdrawn from the scene, to make its appearance again many years later, thoroughly rewritten, as *Uncle Vanya*.

Journey to Sakhalin Island

It was around this time that Anton Chekhov began contemplating his journey to the prison island of Sakhalin. At the end of 1889, unexpectedly, and for no apparent reason, the twenty-nine-year-old author announced his intention to leave European Russia, and to travel across Siberia to Sakhalin, the large island separating Siberia and the Pacific Ocean, following which he would write a full-scale examination of the penal colony maintained there by the Tsarist authorities. Explanations put forward by commentators both then and since include a search by the author for fresh material for his works, a desire to escape from the constant carping of his liberally minded colleagues on his lack of a political line; desire to escape from an unhappy love affair; and disappointment at the recent failure of *The Wood Demon*. A further explanation may well be that, as early as 1884, he had been spitting blood, and recently, just before his journey, several friends and relations had died of tuberculosis. Chekhov, as a doctor, must have been aware that he too was in the early stages of the disease, and that his lifespan would be considerably curtailed. Possibly he wished to distance himself for several months from everything he had known, and give himself time to think over his illness and mortality by immersing himself in a totally alien world. Chekhov hurled himself into a study of the geography, history, nature and ethnography of the island, as background material to his study of the penal settlement. The Trans-Siberian Railway had not yet been constructed, and the journey across Siberia, begun in April 1890, required two and a half months of travel in sledges and carriages on abominable roads in freezing temperatures and appalling weather. This certainly hastened the progress of his tuberculosis and almost certainly deprived him of a few extra years of life. He spent three months in frantic work on the island, conducting his census of the prison population, rummaging in archives, collecting material and organizing book collections for the children of exiles, before leaving in October 1890 and returning to Moscow, via Hong Kong, Ceylon and Odessa, in December of that year.

Travels in Europe

The completion of his report on his trip to Sakhalin was to be hindered for almost five years by his phenomenally busy life, as he attempted, as before, to continue his medical practice and write at the same time. In early 1891 Chekhov, in the company of Suvorin, travelled for the first time to western Europe, visiting Vienna, Venice, Bologna, Florence, Rome, Naples and finally Monaco and Paris.

Move to Melikhovo

Trying to cut down on the expenses he was paying out for his family in Moscow, he bought a small estate at Melikhovo, a few miles outside Moscow, and the entire family moved there. His father did some gardening, his mother cooked, while Anton planted hundreds of fruit trees, shrubs and flowers. Chekhov's concerns for nature have a surprisingly modern ecological ring: he once said that if he had not been a writer he would have become a gardener.

Although his brothers had their own lives in Moscow and only spent holidays at Melikhovo, Anton's sister Marya – who never married – lived there permanently, acting as his confidante and as his housekeeper when he had his friends and famous literary figures to stay, as he often did in large parties. Chekhov also continued to write, but was distracted, as before, by the scores of locals who came every day to receive medical treatment from him. There was no such thing as free medical assistance in those days and, if anybody seemed unable to pay, Chekhov often treated them for nothing. In 1892, there was a severe local outbreak of cholera, and Chekhov was placed in charge of relief operations. He supervised the building of emergency isolation wards in all the surrounding villages and travelled around the entire area directing the medical operations.

Ill Health

Chekhov's health was deteriorating more and more rapidly, and his relentless activity certainly did not help. He began to experience almost constant pain and, although still hosting gatherings, he gave the appearance of withdrawing increasingly into himself and growing easily tired. By the mid-1890s, his sleep was disturbed almost nightly by bouts of violent coughing. Besides continuing his medical activities, looking after his estate and writing, Chekhov undertook to supervise – often with large subsidies from his own pocket – the building of schools in the local villages, where there had been none before.

Controversy around The Seagull

By late 1895, Chekhov was thinking of writing for the theatre again. The result was *The Seagull*, which was premiered at the Alexandrinsky Theatre in October 1896. Unfortunately the acting was so bad that the premiere was met by jeering and laughter, and received vicious reviews. Chekhov himself commented that the director did not understand the play, the actors didn't know their lines and nobody could grasp the understated style. He fled from the theatre and roamed the streets of St Petersburg until two in the morning, resolving never to write for the theatre again. Despite this initial fiasco, subsequent performances went from strength to strength, with the actors called out on stage after every performance.

Olga Knipper

By this time, it seems that Chekhov had accepted the fact that he had a mortal illness. In 1897, he returned to Italy to see whether the warmer climate would not afford his condition some respite, but as soon as he came back to Russia the coughing and blood-spitting resumed as violently as before. It was around this time that the two founders of the

Moscow Arts Theatre, Vladimir Nemirovich-Danchenko and Konstantin Stanislavsky, asked Chekhov whether they could stage *The Seagull*. Their aims were to replace the stylized and unnatural devices of the classical theatre with more natural events and dialogue, and Chekhov's play seemed ideal for this purpose. He gave his permission, and in September 1898 went to Moscow to attend the preliminary rehearsals. It was there that he first met the twenty-eight-year-old actress Olga Knipper, who was going to take the leading role of Arkadina. However, the Russian winter was making him cough blood violently, and so he decided to follow the local doctor's advice and travel south to the Crimea, in order to spend the winter in a warmer climate. Accordingly, he rented a villa with a large garden in Yalta.

Move to the Crimea

When his father died in October of the same year, Chekhov decided to put Melikhovo up for sale and move his mother and Marya to the Crimea. They temporarily stayed in a large villa near the Tatar village of Kuchukoy, but Chekhov had in the mean time bought a plot of land at Autka, some twenty minutes by carriage from Yalta, and he drew up a project to have a house built there. Construction began in December.

Also in December 1898, the first performance of *The Seagull* at the Moscow Arts Theatre took place. It was a resounding success, and there were now all-night queues for tickets. Despite his extremely poor health, Chekhov was still busy raising money for relief of the severe famine then scourging the Russian heartlands, overseeing the building of his new house and aiding the local branch of the Red Cross. In addition to this, local people and aspiring writers would turn up in droves at his villa in Yalta to receive medical treatment or advice on their manuscripts.

Collected Works Project

In early January 1899, Chekhov signed an agreement with the publisher Adolf Marx to supervise the publication of a multi-volume edition of his collected works in return for a flat fee of 75,000 roubles and no royalties. This proved to be an error of judgement from a financial point of view, because by the time Chekhov had put some money towards building his new house, ensured all the members of his family were provided for and made various other donations, the advance had almost disappeared.

Romance with Olga

Chekhov finally moved to Autka – where he was to spend the last few years of his life – in June 1899, and immediately began to plant vegetables, flowers and fruit trees. During a short period spent in Moscow to facilitate his work for Adolf Marx, he re-established contact with the Moscow Arts Theatre and Olga Knipper. Chekhov invited the actress to Yalta on several occasions and, although her visits were brief and at first she stayed in a hotel, it was obvious that she and Chekhov were becoming very close. Apart from occasional short visits to Moscow, which cost him a great expenditure of energy and were extremely harmful to his medical condition, Chekhov now had to spend all of his time in the south. He forced himself to continue writing short stories and plays, but felt increasingly lonely and isolated and, aware that he had only a short time left to live, became even more withdrawn. It was around this time that he worked again at his early play *The Wood Demon*, reducing the dramatis personae to only nine characters, radically altering the most significant scenes and renaming it *Uncle Vanya*. This was premiered in October 1899, and it was another gigantic success. In July of the following year, Olga Knipper took time off from her busy schedule of rehearsals and performances in Moscow to visit Chekhov in Yalta. There was no longer any attempt at pretence: she stayed in his house and, although he was by now extremely ill, they became romantically involved, exchanging love letters almost every day.

By now Chekhov had drafted another new play, *Three Sisters*, and he travelled to Moscow to supervise the first few rehearsals. Olga came to his hotel every day bringing food and flowers. However, Anton felt that the play needed revision, so he returned to Yalta to work on a comprehensive rewrite. *Three Sisters* opened on 31st January 1901 and – though at first well received, especially by the critics – it gradually grew in the public's estimation, becoming another great success.

Wedding and Honeymoon

But Chekhov was feeling lonely in Yalta without Olga, and in May of that year proposed to her by letter. Olga accepted, and Chekhov immediately set off for Moscow, despite his doctor's advice to the contrary. He arranged a dinner for his friends and relatives and, while they were waiting there, he and Olga got married secretly in a small church on the outskirts of Moscow. As the participants at the dinner received a telegram with the news, the couple had already left for their honeymoon. Olga and Anton sailed down the Volga, up the Kama River and along the Belaya River to the village of Aksyonovo, where they checked into a sanatorium. At this establishment Chekhov drank four large bottles of fermented mare's milk every day, put on weight, and his condition seemed to improve somewhat. However, on their return to Yalta, Chekhov's health deteriorated again. He made his will, leaving his house in Yalta to Marya, all income from his dramatic works to Olga and large sums to his mother and his surviving brothers, to the municipality of Taganrog and to the peasant body of Melikhovo.

Difficult Relationship

After a while, Olga returned to her busy schedule of rehearsals and performances in Moscow, and the couple continued their relationship at a distance, as they had done before their marriage, with long and frequent love letters. Chekhov managed to visit her in Moscow occasionally, but by now he was so ill that he had to return to Yalta immediately, often remaining confined to bed for long periods. Olga was tortured as to whether she should give up her acting career and nurse Anton for the time left to him. Almost unable to write, Anton now embarked laboriously on his last dramatic masterpiece, *The Cherry Orchard*. Around that time, in the spring of 1902, Olga visited Anton in Yalta after suffering a spontaneous miscarriage during a Moscow Art Theatre tour, leaving her husband with the unpleasant suspicion that she might have been unfaithful to him. In the following months, Anton nursed his wife devotedly, travelling to Moscow whenever he could to be near her. Olga's flat was on the third floor, and there was no lift. It took Anton half an hour to get up the stairs, so he practically never went out.

Final Play

When *The Cherry Orchard* was finally completed in October 1903, Chekhov once again travelled to Moscow to attend rehearsals, despite the advice of his doctors that it would be tantamount to suicide. The play was premiered on 17th January 1904, Chekhov's forty-fourth birthday, and at the end of the performance the author was dragged onstage. There was no chair for him, and he was forced to stand listening to the interminable speeches, trying not to cough and pretending to look interested. Although the performance was a success, press reviews, as usual, were mixed, and Chekhov thought that Nemirovich-Danchenko and Stanislavsky had misunderstood the play.

Death

Chekhov returned to Yalta knowing he would not live long enough to write another work. His health deteriorated even further, and the doctors put him on morphine, advising him to go to a sanatorium in Germany. Accordingly, in June 1904, he and Olga set off for Badenweiler, a spa in the Black Forest. The German specialists examined him and reported that they could do nothing. Soon oxygen had to be administered to him, and he became feverish and delirious. At 12.30 a.m. on 15th July 1904, he regained his mental clarity sufficiently to tell Olga to summon a doctor urgently. On the doctor's arrival, Chekhov told him, "*Ich sterbe*" ("I'm dying"). The doctor gave him a strong stimulant, and was on the point of sending for other medicines when Chekhov, knowing it was all pointless, simply asked for a bottle of champagne to be sent to the room. He poured everybody a glass, drank his off, commenting that he hadn't had champagne for ages, lay down, and died in the early hours of the morning.

Funeral

The coffin was transported back to Moscow in a filthy green carriage marked "FOR OYSTERS", and although it was met at the station by bands and a large ceremonial gathering, it turned out that this was for an eminent Russian General who had just been killed in action in Manchuria. Only a handful of people had assembled to greet Chekhov's coffin. However, as word got round Moscow that his body was being transported to the graveyard at the Novodevichy Monastery, people poured out of their homes and workplaces, forming a vast crowd both inside and outside the cemetery and causing a large amount of damage to buildings, pathways and other graves in the process. The entire tragicomic episode of Chekhov's death, transportation back to Moscow and burial could almost have featured in one of his own short stories. Chekhov was buried next to his father Pavel. His mother outlived him by fifteen years, and his sister Marya died in 1957 at the age of ninety-four. Olga Knipper survived two more years, dying in 1959 at the age of eighty-nine.

Anton Chekhov's Works

Early Writings

When Chekhov studied medicine in Moscow from 1879 to 1884, he financed his studies by writing reports of law-court proceedings for the newspapers and contributing, under a whole series of pseudonyms, hundreds of jokes, comic sketches and short stories to the numerous Russian humorous magazines and more serious journals of the time. From 1885, when he began to practise as a doctor, he concentrated far more on serious literary works, and between then and the end of his life he produced over 200 short stories, plus a score or so of dramatic pieces, ranging from monologues through one-act to full-length plays. In 1884 he also wrote his only novel, *The Hunting Party*, which was a rather wooden attempt at a detective novel.

Invention of a New, "Objective" Style of Writing

A number of his stories between the mid-Eighties and his journey to Sakhalin were vitiated by his attempt to propagate the Tolstoyan moral principles he had espoused at the time. But even before his journey to the prison island he was realizing that laying down the law to his readers, and trying to dictate how they should read his stories, was not his job: it should be the goal of an artist to describe persons and events non-judgementally, and let the reader draw his or her own conclusions. This is attested by his letter to Suvorin in April 1890: "You reproach me for 'objectivity', calling it indifference to good and evil, and absence of ideals and ideas and so forth. You wish me, when depicting horse thieves, to state: stealing horses is bad. But surely people have known that for ages already, without me telling them so? Let them be judged by jurymen – my business is to show them as they really are. When I write, I rely totally on the reader, supposing that he himself will supply the subjective factors absent in the story." After Chekhov's return from Sakhalin, this objectivity dominated everything he wrote.

A further feature of Chekhov's storytelling, which developed throughout his career, is that he does not so much describe events taking place, but rather depicts the way that characters react to those – frequently quite insignificant – events, and the way people's lives are often transformed for better or worse by them. His dramatic works from that time also showed a development from fully displayed events and action – sometimes, in the early plays, quite melodramatic – to, in the major plays written in the last decade or so of his life, depicting the effects on people's lives of offstage events, and the way the characters react to those events.

His style in all his later writing – especially from 1890 onwards – is lucid and economical, and there is a total absence of purple passages. The works of his final years display an increasing awareness of the need for conservation of the natural world in the face of the creeping industrialization of Russia. The breakdown of the old social order in the face of the new rising entrepreneurial class is also depicted non-judgementally; in Chekhov's last play, *The Cherry Orchard*, an old estate belonging to a long-established family of gentry is sold to a businessman, and the final scenes of the play give way to the offstage sounds of wood-chopping, as the old cherry orchard – one of the major beauties of the estate – is cut down by its new owner to be sold for timber.

Major Short Stories

It is generally accepted that Chekhov's mature story-writing may be said to date from the mid-1880s, when he began to contribute to the "thick journals". Descriptions of a small representative selection of some of the major short stories – giving an idea of Chekhov's predominant themes – can be found below.

On the Road

In 'On the Road' (1886), set in a seedy wayside inn on Christmas Eve, a man, apparently from the privileged classes, and his eight-year-old daughter are attempting to sleep in the "travellers' lounge", having been forced to take refuge from a violent storm. The little girl wakes up, and tells him how unhappy she is and that he is a wicked man. A noblewoman, also sheltering from the storm, enters and comforts the girl. The man and the woman both tell each other of the unhappiness of their lives: he is a widowed nobleman who has squandered all his money and is now on his way to a tedious job in the middle of nowhere; she is from a wealthy family, but her father and her brothers are wastrels, and she is the only one who takes care of the estate. They both part in the morning, on Christmas Day, profoundly unhappy, and without succeeding in establishing that deep inner contact with another human being which both of them obviously crave.

Enemies

Chekhov's 1887 tale 'Enemies' touches on similar themes of misery and incomprehension: a country doctor's six-year-old son has just died of diphtheria, leaving him and his wife devastated; at precisely this moment, a local landowner comes to his house to call him out to attend to his wife, who is apparently dangerously ill. Though sympathetic to the doctor's state, he is understandably full of anxiety for his wife, and insists that the doctor come. After an uncomfortable carriage journey, they arrive at the landowner's mansion to discover that the wife was never ill at all, but was simply getting rid of her husband so that she could run off with her lover. The landowner is now in a state of anger and despair, and the doctor unreasonably blames him for having dragged him out under false pretences. When the man offers him his fee, the doctor throws it in his face and storms out. The landowner also furiously drives off somewhere to assuage his anger. Neither man can even begin to penetrate the other's mental state because of their own problems. The doctor remains full of contempt and cynicism for the human race for the rest of his life.

The Steppe

In 1888, Chekhov's first indubitably great narrative, the novella-length 'The Steppe', was published to rapturous reviews. There is almost no plot: in blazing midsummer, a nine-year-old boy sets out on a long wagon ride, lasting several days, from his home in a small provincial town through the steppe, to stay with relatives and attend high school in a large city. The entire story consists of his impressions of the journey – of his travelling companions, the people they meet en route, the inns at which they stay, the scenery and wildlife. He finally reaches his destination, bids farewell to his travelling companions, and the story ends with him full of tears of regret at his lost home life, and foreboding at what the future in this strange new world holds for him.

The Name-Day Party

Another major short story by Chekhov, 'The Name-Day Party' (also translated as 'The Party'), was published in the same year as 'The Steppe'. The title refers to the fact that Russians celebrate not only their birthdays, but the day of the saint after whom they are named. It is the name day of a selfish lawyer and magistrate; his young wife, who is seven-months pregnant, has spent all day organizing a banquet in his honour and entertaining guests. Utterly exhausted, she occasionally asks him to help her, but he does very little. Finally, when all the guests have gone home, she, in extreme agony, gives birth prematurely to a stillborn baby. She slips in and out of consciousness, believes she too is dying, and, despite his behaviour, she feels sorry for her husband, who will be lost without her. However, when she regains consciousness he seems to blame her for the loss of the child, and not his own selfishness, leading to her utter exhaustion at such a time.

A Dreary Story

'A Dreary Story' (also known as 'A Tedious Story') is one of Chekhov's longer stories, originally published in 1889. In a tour de force, the twenty-nine-year-old Chekhov penetrates into the mind of a famous sixty-two-year-old professor – his interior monologue constituting the entire tale. The professor is a world expert in his subject, fêted throughout Russia, yet has a terminal disease which means he will be dead in a few months. He has told nobody, not even his family. This professor muses over his life, and how his body is falling apart, and he wonders what the point of it all was. He would gladly give all his fame for just a few more years of warm, vibrant life. Chekhov wrote this story the year before he travelled to Sakhalin, when he was beginning to display the first symptoms of the tuberculosis which was to kill him at the age of forty-four.

The Duel

In Chekhov's 1891 story 'The Duel', a bored young civil servant has lost interest in everything in life, including his lover. When the latter's husband dies, she expects him to marry her, but he decides to borrow money and leave the town permanently instead. However, the acquaintance from whom he tries to borrow the money refuses to advance him the sum for such purposes. After a heated exchange, the civil servant challenges the acquaintance to a duel – a challenge which is taken up by a friend of the person who has refused to lend the money, disgusted at the civil servant's selfish behaviour. Both miss their shot, and the civil servant, realizing how near he has been to death, regains interest in life, marries his mistress, and all are reconciled.

Ward Six

In 'Ward Six' (1892), a well-meaning but apathetic and weak provincial hospital director has a ward for the mentally disturbed as one of his responsibilities. He knows that the thuggish peasant warden regularly beats the lunatics up, but makes all kinds of excuses not to get involved. He ends up being incarcerated in his own mental ward by the ruse of an ambitious rival, and is promptly beaten by the same warden who used to call him "Your Honour", and dies soon afterwards. This is perhaps Chekhov's most transparent attack on the supine intelligentsia of his own time, whom he saw as lacking determination in the fight against social evils.

Three Years

In 1895, Chekhov published his famous story 'Three Years', in which Laptev, a young Muscovite, is nursing his seriously ill sister in a small provincial town, and feels restricted and bored. He falls in love with the daughter of her doctor and, perhaps from loneliness and the need for companionship, proposes marriage. Although she is not in love with him, she accepts, after a good deal of hesitation, because she is afraid this might be her only offer in this dull town. For the first three years this marriage – forged through a sense of isolation on one side and fear of spinsterhood on the other – is passionless and somewhat unhappy. However, after this period, they manage to achieve an equable and fulfilling relationship based on companionship.

The House with a Mezzanine

In the 'The House with a Mezzanine' (1896), a talented but lazy young artist visits a rich landowning friend in the country. They go to visit the wealthy family at the title's "house with a mezzanine", which consists of a mother and two unmarried daughters. The artist falls in love with the younger daughter, but her tyrannical older sister sends both her and her mother abroad. The story ends some years later with the artist still wistfully wondering what has become of the younger sister.

Peasants

In 'Peasants' (1897), Nikolai, who has lived and worked in Moscow since adolescence, and now works as a waiter at a prestigious Moscow hotel, is taken very ill and can no longer work, so he decides to return to the country village of his childhood, taking with him his wife and young daughter, who was born in Moscow. He has warm recollections of the village, but finds that memory has deceived him. The place is filthy and squalid, and the local inhabitants all seem to be permanently blind drunk. Since anybody with any intelligence – like Nikolai himself – is sent to the city as young as possible to work and send money back to the family, the level of ignorance and stupidity is appalling. Nikolai dies, and the story ends with his wife and daughter walking back to Moscow, begging as they go.

The Man in a Case

In 1898, Chekhov published 'The Man in a Case', in which the narrator, a schoolmaster, recounts the life of a recently deceased colleague of his, Byelikov, who taught classical Greek. A figure of ridicule for his pupils and colleagues, Byelikov is described as being terrified of the modern world, walking around, even in the warmest weather, in high boots, a heavy overcoat, dark spectacles and a hat with a large brim concealing his face. The blinds are always drawn on all the windows in his house, and these are permanently shut. He threatens to report to the headmaster a young colleague who engages in the appallingly immoral and progressive activity of going for bicycle rides in the countryside. The young man pushes him, Byelikov falls down and, although not hurt, takes to his bed and dies, apparently of humiliation and oversensitivity.

The Lady with the Little Dog

'The Lady with the Little Dog' (1899) tells the story of a bored and cynical bank official who, trapped in a tedious marriage in Moscow, takes a holiday by himself in Yalta. There he meets Anna, who is also unhappily married. They have an affair, then go back to their respective homes. In love for possibly the first time in his life, he travels to the provincial town where she lives, and tracks her down. They meet in a theatre, and in a snatched conversation she promises to visit him in Moscow. The story ends with them both realizing that their problems are only just beginning.

Sakhalin Island

As well as being a prolific writer of short fiction, Chekhov also wrote countless articles as a journalist, and the volume-length *Sakhalin Island* ranks as one of the most notable examples of his investigative non-fiction. As mentioned above, Chekhov's decision to travel to Sakhalin Island in easternmost Siberia for three months in 1890 was motivated by several factors, one of them being to write a comprehensive study of the penal colonies on the island.

Chekhov toured round the entire island, visiting all the prisons and most of the settlements, and generally spending up to nineteen hours a day gathering material and writing up his findings. Chekhov returned from Sakhalin at the end of 1890, but it took him three years to write up and start publishing the material he had collected. The first chapter was published in the journal *Russian Thought* (*Russkaya Mysl*) in late 1893, and subsequent material appeared regularly in this magazine until July 1894, with no objection from the censor, until finally the chapters from number twenty onwards were banned from publication. Chekhov took the decision to "publish and be damned" – accordingly the whole thing appeared in book form, including the banned chapters, in May 1895.

The book caused enormous interest and discussion in the press, and over the next decade a number of substantial ameliorations were brought about in the criminals' lives.

Major Plays

Chekhov first made his name in the theatre with a series of one-act farces, most notably *The Bear* and *Swan Song* (both 1888). However, his first attempts at full-length plays, *Platonov* (1880), *Ivanov* (1887) and *The Wood Demon* (1889), were not entirely successful. The four plays which are now considered to be Chekhov's masterpieces, and outstanding works of world theatre, are *The Seagull* (1896), *Uncle Vanya* (1899), *Three Sisters* (1901) and *The Cherry Orchard* (1904).

The Seagull

The central character in *The Seagull* is an unsuccessful playwright, Treplyov, who is in love with the actress Nina. However, she falls in love with the far more successful writer Trigorin. Out of spite and as an anti-idealist gesture, Treplyov shoots a seagull and places it in front of her. Nina becomes Trigorin's mistress. Unfortunately their baby dies, Nina's career collapses and Trigorin leaves her. However, on Treplyov renewing his overtures to Nina, she tells him that she still loves Trigorin. The play ends with news being brought in that Treplyov has committed suicide offstage.

Uncle Vanya

The second of Chekhov's four dramatic masterpieces, *Uncle Vanya*, a comprehensive reworking of the previously unsuccessful *Wood Demon*, centres on Vanya, who has for many years tirelessly managed a professor's estate. However, the professor finally retires back to his estate with his bored and idle young wife, with whom Vanya falls in love. Vanya now realizes that the professor is a thoroughly selfish and mediocre man and becomes jealous and embittered at his own fate, believing he has sacrificed his own brilliant future. When the professor tells him that he is going to sell the estate, Vanya, incensed, fires a pistol at him at point-blank range and misses – which only serves to compound his sense of failure and frustration. The professor and his wife agree not to sell up for the time being and leave to live elsewhere. Vanya sinks back into his boring loveless life, probably for ever.

Three Sisters

In *Three Sisters*, Olga, Masha and Irina live a boring life in their brother's house in a provincial town, remote from Moscow and St Petersburg. All three remember their happy childhood in Moscow and dream of one day returning. A military unit arrives nearby, and Irina and Masha start up relationships with officers, which might offer a way out of their tedious lives. However, Irina's fiancé is killed in a duel, Masha's relationship ends when the regiment moves on, and Olga, a schoolteacher, is promoted to the post of headmistress at her school, thus forcing her to give up any hope of leaving the area. They all relapse into what they perceive to be their meaningless lives.

The Cherry Orchard

The Cherry Orchard, Chekhov's final masterpiece for the theatre, is a lament for the passing of old traditional Russia and the encroachment of the modern world. The Ranevsky family estate, with its wonderful and famous cherry orchard, is no longer a viable concern. Various suggestions are made to stave off financial disaster, all of which involve cutting down the ancient orchard. Finally the estate is auctioned off, and in the final scene, the orchard is chopped down offstage. The old landowning family move out, and in a final tragicomic scene, they forget to take an ancient manservant with them, accidentally locking him in the house and leaving him feeling abandoned.

Select Bibliography

Biographies:

Hingley, Ronald, *A New Life of Anton Chekhov* (Oxford: Oxford University Press, 1976)

Pritchett, V.S., *Chekhov: A Spirit Set Free* (London: Hodder & Stoughton, 1988)

Rayfield, Donald, *Anton Chekhov* (London: HarperCollins, 1997)

Simmons, Ernest, *Chekhov: A Biography* (London: Jonathan Cape, 1963)

Troyat, Henri, *Chekhov*, tr. Michael Henry Heim (New York: Dutton, 1986)

Additional Recommended Background Material:

Hellman, Lillian, ed., *Selected Letters of Anton Chekhov* (New York: Farrar, Straus and Giroux, 1984)

Magarshack, David, *Chekhov the Dramatist*, 2nd ed. (London: Eyre Methuen, 1980)

Malcolm, Janet, *Reading Chekhov: A Critical Journey* (London: Granta, 2001)

Pennington, Michael, *Are You There, Crocodile?: Inventing Anton Chekhov* (London: Oberon, 2003)